ZOO

OTSUICHI

ZOO

OTSUICHI

Translated by
Terry Gallagher

HAIKASORU
San Francisco

ZOO © 2006 by Otsuichi
All rights reserved.
First published in Japan in 2006 by SHUEISHA Inc.,
Tokyo

Art directors / Mary Ann Levesque and T. J. Walker
English translation © VIZ Media, LLC

HAIKASORU
Published by VIZ Media, LLC
295 Bay Street
San Francisco, CA 94133

www.haikasoru.com

Library of Congress Cataloging-in-Publication Data

Otsuichi, 1978–
    [Short stories. Selections. English]
    Zoo / Otsuichi ; translated by Terry Gallagher. —
1st American paperback ed.
        p. cm.
    First published in Japan in 2006 by Shueisha Inc.,
Tokyo.
    ISBN-13: 978-1-4215-2587-7
    ISBN-10: 1-4215-2587-9
    I. Gallagher, Terry. II. Title.
    PL874.T78A613 2009
    895.6'36—DC22
                        2008040249

Printed in the U.S.A.
First printing, September 2009

CONTENTS

ZOO

1.

The difference between photographs and movies is similar to the difference between haiku and prose.

Not only haiku, but short verse and longer poems as well. Ordinarily these things are much shorter than works of prose. That is the defining characteristic of poetry. In these short chains of words an instant's movement of the heart is clipped and pasted. The writer sees and hears the world, and describes the emotions he feels in his heart. And he does it in a burst of short phrases.

In prose these things are strung together. The heart's descriptions are continuous, and as the number of lines grows, the form changes. Through the many events that take place in a piece of prose, the hearts of various characters are not always the same. But abstracting the essentials from these sentences adds up to a complete description. To make it all hang together, we need to portray "change." Between the first page and the last page, the hearts of the characters have to change into something different. This process of change emerges as a wave, and that is the form of a story. This is simple mathematics. If you take prose and break it down into fragments, it turns into haiku or poetry. If you take a story and break it down into fragments, it turns into description.

Photographs are also descriptive. With a camera a landscape can be captured forever and framed. A photograph can describe a child's crying face. This is close to what happens in haiku or poetry.

There is a difference between words and pictures of course, but both select important moments in time and stop them forever.

So let's say we take a few dozen, or a few hundred, photographs. Not just the same image multiplied over and over again—and not completely different subjects either. Each photograph represents an instant immediately after the previous photograph; one picture after the other, all in a row. And if we flip from one to the next rapidly, the phenomenon known as "persistence of vision" gives birth to time itself.

Let's take that crying child for example: the crying jag may turn into a fit of laughter. Unlike static individual photographs, these form a continuum. The entire intervening process from crying to smiling is there. In this way we are able to witness the changes in the heart. It becomes obvious that "time" is the product of interconnected "instants," and from this we are able to describe "change." In other words, we are able to spin a yarn. And that's what a movie is. That's what I think.

Again this morning there was a photograph in the mailbox. How many times now? This has been going on for at least a hundred days or more. I still haven't gotten used to it and I can't stop thinking about it. Every day I go out in the early morning cold and find a photo in my rusty old mailbox. This gives me simultaneous feelings of dizziness, light-headedness, abhorrence, and despair. I stand absolutely still, gripping the photograph tightly in my hand. Every morning it's the same thing.

The photographs aren't in an envelope or anything, and they haven't come in the mail. They're just there in the mailbox. The photographs are of a dead person. My ex-girlfriend. She appears to be lying in a hole someplace. The photographs show her dead body from the chest up. Her face is decomposing and there is no glimmer of her former self.

In each day's ghastly photograph, the process of decomposition seems to have progressed just a little bit from the one found in my mailbox the day before. It's gotten to the point where I can track the movement of bugs crawling across her face. As she rots, the bugs migrate to other patches of skin.

Clutching the photograph, I return to my room. I scan it into the computer. All the images I have received of her are now in the computer. I have numbered them in sequential order, and she exists as a large volume of graphic data.

In the very first photograph she looks like a human being. In the second photograph—which I received the very next day—the only conspicuous change was a faint darkness in her face. With each passing day the girl in the photographs grew further and further from a recognizable living creature.

I haven't said anything about these photos to anyone. I am the only person who knows my girlfriend was killed. As far as the rest of the world is concerned, she remains an unsolved missing persons case.

I confess, I loved her dearly. I can still remember when we went to see the movie *Zoo* together. It was an arty kind of picture and we both had trouble understanding what was going on.

On the screen were lots of rapidly changing images of rotting vegetables and animals. Apples and shrimp turning black and deforming. Attacked by bacteria, they must have smelled pretty bad. Backed by an inexplicably cheerful Michael Nyman soundtrack, the dead bodies of the animals crumpled in seconds. The decomposition of flesh unfurled like a giant wave striking and receding from the shoreline. The whole point of the film, apparently, was to show the process of decay.

When we left the movie theater she and I decided to visit the local zoo. I was driving and she was sitting beside me reading the road signs. "Look," she said, pointing excitedly out the car window. "Isn't that a coincidence?!"

"ZOO. Left turn. 200 meters ahead."

That's what the sign said. Japanese on top, English on the bottom. I distinctly remember the English letters spelled Z-O-O.

I turned the steering wheel to the left and drove off the main road and into the parking lot. Hardly anybody was there. It was the middle of winter and no one goes to the zoo at that time of the year. It wasn't snowing, but there were thick clouds in the sky, and it was kind of dark. Everything smelled of animals and wet straw—not the most inviting of smells I must admit. My girlfriend and I walked side by side holding hands. I could tell she was shivering the entire time we were there.

"There's nobody here," she said. "I heard something about this. Zoos and amusement parks all over the country are going broke because nobody cares about them anymore."

As we walked through the circuitous pathways of the zoo, our breath turned to white puffs that dispersed into the air. We passed in front of iron-barred cages. The animals huddled in their cages without moving, their dull eyes gazing off into the distance. One monkey, however, a real ugly one, restlessly paced back and forth in its cage. We stood and looked at it for a while. The monkey was kind of scruffy and was missing big chunks of fur. It was alone in the cage with nothing better to do than walk around and around the narrow concrete space.

Having a girlfriend was the best thing to happen to me in a long time. It was the autumn when she disappeared; it seems like such a long time ago.

I told a lot of people about my suspicions that she might have become involved in some sort of weird incident. But the police never really took me seriously, and they treated her disappearance as a simple runaway case. Her family thought the same thing. It was almost like people expected her to run away eventually. Nobody seemed surprised that it finally happened.

After inputting the image files into my computer, I would carelessly throw the original photographs of her rotting corpse in a drawer. By now the drawer was stuffed with more than a hundred of these pictures.

I move the computer's cursor and click on the proper software to play a well-known movie. This software can also be used to edit video. I select the "open image sequence" function and select the very first stored image of her. I select "set image sequence," and then I select "twelve frames per second."

The photos are now ready to be viewed as a video, with each one in sequential order. The photographs of her flit past at a speed of twelve frames per second. This process was originally designed for the purpose of producing animation.

In playback mode I watch her decay. The bugs swarm all over her face, eating her flesh and then moving on. It is like an ocean wave made up of insects.

Each morning when I go to the mailbox to discover another photograph there, the length of the process increases by another one-twelfth of a second. "I will find this criminal," I grumbled to myself.

The person taking these photographs was the person responsible for killing her. I was sure of it.

"I'll make him pay for this," I vowed when the police wrapped up their investigation.

But I had a problem. This problem was absolute, and it had the potential to destroy my very being. And so I was avoiding even acknowledging the problem.

"Shit, where could this criminal be?!"

My words were just lines in a script. Mere theatrics. In my heart I knew something completely different. But if I did not stay in character in this drama, the harshness of reality would come down and crush me.

In other words, I was pretending not to know myself. That's what allowed me to convince myself that I would find her killer. In reality, there was no way I could find her killer.

I had killed her myself.

2.

Since losing her, I continued to live my life as normally as possible. But it was difficult. Looking at my own face in the mirror I could see that my cheeks were sunken, my eyes hollow.

I knew that I had killed her. And I was aware of the contradiction between this knowledge and my passion to find her killer. But I swear to God I did not have a split personality.

I loved her from the very depths of my heart. I did not want to think that I murdered her with my own two hands. I made a decision not to dwell on such disturbing thoughts.

Somewhere in the world there was a murderer who was not me, and if I could make it look like that person had killed my girlfriend, I would feel so much better. I would be liberated from this guilty conscience of mine.

"Who has been putting these photographs in the mailbox?!"

"Why are you showing these photographs to me?!"

"Just tell me . . . who it was who murdered her?!"

The whole thing was a one-man skit. I pretended not to know anything, to detest the murderer with all my heart, and I played the part of myself in the grip of a murderous rage.

My failure to show the photographs to the police was an act of self-preservation. In my mind I convinced myself that I was working with the police to find my girlfriend's killer. That was my reasoning for keeping the photographs to myself. The police, of course, didn't know any of this. They still thought of her as a missing person. I was intoxicated by the image of myself as someone who could take revenge on his lover's assailant without the aid of the police.

As I continued to play out this little script, I found myself at times thinking that in fact I was not the person who had murdered my girlfriend. Someone else had done it. I was innocent, wasn't I?

Unfortunately for me, the photographs that kept arriving in my mailbox every morning prevented me from escaping completely into this world of delusion.

Of course I was the one who had killed her. The photographs kept telling me so.

It was one month after she disappeared, in the first few days of November, that the police ended their investigation. After that

I quit my job to devote myself full-time to my own search for her killer. Of course, I was doing nothing more than being true to my role as the lover of a murdered woman. I had cast myself as the tragic hero, loathing the criminal and rising up to avenge his lover's death.

I started by questioning her friends and acquaintances. I met with anyone who ever knew her—her colleagues at work, her family, the clerks at the convenience store she frequented.

"Yeah, she still hasn't been found. The police think she ran away from home, but I don't believe it. That would be ridiculous, her running away . . . So I'm going around like this, asking questions of people who knew her. Will you please help me? Thank you. When did you last see her? Was there anything odd about her behavior? For example, was there anyone who had anything against her? Were any suspicious people seen walking around in her neighborhood? Did she ever say anything like that to you? . . . She never said anything like that to me . . . What about that ring she always wore? That's right, it was an engagement ring I gave to her . . . Hey, don't look at me like that. I don't need your pity . . ."

Not one person suspected I was the one who killed her. They just thought I was some confused, pitiful guy whose girlfriend had suddenly packed up and left. My acting skills were pretty good, I guess. Some people even shed tears, not for her but for me. The world is kind of crazy. Why didn't anyone realize I'm the one who killed her? Because I am unable to admit this to myself, I have been counting on other people to figure it out for me.

That is really what I want. I am waiting. I want someone to accuse me, to say, "You! You are the criminal!" Even the police—isn't this supposed to be their job?—have failed to uncover my crime.

But now . . . I've been thinking. I want to be free of this guilt. I want to confess everything, to acknowledge my crime. If I don't, I will have to just keep on playing this part forever. I am unable to work up the nerve to turn myself in. The whole thing is too terrifying. Unable to wrench my eyes from this problem, I opt to go on with my deception.

After one week of going through the motions of conducting my own investigation, I ran out of people to interview. At that point I was like a rat in a dead-end maze.

"I have no leads on this criminal! Doesn't anyone have any information?" I found myself grumbling to myself alone in my room sitting in front of the computer.

Once again I played the video of her decomposing corpse. By the end she had completely rotted away, turning into something that was no longer even germ fodder, no longer human, something indescribable.

In all honesty it made me want to puke. I had no wish to watch someone rot away to nothing, much less someone I had once loved. But I had to watch it. Only by watching could I convince myself that I was the one who had killed her. I begged myself to go to the police and make a clean slate of it. But my pleas fell on my own deaf ears.

"You can't just sit there! Go get some new information! On your feet! Investigate!"

I managed to get up and tear my eyes away from the computer screen and the vision of her rotting corpse. I grabbed a picture of her and went out. I walked around town pretending to search for the criminal.

The photograph I took with me was not one of her decomposing body. It was a picture from when she was alive and beautiful. Behind her you could see zebras in their fenced-in area at the zoo. On impulse she had bought one of those disposable cameras. We walked around taking pictures of the smelly, hollow-eyed animals. For the last few snapshots I turned the camera on her. Now, preserved for posterity, I had this picture of her. She was scowling slightly.

I walked around showing this photo to random people on the street, asking if they knew anything about her. These people must have thought I was a nut, or at least some kind of nuisance.

I realized this but I couldn't help myself. I had to do it. I wasn't able to sit around doing nothing. I had no work and no interest in living, and my meager savings were running out. Before long I would be kicked out of my apartment. No problem, I could sleep in my car. If I ran out of things to eat, I could steal some money from somebody. I didn't mind getting my hands dirty. As long as I could find the person who had killed her, or at least act like that's what I was doing.

All morning long I walked around town, asking people questions.

"Do you know this woman? Have you seen her? Please . . . please."

One time a local shop owner reported me to the police. After that experience I learned not to hang around any one neighborhood too long. More than once I attracted the attention of local gangs. Things even got violent. I tried to resist, but a guy pulled a knife on me in a back alley. I wanted him to stab me, one stroke to the heart. Then it would end. Everything would end. I would be able to die, never having admitted that I had killed her. I would end my life not as a murderer but as a victim. That would have been something to preserve my dignity. It was the only escape route that would totally exonerate me from my crime. I could finally stop carrying her photograph, hanging around town asking for nonexistent information, and searching for some nonexistent criminal.

But that young man did not stab me. I grabbed his hand, the one with the knife, and pulled it to my own chest. All he would have had to do was put a little force into it, stick it in a little, and it would have been all over. Instead, he started to shake and apologize. The other members of his gang turned pale. Then the police came, and they all ran away. I called out to them, "Wait for me! Take me with you!"

Some filthy old bag had called the police. She happened to see the whole thing as they surrounded me on the street. She was a tiny little thing and cowered behind the policeman. She was kind of shabby-looking, and from what she was wearing and what she had on her feet, you wouldn't think she was a modern-day Japanese citizen at all. I bet she was poor and had no money. I bet she slept in a tunnel that reeked of piss and shit. The wrinkles in her face were filled with grime. Her hair was filthy. Around her neck hung something that looked like a wooden board. At first I thought it was an advertisement for a pachinko parlor, but I was wrong.

It was a wet piece of wood she must have picked up from the garbage dump or someplace. In simple block letters it read, "Have you seen this man?" Under these words was a photograph of a young man. Compared with the photograph of my girlfriend I was holding, it was almost unbelievably old. She told me her only son had gone missing twenty years ago and now she was standing on street corners looking for him. She stroked the tattered old photograph and mumbled something in an almost indecipherable accent. The picture, apparently, was the only tangible thing she had of her son. She was at her wit's end.

I knelt at the feet of that old woman. I lay down flat out in front of her and rubbed my face in the dirt. I could not stop crying. The old woman and the police officer beside her tried to console me, but all I could do was shake my head from side to side.

3.

My girlfriend and I had a huge fight in an abandoned mountain cabin. She was an impulsive sort of person. That's why we went to the zoo that one day. She saw a road sign and made a snap decision. Similarly, on the day of our fight, we spotted a side road in the foothills. "Let's see where this goes," she piped up. I think she just suddenly wanted to see what was down that road. Being impulsive was one of the things I really liked about her.

After driving for a period we spotted the cabin. The word

cabin isn't exactly correct. It really looked more like a pile of old boards. We stopped the car and went in.

The place smelled of mold. We both glanced up at the ceiling—it looked like it was about to crash down on us. I took her picture with a Polaroid camera. Ever since our visit to the zoo, I had developed quite a fondness for photography.

She made a funny face when the camera's flash flared. "It's too bright," she said bluntly. She grabbed the photo from the camera and crumpled it into a ball. That really upset me. Then she said I should forget all about her. What do you mean, I asked, and she said a whole lot of other hurtful things. She was telling me she didn't love me anymore.

That was the day when, as far as the rest of the world was concerned, she became a missing person. The reason was obvious. She never emerged from that mountain cabin.

That day, she confessed that she had never told anyone we were dating. And now in hindsight I believe her. If she had told her family, her friends, or her coworkers about me, the police would surely have suspected me of murder. And had they asked, I would have confessed. The only call I ever got was from her mother who asked if I knew her daughter. Over the phone I got the sense that she didn't love her daughter very much. She wasn't too worried about her sudden disappearance either.

I was on the verge of confessing to the mother, but the words that came out were different from the ones I was thinking. "What's that? Missing you say? Have you contacted the police? Wait there, I'll come right over." That was the start of my long, meaningless theater performance.

I went to her house and filled out a form for the police. I played the part of a concerned acquaintance. I created a fake self, one who desperately wanted to track her down, one who was going crazy at the thought that she might be dead.

4.

One day, after I had been wandering around town with my ex-girlfriend's photograph, I returned to my car in the parking lot. The day was ending and as the sun sank lower, I looked up at the buildings surrounding me. They cast dark shadows on the ground below.

"Another day finished and nothing to show for it," I grumbled to myself. Every false breath that came from my mouth turned to white mist in the chilly winter air. From the pocket of my tattered coat I took out her photograph and stared at it. I had a cut on my finger and my skin was stiff from the cold, but I gently stroked the image of her face.

My car was the only one in the whole parking lot. My shadow stretched behind me on the concrete surface.

"Tomorrow I'm going to get that guy . . ."

My entire body was exhausted from walking around. I felt like I would topple right over. I opened the car door and sat down behind the wheel. It was then that I noticed something that had fallen under the passenger seat.

"What's this?"

It was a piece of paper, crumpled up in a ball. I picked it up. It was a photograph. I flattened it out to see what it was.

"What the . . . ?" It was her. She looked a little grumpy, but cute nonetheless. Behind her was a ramshackle wall of wooden boards. In the lower right corner was a date.

"What the . . . ?! This was the day she disappeared!" I put on my best puzzled act. This was the very photograph she had gotten angry about and crumpled up that day.

"What the hell is this picture doing in my car? This is too weird. I can't understand it. The criminal must have planted it here. I can't think of any other way . . ."

I opened the glove compartment to put the photo away. There amidst the car registration and manual was a suspicious scrap of paper.

"What's this now?"

A gas station receipt.

"The date . . . also from the day she disappeared! It has the gas station's address! Such lunacy! I never went there that day. I was at home all day . . . Maybe . . ."

My suspicions were leading to an important conclusion. Or at least so I pretended.

"Whoever it was must have used this car to kidnap her! That's it! That's how the criminal managed to entice her. She saw this car and mistakenly believed it was me. She had no fear!"

I turned the key in the ignition and drove away. I knew right where I had to go: the gas station whose address was on the receipt.

"The attendant may have noticed who was driving this car that day! But I wonder if they'll remember. I wonder."

Mumbling to myself, I started the car and headed for the country. Along the sides of the road stood old-fashioned farm houses and untended fields. The sinking sun was red, and its light hit me through the windshield.

It was dark when I finally arrived at the gas station. A middle-aged man approached my car. He was wearing a mechanic's jumpsuit and was wiping his greasy hands with a rag. I rolled down my window, showed him the photo of my girlfriend, and asked him some questions.

"Hey, buddy, have a look at this photo, would you?"

He looked annoyed as he answered.

"Oh yeah, her. She came in a long time ago. Said she was heading west."

"West? What kind of car was she in?

"Who're you kidding? She was in the car you're driving right now."

"I knew it!"

"And you were the one driving. Are we done here? Have we finished the script? I can't believe you still do this every day. Aren't you tired of it yet? How many months now have you been playing this game with me? But of course, you're the customer, so I can't refuse to play along."

"Don't B.S. me. You say I was driving? That's a load of crap."

I was shocked, or so I pretended.

"You mean, on that day, the car she was in? I was driving?"

He made a gesture as if to dismiss me. I stepped on the gas and drove west.

"Shit! I have no idea what's going on anymore!"

I pounded my hand on the steering wheel.

"That guy at the gas station says I was driving . . . But that day I was at home all day! What is going on here?! What is fact, and what is fantasy?!"

That was the instant I started to have doubts about myself. My conversation with the gas station mechanic shook me up. I told myself to get a grip. I had to be prepared for what was to come.

At some point the surrounding countryside turned into a thick forest with tree branches intertwined on both sides of the road. My headlights caught sight of a seldom-traveled side road. I braked hard.

"I've seen this place before, especially this view. But that's stupid. There's no reason to think that."

I turned the steering wheel and entered the side road. It was just wide enough for a single car. After a while the road opened into a clearing. My headlights illuminated the darkness and I could see an old wooden cabin in front of me.

"I know this place . . . I . . ."

I got out of the driver's seat and looked around. There was no one there. The air in the forest was cold and still. From the trunk I grabbed a pocket flashlight and approached the crumbling shack. I opened the door and went in.

It smelled of mold. With each breath I took I felt like something dangerous was invading my lungs. The circle of light from the flashlight lit the inside of the small cabin. The first thing I noticed was a tripod and a camera. It was a Polaroid camera.

The floor of the cabin was bare earth, and a hole was dug in it. The lens of the camera pointed toward the black gap. I moved closer. It seemed filled with blackness like water. I tipped my flashlight downward and the light shone into the hole.

I saw it.

I fell to my knees.

"Now I remember. How could I . . ."

I continued my act. This was a one-man show. I was the actor. I was the audience.

"I killed her . . ."

I burst into tears. They streamed down my cheeks and fell on the parched earth. In the hole beside me, there she lay. She was completely decayed, desiccated, nothing to interest the bugs anymore. There she was, shrunken, small.

"I . . . I . . . her. I must have sealed away the memory . . ."

I had thought out all these lines. The truth is I had forgotten nothing. I remembered everything. But this was the plot of the play I was trapped in.

"All this time I've been tracking down the criminal who killed her. But I am that criminal . . . She said things to me that made me crazy and I burst into a fit of rage . . ." I moaned and screamed. My voice echoed in the hut, where there was no one else but me. The flashlight was the only light in the room.

I pushed my hands against the cold ground and stood up. My entire body creaked from fatigue. I went up to the edge of the hole and looked down at her. Deep in the hole, no longer human, she lay covered in sand and dust, half-buried in the earth.

"I have to tell the police . . . I have to turn myself in . . ." I mumbled to myself as I made up my mind. This too was just part of the script, but it was also what I truly believed in my heart of hearts. From the depths of my soul, that was what I wanted.

"Do I have the courage to do this?"

My fists were shaking. I was asking and answering my own questions.

"Am I ready for this?"

But no matter what, I had to do it. I could not allow myself to run away from the fact that I had committed the crime of killing another person. The fact was, I had murdered someone I loved, and I had to accept the consequences.

"This is a problem . . . To admit this is . . . hard."

I shook my head, grew discouraged, and shed more tears. How would I be able to turn myself in? How would I be able to confess?

"By tomorrow, I will have forgotten how I feel now. I feel like I will have forgotten the truth . . . I will have locked out this memory again, and I will resume my search for the nonexistent criminal . . . I . . ."

I covered my face with my hands. My shoulders shook. Then I remembered something. Or at least I acted as if I did.

"That's right. All I have to do is set myself up! A photograph! If I take a photograph of her I won't be able to forget what I have done.

I walked up to the Polaroid camera and pushed the shutter button. In the brief flash, her body seemed to float up out of the darkness. The camera made its little noise as it spit out the photograph.

"When I look at this picture I will remember my crime. No matter how much I try to turn away from the facts, I won't be able to deny it. This will show me what I have done . . . I will not be able to get out of paying for this."

My voice quavered as I realized what I had to do. I took the photograph and walked back to my car.

"I have to go to the police . . . I will show them this picture and tell them I killed her . . ."

I put the flashlight back in the trunk and got in the car. The image in the photo was just starting to develop, and I laid it on the passenger seat. I stepped on the gas.

I drove through the darkness. The engine throbbed as I pressed my foot on the accelerator. All around me was lonely wasteland. In the headlights the white stripes on the road seemed to float upward. The blackness of the asphalt was surrounded by even more blackness.

On the passenger seat beside me lay the photo, from which my ex-girlfriend's decayed body seemed to rise up to keep me company.

"I will confess. I will go to the police. I will admit my crimes. I will not run away. I must not run away. I was the one who killed her. This cannot be. But this is how it is. These are the facts. I don't want to admit it. I am not the kind of person who does things like that. I loved her. But I was the one who killed her . . ."

This was what I kept repeating to myself, in an effort to keep myself focused.

But I knew. I knew what would happen next. Even as I stuck to the script, I knew I would never go to the police. No, not that I wouldn't go, I couldn't go. The truth was, I wanted to go through with it and be free of all this. But I knew I would not be able to carry out my decision.

This was the pattern I had been repeating every day and every night. Not just this day. This was the play I had been acting out over and over. Around the time the sun began to go down every evening I would discover the photo of her in my car. That is the start of the act about doubting myself. I go to the gas station and I talk to the man there who is helping me act out the scene. Every day I show up at roughly the same time and I repeat the same lines. I go and find the cabin in the forest, I look at her dead body, and I remember what I have done.

And then I make up my mind to go to the police. This part is still an act, but it's also what I truly want to do.

But I never follow through. If I were not so depressed, I would have been in prison long ago living an easier life.

I pass the gas station where I stopped earlier. The lights are out and it is closed for the night. In a little while I will see a certain sign. When I see the sign my determination will crumble. I know this for sure. Every day, every night, this same scenario. "ZOO. Left turn. 200 meters ahead."

That's what I expect to see. Those three letters in English, written at the bottom of the road sign, branded into my retinas: Z-O-O.

In that instant, everything about her comes rushing back into my consciousness. We went to a movie together. We went to the zoo. I took her picture. The first time we met. Telling her about growing up in an orphanage. The fact that she rarely smiled, and the first time she smiled for me. All these things come back to me.

The sign emerges from the darkness and she is sitting beside me in the passenger seat. Not really, of course. But the photograph of her dead body mysteriously takes her form, looks at me, gently reaches out her hand and touches my hair. That's just the way it is.

I must be depressed. It's no good. It can't be true. It can't be me who killed her . . . That's what I will think. A little farther down the road I will stop the car in the middle of the street and cry like a baby. I will go back to my apartment, and I will take the photo from the passenger seat and put it in the mailbox. I will pray that when I wake up tomorrow I will look at this photo and it will inspire me to do the right thing. Otherwise I just hope that the film, now one-twelfth of a second longer, will be the breakthrough I need. I will set the stage for the coming evening by placing the crumpled Polaroid and the gas station receipt back in my vehicle. The show must go on. And that's the end of it.

That's right. In the end, I don't get it. At the end of the day, I never admit to myself that I killed her. Nothing changes. I am no better than that stupid ugly monkey walking in circles in his cage at the zoo. I will relive the same day over and over again. Forever. Tomorrow I will discover the photo in the mailbox, and once again I will be transfixed. For better or worse that's just the way it is.

The car drives through the darkness. The same road I drive every night. How many months have I been doing this now? How many more months like this are in my future? The sign will be coming up soon—the sign that sparks all those memories of her. I grip the steering wheel and wait for the approaching moment.

"I . . . killed her . . . I . . . her."

Mouthing those words, I steel my resolve. In my heart, though, I know it is no use. Still I continue to pray that somehow I can break the cycle. Like believing in God, still in the thrall of revelation, I pray that I can simply pass before the letters Z-O-O.

In my headlights, the white lines of the road seem to go on without end. Along both sides of the road, the withered grass passes by me at high velocity. It's coming soon. The sign will appear—the place where my revelation fails me.

I stop breathing. The car passes the spot. The instant arrives when time itself seems to stop. In the darkness the car seems to be floating through the air, stopped in space. That's the kind of moment it is.

I continue driving from sheer momentum and then I stop in the middle of the street. Leaving the key in the ignition, and neglecting to engage the handbrake, I get out of the car. The breeze cools the sweat that covers my entire body. I look back at the overwhelming darkness behind me.

I think back on what I just saw through the windshield. Actually, that isn't quite accurate. I mean to say, what I didn't see.

I had heard something about this. Zoos and amusement parks all over the country are going broke because nobody's interested in them anymore.

She said something like that at the zoo, I'm sure . . . There was a rumor, I'm sure, that the zoo was going broke.

The sign that said ZOO was not there anymore. In its place was just empty sky. I had passed right by the spot with no landmark to mark it. My past visions of her failed to appear. She was not sitting in the passenger seat beside me and I completely missed the turn. I felt guilty about it, for not remembering. But I also have a feeling that by refusing to appear she was indicting me.

I went back to my car and said a quiet prayer. I don't know if I was praying to God or to my girlfriend whom I had murdered. But I knew I no longer had any need to pretend. I would go straight to the police. I would confess my crimes. My heart was fully at peace.

IN A FALLING AIRPLANE

1.

"I hope you don't mind my asking, miss, but are you familiar with the prophecies of Nostradamus?"

I turned my eyes away from the clouds outside the window. The man sitting next to me wore a drab gray suit and was completely nondescript. If you walked down the street in any town you'd see a handful of guys like him. He was around thirty, so about the same age as me.

"Prophecies? You mean, like, that the world will be destroyed in 1999?"

He nodded.

"Yeah, I know about them," I said. "They were a fad when I was a kid. But . . . I beg your pardon," I said, looking between the seats and up the aisle. "Don't you think it's a little inappropriate to be talking about something like that at a time like this?"

"It's precisely because it's a time like this that I'm talking about it."

Our row consisted of three seats each meant for one person. I was sitting in the window seat, he had the middle seat, and the aisle seat was empty.

"Is this some kind of a come-on?"

"Not at all. I'm a married man . . . although my wife and I are not living together," he said, shrugging his shoulders a bit.

"As I was saying about Nostradamus, I had a lot of faith in his prophecies. I really believed that mankind would be wiped out in 1999. I thought I would die too."

"Same here," I said. "I learned about Nostradamus in junior high school. His prophecies scared me so much I couldn't sleep at night. They really made me believe that I would die, and that my parents would die. Until then, I'd thought of death as something that happened to other people. I thought about how I'd turn twenty-one in the year 1999."

The man lifted his shoulders and looked surprised. He had the body language of a quiz show host.

"So you're the same age as me. The same school year."

"Is that so? I made no plans for my life past the age of twenty-one."

"But it didn't end, did it? The world, I mean. Maybe it's an overreaction, but ever since that time, I feel like I've been given extra years to live," he said, sighing, his voice heavy with emotion. We were sitting in the very last row of the airplane. Through the rectangular window to my left I could see blue sky. Below us was a layer of fluffy clouds covering the land like a dense herd of sheep. It was a peaceful scene, much like I imagined heaven itself would look.

"This is getting a little tiring," the man said, smiling wanly. We were bent forward, hiding behind the seats in front of us. We sat shoulder to shoulder and kept our voices down. We looked like an elderly couple who couldn't stand up straight even if they wanted to.

"I suppose there's nothing we can do."

He nodded and pressed his face against the crack between two of the seats in front of us so he could peer through at the aisle, which was just barely possible due to the angle. As he did this, he said to me, "I've been thinking about this for a long time, long before I got on this plane. All the children who have been born since 1999 when Nostradamus's prediction failed to come true, I wonder what they think about death? I'm absolutely certain their attitude about death is different from yours or mine. Those of us who grew up before 1999 always had that prediction hanging over our heads like a curse, casting its shadow down upon us. Even children who didn't believe that the world was about to end must have had at least a little bit of doubt. But today's kids are different. They never think about what would happen if the world ended or if they themselves were to die."

"You think not?" I said. "Even without Nostradamus, there are plenty of other things to make young people think about death and disaster. Car crashes happen every day, environmental issues are becoming more serious. That's my thinking."

He glanced at me for no more than a second.

"I see your point. Maybe you're right." He pressed his face again against the gap between the seats and looked toward the front with a faint smile of self-deprecation on his face. The plane banked a bit, and at the same time we could hear the sound of a can rolling. This had been happening for some time now. Each time the plane dipped one way or the other, the can would roll back and forth.

"I never imagined, though, that I would die in a plane crash. Did you? Within the hour, this plane's going down somewhere, don't you think?"

"Yeah, it's frightening. There are still so many things I want to do. Dying in a plane crash . . . geez . . . I still can't believe it."

I shrugged my shoulders and raised my head a little bit so that I could just see over the top of the seat in front. The plane would have been packed if it were New Year's or Obon, but at this time of year only about half the seats on the plane were filled. In the aisle between the seats, the hijacker was still standing there with his gun in his hand.

The plane had been hijacked thirty minutes before, shortly after takeoff. It all started when a young guy who looked a little like a college student, sitting near the front of the plane, had stood up and taken something from the luggage rack. One of the cabin personnel approached him and asked him to sit down. He took what looked like a gun from his bag and jabbed it into her ribs.

He had said something incoherent, like, "Forget about it. Forget about it. About me. About me."

He wore a pilly, linty old sweater, and over it a stained white coat. His hair was naturally curly, and he had a single stray curl that stood up like an antenna. The hand gripping the gun was shaking. I have to say the gun looked more like a water pistol than the real thing.

"I can't forget about it. I'm doing my job," the flight attendant answered assertively, ignoring the gun barrel. Apparently she also thought the gun looked like a toy. The young man winced, and it looked like he was about to sit back down.

The flight attendant kept after him as if she had won. "Just what do you think you're doing anyway? The Fasten Seat Belt sign is still on. What do you think that means, that you can just stand up? And what about those clothes of yours? Why don't you take a look at a fashion magazine once in a while. You're a mess!"

All of the passengers were watching the flight attendant scold the young man, and they grinned at his foolishness. Embarrassed, he hung his head and looked at his clothes. Then he pointed the gun back at the cabin attendant and pulled the trigger. There was a single dry pop, and the young woman fell down in the aisle. At once, the expressions on all the passengers' faces changed to pallid stares. There was nothing they could do to help; they could only watch as the disheveled young man made his way up the aisle toward the cockpit.

As he went, he said, "No one move, please. If you move, I'll shoot you. I'm going to have a little conversation with the pilot now. I'm so sorry to have to do this to all of you."

He swung his head back and forth several times, and he had a strange, nervous way of walking. A man seated near the front of the plane stood up. He was a good-looking guy in a nice suit.

"Just hold on there, you!" he demanded in a deep, forceful voice. The young man stopped, looking a bit dazed.

"Wha . . . ?"

"This is no time to be fooling around. Scaring the stewardess with your firecrackers and then not a word of apology!"

"Say what you want, it doesn't matter," the young man responded. "That's a nice suit you're wearing. I bet you went to a good college, and then got a good job after graduation," he said, envy in his voice.

"You'd be right about that. I went to T University—that is, Tokyo University."

The young man raised his gun and shot the man. He faced the other passengers and asked if anyone else had gone to T University. No one raised their hand. The young man turned and disappeared into the cockpit. When he was gone, a commotion started up in the passenger cabin. After a while he returned and the cabin quieted down again.

"Everyone listen, please. I know you're all on your way home or to some vacation spot. I am sorry to have to tell you this, but I have changed the destination of this flight from Haneda Airport to the hallowed halls of T University."

He paused for a moment to let the meaning of his words sink in before continuing. "In about an hour and a half, we will crash into the buildings on campus. I am asking you to please die with me. Please. I have failed the entrance exam for the university five times now. There is nothing left for me to do but die."

The young man who looked like a college student was not really a college student at all. He was unemployed and desperate. We, the passengers on the plane, had become ensnared in his suicide plot.

When the next shot rang out, the man in the dull gray suit and I looked intently up the aisle. The young man stared, confused, at the body slumped over in front of him. "I asked you not to move! Why did you have to move?!"

He apologized to the passengers who had covered their ears
at the gun blast. Sensing an opportunity, several passengers tried
to get the gun away from the young man. They stood up from
their seats and attempted to jump him from behind. His restless
pacing, his nervous look and gestures all seemed to say, "Come
on, just try it!" It seemed like it would be an easy task to take
him down. Even I, who had little arm strength, was tempted to
try. There was just something about him that suggested he had
been picked on all his life.

Somehow, though, everyone who tried to grab him ended up
slipping on the empty can rolling around the cabin. Then the
young man shot them and they stopped moving.

The can rolled from one end of the cabin to the other. After
one person tripped on it, it would ricochet off to another spot
among the seats.

"That kid is really lucky," said the man next to me, still hiding behind the seat back. Nearly all the passengers were keeping
their heads low to avoid being hit by a stray bullet.

"Why is everybody stepping on the empty can? They must be
so intent on what they're doing they're not paying attention to
their feet."

I had no idea what the hijacker would say to us if he heard our
discussion. But I felt sure we would not draw his attention as long
as we kept our heads low, hidden in the shadow of the seat.

"I guess only things without feet don't get tripped up by empty
cans," the man remarked. "Like ghosts. Still, I can't believe this
guy is forcing us to accompany him on this suicide trip."

"You think this plane is really going down?"

"If this were fiction, some sort of action hero would show up
and take care of the situation."

"You mean, and save us?"

"Well, if this were the kind of dashed-off story that's simply
tagged on near the end of a short-story collection, it might not
have that kind of proper ending. I'm pretty sure we're all going
down. The buildings of T University will be made to taste a terrible fear."

The man pressed his index finger to his forehead and shook his head from side to side as if he were grieving. It was a theatrical gesture. I sighed. There was a reason for me getting on this plane, and it was not to get hijacked.

I hated the thought of dying in an airplane crash. From my earliest childhood I had dreamed that my life would end in a peaceful manner. If I saw a falling star, I wouldn't wish for a happy marriage or a fulfilling career. Instead I would wish to die in my sleep.

"I can't bear the thought of falling to my death. Isn't there anything we can do?"

"I know what you mean. The second we hit we'll be in incredible pain. Our bones will break, our insides will come flying out, we'll be consumed in flames. It'll be just awful."

"At the very least, I hope to die quickly . . ."

"Well, that's an easy one!" he said enthusiastically, his voice kept low lest the hijacker overhear us. "Wanting to die quickly is not a very tall order. Who knows what'll happen? If he screws up we might all be fine, or we might end up suffering for hours with branches stuck through our guts."

I had a sudden vision of myself writhing in agony, nauseated, my armpits stained with sweat.

"If it is at all within my power, I wish to die a peaceful death."

Hearing my desperate murmurings, he tapped his fingers so that the young man could not hear.

"Those are the words I was waiting to hear," he said.

I moved a little away from him.

"What are you talking about? Drumming your fingers like nothing's happening! Even uncommon sense has its limits."

"Pardon. I haven't told you yet, have I? I'm a salesman."

He pulled something from his suit pocket and brought his face closer to mine.

"Have a look at this."

In his outstretched hand he held a small hypodermic needle containing a transparent fluid.

"One shot of this and a person will die a painless death. This is my last dose. Would you like it? Will you buy it?"

Someone else got up from their seat and tried to take the gun away from the young man, and then we heard the sound of the rolling can and the gun firing in the plane.

2.

"You're saying this syringe contains a euthanasia drug?"

"Exactly. If you take this injection before the plane crashes, you will be able to die without fear, without feeling anything. This is the perfect product for this occasion. But if you're going to buy it, you'll have to be quick about it."

"Why is that?"

"Because it takes about thirty minutes for the drug to work. Assuming this plane is going to crash in about one hour, you have about a half hour to decide whether you want to buy the drug and then inject yourself with it. Otherwise, before the drug has a chance to do its work and send you on a trip to the next world, you'll find yourself paying a visit to T University. So don't waste any time making up your mind."

"Who are you, the grim reaper or something?"

"I'm just an ordinary salesman. You probably think it's strange that I just happen to have a euthanasia drug. Well, I don't mind telling you now. I'd been planning to use this to kill myself."

As he returned the hypodermic needle to his suit pocket, he got a far-off look in his eye and began to tell his story.

"Ever since I was a child, it was always my dream to be a salesman. Not the usual dream, is it? My teachers told me that too. What's the attraction, you might want to know, and all I can say is that it's talking to people, selling them products, the little bit of haggling."

"So your dream came true, and you became a salesman."

The man nodded, but his expression was none too cheerful.

"But the truth is, I had no great talent for it. I've been a salesman for ten years now, and I don't seem to be getting any better at it. Even people who got their start after me are doing better. My position in the company is lower than a new hire fresh out of school. My wife even gave up on me. She ran away and is living with her parents in Tokyo."

"So you felt like your life was falling apart, and you decided to commit suicide?"

He nodded.

"I went to an acquaintance of mine who understands these things, a doctor, and I paid him a lot of money to get this euthanasia drug."

"What kind of awful doctor would do a thing like that?"

"A very old and slightly senile one. Once I had the drug, I boarded this plane and set off for the place I wanted to die."

"Your plan was to travel somewhere and inject yourself?"

"Yes. I planned to kill myself on my in-laws' front steps out of spite. I can see my wife leaving the house and tripping over my dead body. That would really give her a shock. And it would cause her all sorts of problems. The neighbors would never look at her the same way again, you can bet that."

"That's horrible!"

"Spare me your criticism. Now, of course, that plan is out the window. Because of the hijacking, I mean. The only thing left now is this hypodermic needle in my suit pocket. So how about it, you want to buy it? My last wish as a salesman is to be able to sell somebody something. Won't you buy this syringe from me, so I can have some sense of satisfaction in these final moments of my life?" he said, with sad eyes, like those of a dog that's gotten soaked in the rain.

I thought for a minute. It didn't seem like such a bad idea. "But that drug, it must be very expensive. How much?"

"How much do you have in your purse?"

Taking care not to raise my head above the seat, I pulled my wallet from my handbag. I opened it and showed him what I had.

"Three ten thousand-yen notes and some change. You have a bank card, I see. How much is in your account?"

"About three million yen."

"So all together that would be about three million thirty thousand yen."

"That's too expensive. That's everything I have."

"Well you can't take it with you if you die. How about it? Just hand over your bank card. And your PIN number too, of course."

"Hang on a minute. I get it. You and the hijacker are a team. Your scheme is to hijack the plane so that you can sell this euthanasia drug for all the money you can get."

The salesman snorted. "You think for the sake of a fraud like that I would commit murder?" He was pointing with his chin at the cabin attendant who still lay fallen in the aisle.

"All right. I believe you. But still I think everything I have is too high a price to pay for one hypodermic needle. I'll give you ten thousand yen. I think even that's too expensive."

The truth was, I really wanted it. If I was going to die anyway, what was money to me but scraps of paper? As soon as I gave him the bank card he was going to die anyway without being able to withdraw the money. Like me he was in an airplane that was about to fall out of the sky. There was no way of escaping our fate. But I was stubborn.

"You're out of your mind. Three million thirty thousand yen! That's too much!"

"You're haggling about price at a time like this? If I sell you this for ten thousand yen, my soul will not be able to rise again in the next life!"

"I don't know a thing about your soul," I said, "but my whole life has been about getting people to cut prices for me. Day after day, I go to the vegetable stand or the fish market, and my sole pleasure is to get people to cut prices, cut prices, cut prices. I'd tell them there was a wormhole in the cabbage, or that the fish fillet was a little light. I would make up any old flaw to get something a little cheaper. That was the only time in the whole day that I would genuinely interact with other people."

"What a sad life. Don't you ever talk to people at work?"

"No, I don't. I work part-time in a manga cafe. If someone spoke to me I would ignore them. I'm just the sort of person who is always afraid of other people. That's why I never got married, and I still live alone."

"What a waste. Perhaps I shouldn't be saying this, but you're not bad-looking. You have nice features . . ."

"I know."

"I knew I shouldn't have said anything."

"But I suffered some trauma that made me completely terrified of other people. Men in particular. A long time ago a man did some nasty things to me."

"Nasty things . . . ?"

"That's right. The kinds of things people think twice about writing down and putting in books."

He was clearly anxious to hear more about this, so in a very low voice I told him about what had happened when I was in high school. I could still clearly remember the name and the face of the man who had scarred both my heart and my body.

The salesman listened intently, sweat beading on his brow, holding his hands to his mouth as if he were about to be sick. His eyes turned red, and he looked like he might cry.

"Oh, that's terrible. It sounds like one of those true-life mystery novels where the criminal was a young woman whose motive for her crimes was the fact that she had been brutally raped in the past."

"You see?" I said. "The truth is, just a few days ago I discovered the address of the man who did those things to me. I hired a private investigator who lives in Tokyo."

"Why in the world would you want to find him?"

"Isn't it obvious? Revenge! According to the investigator, he has a wife and child now. Who would be able to stand idly by while he enjoyed a happy life? That's why I got on this plane. I want to get off this plane at Haneda Airport, go to his house, and hurt his children right in front of him."

"And you called me horrible! What about you?"

"Leave me alone. Leave me out of this."

Once again we heard the rolling of the empty can, and the sound of gunfire rang through the plane. We didn't bother looking this time. It was pretty clear that once again someone had stood up and tried to jump the young man and slipped on the can and gotten shot.

"All that aside, ten thousand yen is just not enough. Although I hesitate to even suggest such a thing to someone like you, whose only pleasure in life is bargaining for lower prices."

"Listen. This could be it for us. I can't be so worried about getting a good deal. How much did you pay that doctor anyway?"

"For this one hypodermic, I paid the doctor three million. That stupid doctor. This stuff is completely illegal for ordinary people to use. It was expensive. But even at that, it was exactly the same amount as you have in your bank account. A perfectly balanced transaction."

"I don't know if I trust you. How do I know you bought this stuff for three million yen or if you just made that up."

I looked at the salesman's eyes, trying to figure out whether he was lying. He quickly averted them.

"The higher the original price, the better, right?" he said quietly, annoyed, still not making eye contact.

I wondered what the value of that euthanasia drug he had might be right now. I bet the more afraid a person was of dying in an airplane crash, the more they would be willing to pay. But was that the only thing determining the value of that drug?

"Tell me, why don't you use the drug yourself?"

"Surely you of all people can understand. I want the satisfaction of having sold someone something in the very last moments of my life."

As I pondered this, I raised my head above the top of the seat to get another look at the young man with the gun. He was standing in the middle of the aisle, clumsily reloading his weapon. Two men, pumped up with a sense of heroics, took the opportunity to try to jump him. But as luck would have it, the first one slipped on the empty can, and the second one stumbled over him. We heard two shots, and then all was quiet again.

"I get it. This isn't a business negotiation; it's simply gambling."

I turned back to look at the salesman. His face showed shock.

"You said it would take thirty minutes from the time of the injection to the time of death, and that I should make up my mind quickly. If I am to escape death by crashing, I have to inject myself before the plane actually starts to fall. Here's the rub. What if after I take the drug the young man with the gun is captured and the plane lands safely at Haneda Airport?"

I looked at the salesman in the seat beside me keeping his head low. He nervously cleared his throat.

I continued. "In that case, having taken the injection, I would simply die in peace, never knowing that the plane had not crashed. I would never know I had purchased a product for which I had no need. And you, having survived, would get off the plane and go directly to my bank and drain everything from my account. It would be a sweet deal for you. If we assume you actually paid the doctor one hundred yen for this shot, your profit would be two million nine hundred ninety-nine thousand nine hundred yen."

"Well, I must admit that is one possibility," said the salesman. "Though I hadn't really thought of it that way until you pointed it out."

"You're a bad liar."

"Well, yeah, like you say, there's certainly a possibility that this plane won't crash. Look at that guy and the clumsy way he's handling that gun. He looks like he might just shoot his own foot off. But so far luck's been on his side. Nobody has been able to bring him down, and he's still in control. If things continue the same way, I have no doubt that we'll crash into the buildings of T University within the hour."

"Whatever. I think you're just saying that so you can sell that drug. In your heart of hearts, I think you're betting that someone's going to be able to take that kid down."

"Well, I wouldn't know about that."

On his lips was the trace of a smile, like a cunning fox.

"I might bet that way if I thought it was to my advantage," he said. "But now it's clear how you might decide whether or not to buy the medicine: if you think that nothing will deter that young man from carrying out his desire to kill himself, then you should buy the drug. If you're going to die anyway, it's better to die a peaceful death rather than a violent death. If on the other hand you think he doesn't really have what it takes and that his effort will fail, then you shouldn't buy the drug. It would be foolish to die even a peaceful death if the plane weren't going to crash."

"You're just saying that to antagonize me. This is a bad deal all around."

I looked out the window. As before, all I could see was blue and white.

"This is interesting. I think I'll watch him awhile before making my decision. Shall we talk a little bit more about the price?"

"We've already discussed whether or not to cut the price, but I don't really see what the problem is. It's simply a matter of you telling me your PIN number."

As soon as he said that, I realized that once I was dead, he would be free to search through my luggage for whatever he wanted. I would lose the thirty thousand yen for sure. Giving him my PIN was the key factor in determining his take. In other words, he stood to make either thirty thousand or three million yen.

"Tell me, your PIN wouldn't happen to be your birthday, would it?"

"And if it is, would that be so awful?"

He shrugged both his shoulders and looked surprised.

"You know, it'll be easy for me to find out your birthday by looking at your driver's license. So in effect you've already set the price at three million thirty thousand."

"You win. My life will be over anyway."

Seeing my smile as I said this, he smiled too.

"Say, you two," said a voice from above. "You seem to be having a nice time down there."

"Hang on a minute, will you?" said the salesman. "We're having an important business discussion, and we're just about to wrap things up." He lifted his head and saw who it was that had addressed us. His voice came out like a strangled duck.

"Oh! I'm sorry . . ."

"Not at all. I'm sorry for having disturbed you. Please continue your business discussion."

The person who was speaking to us was the hijacker himself. He stood in the aisle, his gun gripped tightly in his hand. I couldn't take my eyes off it.

A big man from a nearby seat approached the hijacker. He looked like he might have been a judo instructor. The salesman and I stiffened and prepared ourselves for the battle between the judo expert and the weakling with the gun. But, as we should have guessed, the judo fighter slipped on that damn can. He cracked his head on the corner of a seat and collapsed. The young man chopped him in the neck and checked to make sure he was dead.

3.

"I've been keeping an eye on you two," said the young man, sitting down in the empty seat in our row. From right to left it was me next to the window, the salesman in the middle, and the hijacker in the aisle seat. About forty-five minutes had passed since the hijacking started.

"You've been hiding behind the seats and talking about something. I can only speculate that you've been cooking up some plan to spring out at me and try to get the gun. Or maybe you were talking about my cowlick, or my clothes, or what nicknames I had in school, and you were laughing at me. That's what I thought at first. But then I realized . . . how should I put this . . . you two are behaving very differently from the other passengers."

"Is that so?" I asked, leaning forward so I could get a better look at the young man. "What do you mean?" The salesman pressed himself back into the seat so that I would get a clear view. The hijacker seemed a bit embarrassed and stroked his hair with his free hand. Once his hand had passed over his cowlick, though, it always sprang up again, just like an antenna.

"All the other passengers are practically paralyzed with fear, even the people who are trying to be heroes. Some people are sobbing uncontrollably, and others are white as ghosts. But the two of you look like you're sitting in your living room having a pleasant conversation. Aren't you afraid of my gun and me? Or are you not afraid because I don't look like someone who could pull off a stunt like this? Are you thinking that someone who couldn't get into T University shouldn't even try to hijack a plane?"

"Not at all," the salesman began. "We are plenty afraid. For example, that—"

"—I mean, your words and actions suggest you have a complex about all kinds of things, so that makes you seem a little unbalanced, and that's scary enough," I finished.

"Complex? I wouldn't go that far. But I do always feel like people are laughing at me. Dogs that pass me on the street, high school girls on TV shows—I feel like everybody knows I failed my college entrance exams, and they're secretly laughing at me."

"Ha ha . . ." the salesman said, looking at me in a way that suggested he thought this kid was truly dangerous. "You're just too sensitive," he added in an artificially kind voice.

I looked around. Everyone on the plane looked sick with fear. No one was directly looking back at us, but clearly everyone was worried about what was going on. The people sitting closest to us seemed to be straining to hear our conversation. I turned again to the young man and said, "If we don't seem to be as worked up as the other passengers, it may be because we don't have as much to lose."

The young man tilted his head in a way that suggested he wanted to hear more.

"Yes, I'm terrified of dying in a plane crash, but compared with everyone else, it may be that we two are just better prepared to accept our fate."

I pointed at the salesman and explained that he already intended to commit suicide himself. For my part, I told him, a man had abused me when I was in high school, and I was on my way to exact my revenge. The young man pressed his hand to his mouth just as the salesman had before him.

"Ever since that time, I haven't been able to trust men."

The young man's eyes reddened a bit, and he stared at my face. Several times he looked about to speak, then hesitated, before he finally managed to say, "The man who did those terrible things to you, do you wish you could kill him?"

"I suppose. I do hope he dies an excruciating death. I don't know how else I'll get over it. Anyway, that's why this salesman here and I are somewhat removed from the whole idea of happiness. Even if we do find ourselves faced with an unhappy reality, like being forced to die in a plane crash, our only feeling is, well, such is life."

"So that's why you've been able to sit here talking calmly," the young man said.

He sat thinking in silence for a while and then, head hung low, said, "You're strong. Terrible things happened to you, but you kept going. You plotted your revenge, and you've been able to go on living."

"But it looks like now I'm about to die."

When I said this the salesman next to me said, "Ha ha ha, good one."

I leaned forward some more and looked into the young man's

eyes. This took him a little by surprise and he recoiled a bit.

"Tell me, what are your feelings now—now that you've hijacked an airplane full of innocent people?"

"Don't ask him that!" the salesman said, pushing me roughly back into my seat.

"Wait a minute, this is important. The question of how badly he wants to do this speaks directly to my decision about whether or not to buy the drug."

"Ah yes, I see. You have a point," the salesman said, nodding.

"Drug? What are you talking about?" the young man asked. The salesman and I exchanged glances, wondering whether we should tell him about the euthanasia drug. In the end we told him everything, about the hypodermic, about the plan that I might buy it, and about what the salesman stood to earn if the hijacking failed.

"So, you're agonizing about whether or not you should buy the hypodermic?" asked the hijacker. I nodded. The salesman cleared his throat several times, and then he asked the young man, "What do you think? How much are you into this shooting business? I mean, it's one thing to commit suicide, but why do you want to drag all of us into it?"

The expression on the young man's face was firm as he returned the salesman's gaze. The salesman shrank back a little at the look in his eyes.

"Everything was already unbearable," he said.

"My mother brought me up to believe I had no choice but to go to T University. Any other life was unthinkable. My mother said anybody who couldn't get into T University was subhuman. Getting into T University became my sole purpose in life."

"What about after graduation?" the salesman asked.

"What are you talking about? That didn't even enter my head. All I was concerned about was being admitted to that fucking university. Nothing else mattered at all. That was why I stayed

home at night and studied. While everybody else was playing
games or hanging out with girls, all I ever did was study."
"What did you do when you weren't studying?" I asked.
"I made pickles."
The salesman and I exchanged glances.
"My hobby was making Japanese pickles," he said. "There's
more to it than you think." He went on about the right way to
cut the vegetables, the kind of crunch they had, the variations in
pickling times, the amount of salt needed, and things like that.
As he talked about this, his face was open and cheerful.
"When I was alone and the house was dark and quiet, making
pickles was comforting to me. I started when I was in primary
school . . ."
In a low voice the salesman said to me, "Sounds like this guy
has been off his rocker ever since elementary school. Don't you
think?"
"Everybody at school thought this was funny. They said my
clothes were old-fashioned. I was too scared to go buy new ones.
I thought the clerks in the store would laugh at me. I was too
weird to be fashionable, right? I just wore whatever clothes my
mother bought for me. The only things I ever bought for myself
were notebooks and writing implements. When other kids were
saving their money to buy CDs, I was using my allowance to
buy a fountain pen. All I ever did was study, so nobody at school
wanted to play with me. They all secretly called me 'Stinky,' but
I took a bath every day!"
"Not a very original nickname," I said, though I noticed he
did smell vaguely of pickles.
"My mother and all my relatives were so sure I would get into
T University. But I couldn't."
"Why not?"
"They didn't let me in."
"But I mean, why not? Did you have a cold every year on the
day of the exam or anything like that?"
"No."

"Were you helping some lost kid and that made you late?" asked the salesman. "Were you saving a drowning child? Were you holding the hand of some child dying of a brain tumor?" The young man just kept sadly shaking his head from side to side.

"I can't understand it either. I didn't get it, so I asked my teachers why I wasn't making the grade. And they told me I just wasn't good enough to be admitted to T University, no matter how hard I tried. I should give up, they said."

He just wasn't smart enough. No one in the plane said a word, but the thought was on everyone's face. The young man himself said, "It just isn't fair." He started crying silently.

"My mother, my relatives, they all looked down on me. Can you understand how I felt? How can I put this? When people first told me I would never get into T University I didn't believe them. But this year, when I failed the entrance exam for the fifth time, I finally came to accept that I would never make it. So what am I supposed to do? What about the twenty-three years I've lived for this? Everything my mother taught me about life depended on my getting into T University. Now I'm just pitiful. Pitiful. Wherever I go, I feel like everyone's laughing at me."

He hung his head and leaned forward in the seat. With the hand that was not holding the gun he covered his face.

"Ah, it's horrible," he groaned. His voice was low, with a resonance that could peel paint. Because his hand was over his face, I could not see his expression, but I could hear him muttering.

"I can hear them laughing. I can hear my classmates' voices. Everyone is laughing at me . . . My cowlick . . . The fact that I've never even held hands with a girl . . . In their hearts, everyone is laughing at me. Ah . . . I can't . . . Leave me alone . . . Leave me alone . . . Ah . . . I can't . . . I want to go around killing everyone in the whole world . . . It's no good . . . Somebody help me please . . . I can't bear it, I can't bear it any longer. There's no way out . . ."

Now would have been a good time to catch him off guard and grab his gun. But nobody did. He was so pathetic and his behavior so odd that no one thought about attacking him. The darkness in his heart came out in the words he spoke; the pain in his voice was piercing.

"Hatred . . . hatred . . . the emotion I feel toward everyone, that is its name. Everyone is . . . unbearable. I want to kill you . . . I want you to taste my desperation, my hopelessness . . . Everyone in the entire world . . ."

The young man finally removed his hand from his face. His face was blank, but I thought I saw a flicker of heat coming out of his eyes.

"But it would be impossible to kill everyone in the world. That's why hijacking this airplane made sense to me. Actions at this level are manageable by an individual acting alone. The passengers on the plane, the people in the buildings of T University where the plane will crash, will die for no reason. And then this dreadful news will be broadcast around the world. That is my hope. Just a short while ago, I started selling my homemade pickles over the Internet. Sales were terrific. They were flying out the door. In just one year, I made three million yen."

"That's more than I make," the salesman said.

"But my goal in life was to go to T University. It was not a matter of money. I used the money I made to buy this gun."

"From whom?"

"Some vendor who lived in a back alley. He spoke broken Japanese. He might have been Chinese."

I wondered if that Chinese person really existed, but I said nothing.

"I bought the gun and ammunition from him, and then I got on this plane."

"How were you able to bring the gun onto the plane? What about security?"

"I slapped him on the cheek with a wad of bills, and he waved me right through with a very cheerful expression on his face."

"Really . . ."

The power of money is a terrible thing.

"And that's how we got to where we are right now."

The young man checked his watch.

"Wow, look at the time. Thirty-five minutes until we reach T University."

He looked directly at me.

"I am going to crash this plane. If I don't, I don't know how I'll ever get over it. All the unhappiness I have caused people . . . I need to show the people of this world how absolutely, overwhelmingly meaningless death is."

All traces of awkwardness and nerves had left the young man. His eyes blazed with a terrible resolve. He was hell-bent on his mission of death. I made my decision and turned to the salesman.

"I will buy the medicine. I'm gambling that this plane is going down, and I want to die a peaceful death, the sooner the better."

4.

"Are you sure?" the salesman asked.

"I don't care anymore." I looked around the cabin, at the people and the bodies slumped in the aisle.

"Just now when I looked in his eyes, I felt something profound. And in my heart I made up my mind. I'm certain that this plane is going to crash and everyone in it is already in hell."

"What the . . . ? She's lost it," said the salesman to himself.

"I'll buy the drug. I won't change my mind."

I handed my wallet over to him. I had no regrets about giving up my cash or my bank card.

The salesman took the hypodermic needle from his suit pocket. The narrow glass tube contained a clear fluid. The eyes of all— myself, the young man, and all the people in all the seats on both sides of the aisle—were focused on this object.

"All the death that is needed to end the life of a single human being is dissolved in the clear liquid in that small syringe?" asked the hijacker.

"A sweet, painless death," the salesman said as he handed me the syringe. I took it carefully in both hands to be sure I wouldn't drop it. Even as the needle rested in my hands, I could hardly feel that it had any weight at all. I held it level with my eyes and looked through the clear fluid at the world beyond, distorted by the curvature of the glass syringe, like pulled taffy. The syringe held the gaze of the people around us. Some were even getting up out of their seats to get a better view.

"Being the center of attention like this is going to make it hard to die."

At this some of the still living passengers coughed and looked the other way.

"You can't waste any time. They say it takes thirty minutes for the drug to work."

I rolled up my left sleeve to the elbow.

"I've never injected myself with anything before. What do I have to do?"

"Just do it. The doctor said no matter how you inject yourself you'll die."

The salesman's words boosted my confidence, and with my fingers I removed the cover from the needle. The long silvery needle came in contact with the air. I gazed at the point for a while, and then I looked at the young man.

"I'm betting that you are serious about crashing this airplane. I am counting on you to do your best to plunge everyone here into the depths of terror."

The young man nodded vigorously.

"Your peaceful death will not be in vain."

"This has been the most gruesome conversation . . ."

I ignored the salesman's interjection. I pressed the syringe and a few drops of liquid squirted out. I touched the tip of the needle to the inside of my left arm and pushed. The point pierced my skin and caused a twinge of pain. As I pressed on the plunger I could feel a cold sensation spreading down my arm.

When nothing was left in the hypodermic, I removed the needle from my arm and returned the empty syringe to the salesman. I rolled my sleeve back down, closed my eyes, and said, "That's that." A deep darkness spread out before me.

"Look at that. After the first spasm she's not moving at all . . ."

"I lied when I said it takes thirty minutes to work. The truth is it works right away. That's what the doctor said."

"Why did you lie about a thing like that?"

"I didn't want her taking too long making up her mind. I mean, if you were captured, that would be too late to make a deal, wouldn't it?"

"I see your point. So does that mean you're still hoping that I'm going to be caught?"

"That would be in my best interest, don't you think? If that happened, I'd be able to go to the bank and withdraw her life savings. The truth is, I got that drug from the doctor for practically nothing. So it's pure profit. I might take the money and start a new life, or I might just have a good time for a while and then think again about whether to kill myself . . . Ah, a whole new life. Did you never think you might like to just make a complete change and restart your life all over again?"

"No. My hatred was always too strong for me to think of anything so positive. It's hard to think of starting a new life if you think of yourself as already dead . . . Too hard for me at least . . . But I have a favor I'd like to ask you. Not just you, but everyone who can hear my voice right now. I would like you all to stand up and move toward the front of the plane. Some seats were empty from the beginning, and some no longer have occupants, so about half the seats are empty. I'd like you all to sit in a tighter group, to make it easier for me to keep an eye on you."

"No problem. Let's all change seats. But if we're all bunched up at the front of the plane, won't that throw off the balance and make it crash?"

"We're going to crash anyway, so I'm not worried about that."

"I see. What about her?"

"Leave her here. And the people lying in the aisle. Just all of you who are still alive, please move forward. This is an order. Or do you not want to take orders from someone who couldn't get into T University?"

I was dead, but when I opened my eyes I had a good stretch. I moved my head around and massaged my neck and looked out the window. I was still sitting in the same seat. It seemed I had become a ghost but was still on the plane.

I glanced beside me, but the salesman was no longer there, and neither was the hijacker. I recalled their conversation that I could hear in the darkness just before I died. The young man was ordering everyone toward the front of the plane.

I, now a ghost, stood up and looked over the top of the seat in front of me. There, densely packed in the front half of the plane, were all the passengers, their backs to me. From about the middle of the plane to the very back, where I was, the seats were empty.

The back half of the plane was empty of living passengers, but there were still dead people cluttering the aisle where they had fallen. The front half of the plane was the land of the living. The back half of the plane was the land of the dead.

I spotted that distinctive cowlick up ahead. The young man had taken a seat in the rear half of the plane. As the only living person sitting in the land of the dead, he looked lonely.

No one spoke. The engine noise was the only sound to be heard. Quietly I walked up the aisle toward the young man's seat. I stepped over the people lying in the aisle. I picked my steps carefully so as not to stumble on the rolling can when it skittered near my feet. I came up behind the young man and put my hand on the back of his seat. I looked straight down at his cowlicked head. He was staring intently ahead so as not to miss a thing. I could feel the intensity radiating from him.

With my fingertips, I plucked at his antenna-like cowlick. I realized it was true what they say about ghosts, that they can touch whatever they want, from any angle they want, and no one will notice. I realized I was going to like being a ghost, able to bang away at any old man's baldpate to my heart's content. Gazing around the cabin like an eagle hunting its prey, I found the bald one I was looking for. Without lingering a moment, I went off to rub it.

Just then, the young men stretched his spine and placed his gun on the seat beside him. Casually I picked it up to see what it felt like. It was surprisingly heavy. It seemed so hard and real—like I was really gripping a piece of metal. I was impressed to discover that ghosts could actually pick up material objects. I struck a few action poses.

"Huh? What's going on?" the young man burst out in a perplexed voice. Having finished his stretching, he had turned back to look in my direction as I pretended to be a female police officer. I was surprised that he was looking straight at me.

"You can see me? You can see a ghost?"

All the heads assembled in front of us swiveled around. One person stood up. It was the salesman. He opened his mouth wide and yelled, "Why are you still alive?" I stopped pretending to be a policewoman and said, "Gee, I thought I was dead . . ."

"Well, it sure looks like you're not! Take a good look at yourself! You've got feet for goodness' sake!"

I looked down at my own two feet, verifying that they were there. I was indeed still alive, just as the salesman said. I had injected myself, but I failed to die. I turned the gun on the salesman.

"You tricked me! That was no euthanasia drug!"

The salesman slumped down in his seat to get out of the line of fire. The people sitting in his row started screaming and trying to get away from him. This caused a great commotion in the cabin.

"Hang on a minute! I don't know what's going on here either," he blurted out, just his head protruding from above the seat back. After a moment's pause he took a big gulp.

"That sneak of a doctor! He tricked me and sold me a placebo!"

I kept the gun trained on him and put my finger on the trigger.

"Forget about that! What are you going to do for me now? I didn't get my peaceful death, and now I'm going to crash in this plane with the rest of you."

Still using the seat back as a shield, the salesman shook his head violently back and forth.

"Wait! Wait! Calm down. Do you realize what it is you have in your hand?"

"Don't be stupid!"

"If you know what it is, why are you pointing it at me? You should be aiming at someone else, shouldn't you?" The salesman pointed at the young man beside me. "Point the gun at him and tell him to surrender!"

I looked again at the young man. He was rising from his seat and glaring at me.

"Why should I tell him to surrender? I was betting he was going to crash the plane!"

"You're an idiot!"

The other passengers started booing. I started to think more clearly and finally understood their reasoning. The fact that I had relieved the young man of his weapon meant the plane no longer had to crash.

I took the gun off the salesman and aimed it at the young man. The salesman was visibly relieved.

I apologized to the young man. "Sorry. Not long ago I was on your side."

He simply shook his head, showing no sign of even noticing the gun aimed at him.

"No worries," he said, shrugging his shoulders and putting his right hand in his jacket pocket. "I have another gun right here."

The tension in the cabin heightened to a fever pitch. None of the passengers moved or uttered a peep. Only the young man's expression seemed to suggest he was on top of things. Keeping his hand between his jacket and his sweater, he looked me straight in the eye.

"I have a gun in the inside pocket of my coat. Now I'm going to draw that gun with my right hand and shoot you."

I could not get a clear view of his right hand. "Don't move," I said. "Leave your right hand right where it is."

"If you don't want to get shot yourself, you'll have to shoot first," he said with a calm smile. He spoke again.

"One winter's night I was studying, and before I knew it, the sky began to grow light. I opened the window, and the chilly night air filled the stuffy room. I could see my breath turn white. As morning came I could see the landscape touched with frost, sparkling. I was very happy, because I had really studied with all my might. I loved that morning. Now I've killed a lot of people, and I will never again be allowed to see such a beautiful scene."

So saying, he pulled his right hand from inside his jacket and pointed it at me. Without hesitation, I pulled the trigger. In the palm of my hand I felt the recoil, as if a heavy ball had struck me. A wind struck my cheek, as if the air itself had exploded. All the people in the plane crouched down. The young man collapsed in the aisle. The only thing in his right hand was a fountain pen.

5.

As the sky colored from late afternoon into twilight, I sat in his house with his child on my lap, watching television. His child was a girl, kindergarten age. She was alone in the house. She showed no shyness of strangers and took to me right away. She sat in my lap, and we watched the TV news. A short while later she fell asleep.

On the TV, which stood in the corner of the room, was the news of the hijacking incident that had started around midday. Images flickered rapidly from one to the next: the airplane just after it touched down; the passengers disembarking from the plane and being led away; the police entering the aircraft; and more. I caught a glimpse among the passengers leaving the plane of the salesman, and of my own face.

"That was the worst flight ever," I remember the salesman saying just after he left the plane. He stomped both his feet, confirming for himself that there was solid ground beneath him once again. "I hope I don't have to contemplate death again for a long time."

I was taken in an ambulance to a hospital. Because I had injected myself in the arm with an unknown fluid, I had to be examined. Other passengers besides myself were also taken by ambulance to the hospital, mostly because they had lost consciousness at some point.

I must be dreaming, I thought to myself as his little girl, asleep in my lap, moved. Her sleeping face pressed against my chest, she looked happy. His apartment was on the third floor of a condominium building. The windows faced south, making the rooms very sunny. A vase of flowers stood next to the window, and as I looked at it I could hear the sound of the front door opening.

"I'm home." It was a man's voice that I hadn't heard since high school but that I still remembered clearly. I heard his footsteps in the hall, and then the door to the living room opened. He stopped on the threshold and saw me sitting on the floor with his daughter on my lap. Our eyes met. His face had not changed much from what I remembered. I will leave out the details of the terrible things he did to me so long ago, but the scars were still clearly there, in my heart and on my body.

"Welcome home," I said. For a moment he looked at me with suspicion, but it didn't take him long to remember me, and he took a step backward.

"What are you doing here . . ."

"I tracked you down," I said, picking up the knife that lay beside me. "Getting here was quite an adventure though. My plane was hijacked, shots were fired . . ."

"Where is my wife . . ." he asked and stopped in his tracks

when he saw the knife in my hand.

"Shopping, it seems. She left your daughter here alone." I held the blade of the knife to the sleeping girl's neck. Just at that moment, my name was spoken on the television. I turned to look at the screen and saw a close-up shot of my own face. The news announcer was saying that I was one of the rescued passengers and had been taken to the hospital, but that now I had gone missing. I remembered that the police had waited outside my hospital room to ask me some questions. I said I had to go to the toilet, and I made my way straight out of the hospital. He compared the image of me on the TV with the me he saw before him holding the knife.

"What are you planning to do?"

"Surprising developments, followed by unjustifiable unhappiness. Did you ever suspect something like this might be happening to you?"

"Please. Let my daughter go." Kneeling on the floor, he apologized tearfully for the terrible things he and his pals had done to me in high school. In the whole room, the only sound to be heard was his sobbing voice. Then, the front door opened and his wife entered the apartment. Carrying her shopping bags, she came walking down the hall to the living room, where she stopped at the door. She saw her husband kneeling and me with the knife, and I could tell she did not understand what was happening. The girl's sleeping face still rested against my chest. For a long time no one said anything, and no one moved. With the knife pressed to the girl's neck, I continued to watch the news.

Finally on the screen appeared the face of the young man. The newscaster told the story of his crimes, how he had hijacked the plane, killing passengers and cabin attendants. I remembered what he said to me before I shot him and he died, the story of the beautiful morning, covered in frost. I took the knife away from the girl's neck.

"I can't kill two people in the same day."

I removed the girl from my lap and headed for the front door.

As I walked through the living room door, I passed the man and his wife. He did not turn to watch me leave, but his wife followed me with confusion in her eyes.

I left his apartment and left the building. The sun was setting and the sky was red. I ran, bumping into people along the way. I didn't know where I was headed, but I knew I had to run.

THE WHITE HOUSE
IN THE COLD FOREST

1.

I used to live in the stable. Not in the house. In the stable were three horses. They used to shit all over the place.

"If it weren't for you, we could fit another horse in there," said my aunt, very annoyed.

The lower halves of the stable walls were made of stones, piled on top of one another. The top halves of the walls were made of wooden boards. The stones were not cut into square blocks. The still-round stones had been piled randomly and stuck together with mortar. I always slept facing the stones. If I didn't curl up in a corner of the stable, the horses would have trampled me. I used to count the stones that were right in front of my face. The stones were different shapes, but they all looked like human faces. Or arms. Or heels. Or breasts. Or the nape of a neck.

The stench of horseshit was overpowering and constant. But the barn was the only home I had. Winter nights were cold. I slept beneath a pile of straw, but that was not enough to stop me from trembling.

It was my job to muck out the stable. It was a never-ending chore. At the back of the stable was a huge pile of manure, and I would pile more horseshit on top of it every day. Heaping double handfuls of shit. I also carted the manure to the fields. I did as my uncle told me. My uncle never came close to the stable. He held his nose and barked orders.

There were three kids in my aunt's house—a couple of boys and one girl. The two boys often came to the barn to play. The older one would hit me with a stick. The younger one would try to hold back his laughter. Before long, however, there would be blood.

The worst was when they tied me to a horse with a rope. I was trampled pretty severely when the horse bolted from its stall. My face would never look the same again. The brothers got all worked up about it and ran away. Afterward they pretended not to know anything about it.

I was missing a chunk of flesh from my face. I scooped up the red fleshy pulp and walked out of the stable. I went up to the main house to ask my aunt for help. It was light outside. A fresh breeze blew away any whiff of horseshit that might have been in the air. The lawn was a sea of green. My face dripped as I walked.

My aunt kept chickens and dogs at her house, and they were lying restfully in the yard. I knocked on the door of the house, but I said nothing. Whatever it was that had fallen from my face, I gripped it tightly in my hand.

My aunt opened the door and stepped out. She screamed. She didn't want me anywhere near her home.

"I have guests now," she said. "Stay in the stable. If they see you, they'll surely be disgusted."

She shooed me back to the stable. Night fell. I bathed my wound in the horses' drinking water. I was not permitted to use the clean water from the well. I blacked out repeatedly and I slept.

My cousins avoided the stable because they were afraid. I nibbled on horse fodder to stave off starvation.

My aunt, who brought me daily table scraps, looked at me with revulsion. "What? Are you still alive? You must really be made of tough stuff."

I passed a whole month trying to make sure my face never

touched anything. The pain endured for half a year. I saved the piece of my face, but it rotted in time. It turned black and smelly. I kept it right by my side for a long time. The walls of the stable were made of stones. The stones looked like faces. Sometimes, I indulged my imagination by sticking the piece of my face onto one of the stones. My own face retained its gouged form as it firmed back into shape. Eventually it stopped oozing.

Once in a while, the little red-haired girl who lived in my aunt's house would come and visit me in the stable and we would talk. Unlike my aunt or the boys, she never hit me. Occasionally she would bring a book and leave it for me. Because of her kindness I was able to learn to read. It didn't take me long.

"What a liar!" she said to me one day. "Nobody can learn to read that easily!"

To show her that I wasn't lying, I opened a book and read a passage. She was surprised.

I learned to memorize books. There was no light in the stable at night. I had to read during the day by the rays of sunlight that shone in through the gaps in the barn wall. The girl told me the books mustn't be discovered. In many cases I could memorize a book just by reading it once.

The red-haired girl also taught me about numbers. I learned arithmetic. I read books with lots of equations. I learned to do calculations more complex than even she could do.

"You're really smart!" she said.

Once, my aunt came into the stable while I was reading a book. I had no time to hide it in the straw. My aunt snatched the book away from me. She told me books were valuable and I mustn't touch them, and then she beat me with a stick. She couldn't understand how a book came to be here.

"Mom, stop it!" yelled the red-haired girl, who had just stepped inside the stable. "This kid is smart! He's smarter than my two brothers!"

My aunt could not accept this. To prove her point, the girl

commanded me to recite from memory a verse from the Bible. I did as I was told.

"So what?" said my aunt, jumping up with indignation. She tripped and fell in a pile of horseshit.

We all grew older, and the brothers still stayed away from me and the stable. They only came around when they needed a horse to go hunting with. The red-haired girl went off to boarding school, so she was never around anymore. Even my aunt stopped bringing me table scraps. My uncle slowly sold off his fields to other people.

I stayed in the corner of the stable, forgotten, seldom seeing anyone. For years I lived hidden in the straw. I think people came to believe I had run away long ago. I continued to muck out the stables at night. If anyone ever ambled into the stable, I would hide. The stones on the walls continued to remind me of human faces. I could still see arms and heels. This is what I looked at as I fell asleep.

In the middle of the night, I would crawl out and scrounge a meal at the pit where leftover food was tossed. One night my aunt discovered me.

"Are you still around?" she asked. She threw a little money in the dirt. "Take that and get out of here."

I went into town. There were tall buildings there. There were many people. Everyone I made eye contact with was shocked because of my disfigured face. Some people stared, unabashed, while others averted their eyes.

I kept my aunt's money in my front pocket. At night while walking through the back streets, several men came up to me. Terrible things were done to me, and I learned to stay away from towns. I chose to follow unmarked roads and forgotten trails. For many years I walked.

At long last I entered the forest in hopes of starting a new life for myself. I lived in such a way that people would not be able to find me. Whenever I had encountered people, terrible things had resulted. I knew I had to build a house. I remembered the stone walls of the horse barn. I thought I should build something like that. I searched for stones that resembled faces, or arms or legs. I wandered the entire forest. I found hardly any stones. No matter how far I wandered, the forest was nothing but trees. A thick layer of humus, made of decaying leaves, covered the forest floor.

On my search for stones, I encountered a young man walking a mountain trail. I thought people were all horrible, so I decided I should kill him.

So that's what I did. I killed him.

His face seemed somehow familiar. It resembled one of the stones of the stable wall. I carried his corpse deep into the forest. I had found something with which to build my house.

2.

I built my house of dead bodies. I built up the walls by stacking up corpses. To gather the bodies, I had to leave the forest.

A woman, clutching her cloth bag to her chest, was walking along the road. I hid in the hedge at the side of the road and watched as she passed right in front of me. I stood up out of the hedge and followed her. Hearing the sound of my footsteps, she looked back. Her scream was very loud. Most people, seeing the gouge in my face, either screamed or flew into a rage. I put my hands around her neck. The woman dropped the cloth bag she was clutching. Its contents scattered. Vegetables. A potato struck my toe.

The bones of her neck were easy to break. At that instant, the scream disappeared from her mouth. Her eyes were wide open. Even in death, they were trying to probe the depth of the gouge in my face. I pulled her body into the hedge, and I gathered up the scattered vegetables. Later, her cold body would become the foundation of my house. I would lay it down in the cold, rotting leaves of the forest, and it would support the walls of stacked corpses.

A man was crossing a bridge. He was wearing a cap and pulling a handcart. It was a small wooden bridge. Weeds grew at the edges of the brook, and the wooden bridge was reflected on the surface of the water. I hid beneath the bridge. Just as the handcart passed over my head, I jumped aboard. I was careful to made no sound. At first, the man did not notice. But sensing that the cart had suddenly grown heavier, he turned around. With a rock gripped in my hands, I split his head open. He didn't even have time to scream.

I put his body into the handcart. It seems the man had been taking some produce to the next town. The floor of the handcart was stacked with wooden crates. On the lids of the crates were branded letters indicating what kinds of fruit were contained inside. I took the whole cart deep into the forest. Stacked together with countless other corpses, this dead man would become part of the walls of my house. His lifeless body was building material for my house.

I gathered the building materials for my house from many different places. The least fuss was made when I gathered my materials in villages that were far removed from the forest. I would kill people and gather them in a place away from the town. When I had plenty of them, I would load them in the handcart and take them to the forest. I would load the bodies on the bed of the handcart and cover them with straw to hide them. I would return to the forest under cover of darkness.

One night as I was pushing the handcart full of building materials back to the forest, a voice from behind me called, "Halt!" It was a man's voice. Quickly, I hid my disfigured face. I mustn't be seen, I thought, or bad things would happen.

"What do you think you're doing walking around here like this in the middle of the night? They say there's been a kidnapper around here lately."

The man held an electric lamp. He was old, but not too old. He approached me. He put his hand on the rim of the handcart. He looked at the straw in the cart and said, "The kidnapper has been in the next village, and also in another village farther away. Nobody knows what's happened to the missing people. My grandchildren say they've been eaten."

The man's gaze came to rest on a woman's white ankle jutting out of the straw. He tilted his head and reached out to touch it. He could feel the coldness from the dead body and was shocked. I strangled him and loaded him into the cart.

It was quiet in the forest. Tree trunks, hard as steel, went on forever. It was the cold time of the year, so the leaves had lost all their color, and most had fallen. I laid the corpses out on the leaves on a spot where I could build a wall.

I built a simple house, the shape of a rectangular box. To make the walls I stacked up bodies with no gaps between them. Some were male and some were female. Some were villagers and some were travelers. When I got them to the forest I removed their clothing. They were all naked and very white.

Some bodies were fitted into the walls lying down, and some were fitted into the walls sitting up. Some were hugging their knees, and some had their hands around somebody else's throat. The walls were not thin. If the walls were just one person thick they would have been weak, so I had to make them a few people thick. In places I had to use wood for additional support. The house was nearly complete. When I ran out of building materials, I went to get more. The walls were nearly tall enough. The materials were white, so the house was white.

The cold days continued. I slept huddled against the unfinished walls. I kept myself fed with the food in the bags the people carried. Once the walls made of piled-up humans were completed, it would be time to build the roof. I set several large tree branches across the top of the walls and laid more bodies over them. That kept off the snow.

The house was finished. It was a small white house in the quiet forest. The skin of the corpses was a cold, frightening white; when bathed in moonlight, the house gleamed as if draped with a veil. The bodies at the base of the wall, pressed beneath the weight of those on top, were sinking steadily into the decaying leaves.

The house was big enough to stand up in. It was a simple structure, just a roof, walls, and an entryway. But it was enough to keep out the wind. I entered and hugged my knees. Looking around, I saw faces all around me. The human bodies that made up the walls were jammed together in complex contortions, all piled on top of one another. All their eyes were open and looking at me. It was just like the walls of the horse stable. One woman in the wall had very long hair that hung down and hid the faces of the others below her.

I lived in this house. Mine was a quiet life. There were not even any birds in this forest. There was just my white house. All the eyes in all the faces were open and looking at me.

The bodies in the walls were all entangled with one another. One man had his elbow bent, and the body of the person right next to him was twisted and bent to match up with the elbow. One young person stood straight up from the earth, supporting the men and women above him on his head. The way the arms and legs of the people were intertwined, it looked like a lot of snakes had been assembled, writhing around in one place. Hugging my knees, I slept. The cold nights continued.

I often remembered the time when I was at my aunt's house. Whenever I closed my eyes I was there again in the stable. I also remembered the little red-haired girl. I began to think about the house where I had lived with my parents. We were not a rich family. During the winter my father would venture out to the cold, frozen fields and swing his hoe. My mother would help him until her hands were red. One rainy day my parents were in a fatal accident. They were struck by a runaway horse cart. That's what I was told.

As a result my aunt took me in, and I was allowed to live in her barn. I was not allowed to enter the main house. That was because I always smelled like horsehit. The bottom half of the barn walls was made of round stones, piled up, looking like a row of human faces.

After I had lived in my house for a while, a girl came to visit me.

∃.

I was in my house thinking when I heard the sound of footsteps on fallen leaves. I realized someone must have wandered deep into the forest looking specifically for this house. A feeble sun in the gray sky shone in through the entryway of my little house. A small shadow covered the entrance, and I lifted my head to see who it might be. The girl stood with one hand gripping the edge of the entryway.

She was just a small child. Her face was full of fear, and her clothes were very dark blue, almost black. Her skin was an unhealthy white, and her lips were blue, not from the cold, or from hunger, but from fear.

"Do you live here?" she asked, her voice trembling. Her arms were folded tight across her chest, and her head was recoiling. "Your house is made of people!"

She walked around the inside of my little house while looking at the stacked-up white bodies. I walked around behind her. When she turned to look at me, a look of surprise came over her face. "You've got a hole in your face."

She looked concerned as she approached me.

"It's a big hole. Big enough for a bird to build a nest in. It's so deep and dark, I can't see it properly." She seemed to be truly worried about the gouge in my face.

"Are you the one who took them all away?" She was so tense she looked as though she might faint at any moment. "I always thought the person who took my brother away would be here, deep in this forest. Give me my brother back! I came all the way here to find my brother."

She looked like she was about to cry as she stared at the wall of stacked bodies. In the cold forest, in the pale sunlight, the white bodies appeared almost phosphorescent.

"I'm sure my brother is here. My brother is very smart and very handsome."

The handsome, smart-looking boy was part of the inside wall.

He was the one holding up the bodies above him with his head. I showed the girl inside, and when she saw the face of her brother standing, she called his name. The sound of her voice surprised me. She grabbed the shoulder of her brother's corpse and tried to pull him out of the wall, but I made her stop. Without that boy my house of corpses would fall down.

"But I have to take my brother home!" She was crying. "My father likes my brother better than me. He always hits me. And he always has a mean look on his face. Ever since my brother disappeared, my father has been very sad. He always loved to eat his meals with my mother and my brother. Now my mother is working in a foreign country, and before she gets back I want to bring my brother home. Please, please give my brother back to me."

She knelt in the dead leaves and begged me. I had to turn her down, because without her brother, my house would fall down. Her eyes were full of tears. She said to me, "Let me take his place."

And so I removed his body. Quickly she squeezed into the space where his body had been. Still in its rigid standing posture, his body toppled into the room. She filled the space where her brother's body had been perfectly. She remained clothed and provided the only color in a wall of white bodies.

"Please, please take my brother back home . . ."

In a voice filled with pain, she explained to me how to get to her house. I was able to remember it easily.

"You're a quick learner."

Buried in the wall of bodies, she wore a shocked expression. I took the boy's body out of the house and made as if I were set-ting off for her house. In reality, I only went a few paces down the path before dropping his body. I sat down beside it, clutching my knees, and kept an eye on the entry to my house. I had no intention of taking his body home. While I was gone, I was sure she meant to escape from the wall.

I waited for some time, but she did not emerge. A whole day went by. That would have been enough time for me to go all the way to her house and back again. So I went back into my house, pretending I had taken her brother's body home. She was still there in the wall, not having moved an inch.

"Thank you so much for taking my brother home. I'm sure that will make my father happy. When my mother comes back from abroad, she won't have to be so sad either," the girl said with tears of joy in her eyes. Wedged into the wall among the stacked-up white corpses, she stood tall and supported the dead bodies on her head.

Thus began my life with the girl. She liked to talk. The small house was filled with her voice. In the faces of the bodies lined up in the wall, the eyes were still open. With each passing day, the bodies at the base of the wall began to lose their form.

At first, she was very timid when she talked, but over time she began to smile. In the cold, white, little house in the quiet forest, her smile was like a ray of sunshine.

"Tell me, how did you get that gouge in your face anyway?" she asked. I told her about my aunt's house.

"That's so sad," she said, sobbing with empathy. She had been beaten by her dad. And she too had run away to the horse barn. Remembering the smell of the horseshit in the stable, she grimaced.

"The smell of this house is pretty overpowering too, but not like the smell of the stable."

And so we passed the time with me telling her stories. I did not forget to tell her about the books I had read at my aunt's house.

Those were strange days. Until that time I had been alone in the house and all I had to do was hug my knees among the many open-eyed faces lining the walls. The fear I had felt before had by then faded. Soundlessly, peacefully, my heart was full.

4.

She slept standing upright. After a while she spoke less and less. Her face grew whiter and eventually became the same color as the corpses around her. I thought she would die of cold and hunger.

"Tell me a story," she would say to me, and I would recite to her one of the books I knew by heart.

Eventually she stopped blinking, and her eyes remained wide open. A gentle smile floated on her face.

She grew shorter. I knew that little by little she was being crushed down by the weight of the dead bodies on her head. She had started out a little bit taller than her brother. Her face turned a cold white, and now the deep blue of her clothing was the only color in the room. Hugging my knees, I sat still in the middle of the room. With no one to talk to, there was no need to speak. The house built of stacked-up bodies was once again quiet, as it had been before. I felt a stab of regret.

I stood up and decided to go to her house. I had not kept my promise to her. I had to take her brother home.

The boy was still lying near the house. His body was decomposing from lying in the sun. When I tried to lift him he was soft and falling apart. I wanted to take the girl home too because she had loved her parents so deeply.

I did not hesitate to pull her from the wall. I grabbed her shoulder and tugged. The house started to lean. Just as I emerged from the entryway holding her lifeless body, my white house made of stacked-up corpses fell apart. All the bodies of the walls, and all the bodies of the roof, fell into a heap. The tangle of bodies were no longer recognizable as human beings. They were now just one great big pile of muck.

Deep in the frozen, cold, quiet forest, where the tree trunks went on like an endless row of columns, was a mountain of flesh. The wooden box that I had used to transport dead bodies through the forest sat nearby. Once upon a time it had held fruit. Labels were affixed to the lid of the box indicating what types of fruit it held. I put the body of the girl inside. I put her brother's decomposed body in there as well. The brother's body oozed comfortably into the gaps left by the girl's crumpled body. I put the lid on, picked up the box, and headed for their house.

It took me half a day to reach my destination. The house was on the hilltop of a small village. I knocked on the door but nobody was there. I left the box with the bodies of the two children at the doorstep and turned to leave.

As I walked away, I noticed a woman heading toward me. The woman carried a big bag. She was getting closer to the house. I was sure it was the girl's mother coming home from abroad.

I stood where I was and waited for the woman to come closer. Finally she reached the front porch and stopped. Her smile filled her whole face.

"Oh, thank God."

She put her arms around my shoulders.

"You're alive. Your face is just as it was when that horse kicked you. I've been worried about you for all these years."

Even though she was older, her hair was still red. "That's right," she continued, "you can start working here again. I've just returned after being away for a long time. I can't wait to see the children." She looked down at the box by the door. She bent down to open the lid, but I stopped her.

"What's that smell? This fruit must be rotten. Would you take it back to the compost pile for me?"

I picked it up and started walking to the compost pile behind the stable. I saw the mountain of manure, just as it was when I was a child. I buried the boy and the girl in the pile of horseshit. I entered the stable. It was just as it had always been. I huddled my body against the wall and went to sleep.

FIND THE BLOOD!

1.

When the alarm clock rang, I (sixty-four years old) opened my eyes. I silenced the noisy clock, and with the same hand I rubbed the sleep out of my eyes. It was five in the morning. The sun streamed through the curtainless window beside my bed. The window was so badly fitted that not only would it not lock, it would never open more than three centimeters no matter how much you pushed or pulled on it. The only way out of the room was through the door.

When I looked at my hands, I gasped. They were solid red. Some dried red stuff was smeared all over them. It scared me and I cried out. I had had an awful experience in the past and I thought (perhaps) it was happening all over again.

"What's wrong, Dad? Let me in!" There was a banging on the door. It was the voice of my second son, Tsuguo (twenty-seven years old). The door (it seemed) was locked and he couldn't get in. I got up from the bed and tried to determine what part of my body was bleeding.

"Whe . . . whe . . . whe . . . where is it? Where is the blood coming from?"

I was shaking uncontrollably, but I could not for the life of me figure out where I was wounded. There was blood in my eyes, so my surroundings were blurry. For the moment I gave up trying to

figure out where I was bleeding from and (somehow) managed
to walk to the door and unlock it.

"Dad!"

Tsuguo opened the door and rushed in. When he saw the state
I was in, he cried out, "Ah!"

"Whe . . . whe . . . whe . . . where am I bleeding? Quickly, take
a look, Tsuguo! Find it!"

I had always despised Tsuguo for being a coward, and for
an instant I thought he would run away. But he (surprisingly)
obeyed my plea and examined my back. I could hear him emit
little gasps the entire time—*ughs!* and *icks!*

"Ah! Here it is!" he said. "You've got a cut on your side,
Dad!" I groped for the spot with my hand and felt something
hard sprouting from my body.

That was about the time my second wife Tsumako (twenty-five
years old) and my first son Nagao (thirty-four years old) arrived.
With blood in my eyes I couldn't see very well, but I could see
that they were standing in the doorway wondering what was
going on.

I could hear their cries:

"Aiyee!"

"What the . . . !"

"Tsuguo, can you tell what this is, this hard thing sticking
out of my side?"

"Uh . . ." he said in a tone that suggested both reluctance and
slowheadedness.

"As far as I can tell . . . well . . . the thing sticking from your
side seems to be . . . a kitchen knife."

I felt faint. Blood flowed unstaunched from my right side, and
a stain forming on the carpet spread slowly outward. I had no
recollection of being stabbed with a kitchen knife.

己.

Ten years ago I was the cause of a terrible traffic accident. The car I drove was bulletproof and was even equipped with sprinklers. It was my "money talks" car and was built like a tank. My first wife was sitting in the passenger seat at the time.

It was a horrible accident. My car, which I was so proud of, was reduced to a mangled heap of crunched metal. Afterward I had the (unaccustomed) experience of feeling lucky to have survived.

I awoke in a hospital bed. My entire body was swathed in bandages, but I felt no pain anywhere. I got up and walked around the hospital, trying to find out what had happened to my wife.

Seeing me, a male nurse cried out. I could tell that there was something different about my body, and then one of my legs buckled under me. I was told I had broken many bones and should be lying quietly in bed.

I found that hard to accept. I felt no pain, so why should I rest quietly?

The next day the doctor explained the situation to me. In the accident I had hit my head hard. This had done some damage to my brain, and I was still suffering from the aftereffects. I had (completely) lost the ability to feel pain.

Ever since that time, I was terrified of wounds. I might be reading the newspaper comics (for example), and the fourth frame of *Honobono-kun* would be covered in red. It would set me off: Who the hell would do that and ruin the punch line? What the hell kind of cartoon is this anyway? Who knows if it even had a punch line? And then I would realize that I was bleeding from a cut on my finger, my own blood staining the newspaper. Maybe my dog (a Tosa breed) took a bite out of my finger because I forgot to give him his breakfast. I could never be sure.

Or I might be getting ready for my bath, stripping down to my underwear in the anteroom, and notice bright red polka dots on my clothing. I would get angry, wondering who had bought me such tawdry-looking underwear, before realizing that the splotches were my own blood. Wall tacks (I later figured out) had pierced my back in two or three places while taking a nap. I was such a restless sleeper that (it seems) I had rolled back and forth over some tacks.

And that's how it would be for me. From time to time I would simply notice that I was bleeding. I might nick myself on a nail and not notice. Once I even stubbed my little toe on the corner of a dresser so hard it broke the bone. I didn't notice anything was wrong for two whole days.

I was fearful for my own safety. I decided that every night before I went to sleep I should have the family doctor, Dr. Omoji (ninety-five years old), give me a quick exam. I wanted to make sure I wasn't injured somewhere.

Even so, I was unable to fully erase the last traces of my anxiety. What would I do if tomorrow I were to awake to find my body covered in blood? That was always my fear as I drifted off to sleep.

In the year following my accident I lost my zest for living. Losing my wife, and saddled with my good-for-nothing sons, my only joy in life was seeing my company grow bigger and bigger.

But even this success was a double-edged sword. Because of my company's good fortunes, I got wealthier and wealthier. But because I couldn't count on my sons to succeed me, I could never think about retiring. I had little to smile about. I lived in fear of injury in a world without pain.

3.

From my window I could see the mountains in the fresh sunlight of early morning. It was a spectacular view. The twittering of birds outside on the windowsill, however, was annoying. Tsuguo and Tsumako sat at my bedside table.

"You're really bleeding a lot. Like a fountain," Tsumako said, pressing her hand to her mouth. Nagao finished his phone call and came back to the table.

"Dad, I called an ambulance. It'll take them at least thirty minutes to get up here from the base of the mountain. What do you want to do?"

I grumbled about the thirty-minute wait, and then I looked down at the knife stuck savagely in my side. I had to twist my body to see it because my fat got in the way. I had been stabbed; there was no doubt about it.

"Dad, don't do that! You're making the blood pour out of your body like somebody squeezing a rag!"

"Oh, you're right, you're right." Hearing Tsuguo's admonition, I stopped looking at my wound. If I kept bleeding like this I wouldn't last thirty minutes. Here at our mountain lodge there was no hospital in the immediate vicinity.

"Tsumako . . ." Nagao called my wife by her first name because she was younger than he. "Why are you pressing your hands to your mouth? Are you not feeling well?"

Tsumako shook her head. "That's not it. I'm just trying to contain my laughter. I am so happy. Finally this old husband of mine might actually die."

My beautiful young wife had married me for my money.

"What the hell?" Nagao turned to me with an insincere attempt at an ingratiating smile on his face. I always thought of my older son as a hypocrite. "Dad, you can't be expecting us to share our inheritance with this woman. Leave the company to me and you can die in peace."

"Just listen to you. You're so in debt you can't wait to get your hands on that money."

"I can't believe these two," said Tsuguo, my cowardly son, as he pushed his chair farther away from the other two.

"Listen to yourselves, all of you, talking nonsense as I'm dying."

"It's *because* you are dying," said Tsumako lightly under her breath.

That bitch, I'll have her dropped from the will.

"Dad, you shouldn't get angry. If your blood pressure rises the bleeding will get worse." The sound of Tsuguo's voice brought me back to the present situation. I took some deep breaths and reined in my anger. Then it occurred to me I hadn't yet seen a certain person that morning.

"Speaking of which, where is Dr. Omoji?" I never traveled without him and this time was no exception. All five of us had come to the cabin on holiday.

Dr. Omoji was a fossil. To give you an idea just how old he was, most people who went to see him said things like, "Does that old coot still have his medical license? I'm not putting my life in the hands of some geezer who's been around since the days of the shogun." For this reason, Dr. Omoji's calendar was always empty, and if I asked him to go on a trip with me, he was always quick to say, "I'd be delighted." He had no reservations about dropping everything (nothing?) and coming along.

"I think the doctor is still sleeping in his room," Tsuguo said, shaking his head in dismay. "I'll go wake him up."

Dr. Omoji's room was on the first floor right next to mine. With all the screaming he should have been the first one up. But he was so hard of hearing he probably didn't notice. Maybe he'd passed away in his bed during the night. Anything was possible. The door to his bedroom opened into the living room, so I had a clear view as Nagao rapped on the door and called for the doctor.

After a while he emerged, scratching the back of his head. He and Nagao walked to the table where we were all sitting. The whole time blood continued to flow from my body, soaking into the carpet.

"Dr. Omoji. So sorry to disturb your sleep. Could you please have a look at me. Someone seems to have stabbed me in the back."

Nagao shook his head from side to side.

"No, Dad, you're wrong. The doctor was already awake."

Dr. Omoji, who was dressed all in white, shuffled up to me. He almost always wore white, even when he traveled.

"I . . . I'm so sorry. I heard you yelling, but every morning at 5:14 there's this travel show I like to watch. I decided the program was more important to me than whatever troubles you were having."

"What an old quack!" Tsumako blurted.

"Never mind about that. Just have a look at me," I said. Omoji bent over and examined my wound.

"A-ha!" he said. "You've been stuck with a kitchen knife! Nothing I can do about that here."

"Wow, a chance to see a real autopsy with my own eyes. Never thought I'd get the opportunity to do that," Nagao said.

What was he talking about, autopsy? I wasn't even dead yet.

"Can't you do anything to help me, Doctor?" I said, trying my best to ignore my stupid son.

"Well, let me think now. With a wound like that, you won't last until the morning TV news show. Too bad about that."

Across the table, Tsumako's eyes were tearing up, and she was pounding her head with her open palms.

"What is going on here? What is the point of having your own doctor if . . . ?"

With one hand I pointed a finger at her, and with the other I grabbed at Dr. Omoji's sleeve.

"My wife is frightened. Isn't there some way I can live through this?"

A smile came to the doctor's wrinkled face.

"Don't get so upset. I anticipated that something like this might happen someday. Whenever we go on a trip I always bring along enough blood for a transfusion."

Hearing his words, I fell to my knees. Every so often he would stick a needle in my arm and draw some blood. He did this so often I used to wonder if he wasn't selling it somewhere. Now I realized he was saving it up for something like this. I started to see a halo above his head.

"If we start a transfusion now, you should be able to stay alive until the ambulance arrives. Someone did call an ambulance, I presume?"

We explained to him that the ambulance would take thirty

minutes to get to this mountain lodge.

"Well, it'll be a close call. At any rate, I have a big supply of your blood in my room. I'll go and fetch it for you."

And Dr. Omoji shuffled off to his room.

"Well, I'm glad to see you still have an interest in staying alive, Dad."

"Yes, I must say so too. It will be most gratifying if you decide to stay on and live a long life with us."

I found Nagao's and Tsumako's sentiments extremely tiresome. Somebody made a *tsk!* sound with their tongue.

"Dad, if you die, I'll have to live with these two? That's too scary," said Tsuguo, nearly in tears. He shook my shoulders to emphasize his point.

Knock it off, I thought to myself, you'll only make the bleeding worse. I (finally) got his hands off me just as Dr. Omoji returned. His smile stretched from ear to ear.

"Please, Doctor, give me the blood. I'm starting to feel faint."

"I'm afraid I won't be able to do that."

What?

"I'm sorry, but I seem to have misplaced the bag that had all your blood in it."

It was a rare sight to see a ninety-five-year-old doctor turning red with embarrassment.

4.

Left it somewhere?!

"I don't understand what happened to it, but it doesn't seem to be in my room."

Nagao and Tsumako looked happy.

"When we left the house you had the bag with you, right? Where could you possibly have left it?"

"No idea," Dr. Omoji said, shaking his head. "I don't even remember clearly if I had it when we arrived here. I might have left it on the last train we took. It might have gotten mixed up with somebody else's luggage."

I ordered my wife and son to go check their bags.

"Even if Tsumako or Nagao find the bag with your blood, they'll probably just hide it," Tsuguo said. He was right, of course.

"All right then, let's do this: To the person who finds the bag with my blood, I will give my entire fortune—the company, the property, everything. If money is what you want, go and find the blood!"

Nagao and Tsumako looked at me, astonished.

"Now don't you worry, dear! I'll find it right away!"

"Me too!"

The two of them scrambled up to their rooms on the second floor. Tsuguo did the same. Dr. Omoji rolled up the sleeves of his white coat and looked like he was about to get down to business.

"Not you, Dr. Omoji. If you find the blood, I'm not giving you everything I own."

"I thought not."

"Would I be able to accept blood directly from anyone in this house?"

"You're type O, right? Everybody else is A, B, or AB. Sorry, no way."

From upstairs I could hear the sounds of three people rummaging through their luggage. All the while, blood continued to drain from my body.

"Couldn't you at least do something to staunch the bleeding?"

He nodded. "I have my favorite scalpel with me and thread for stitches. I can do a simple operation. Luckily, we won't need any anesthesia."

"I'm begging you. I have to live at least a little longer. Who could depend on the three of them for anything? I spent years building up my company. Do you think I could let them just destroy it?"

"Don't worry. You're not dying yet."

The doctor drew a rusty scalpel from his pocket.

"Hang on just a minute! What's with that scalpel? It's covered with rust!"

"Why are you worried about a little bit of rust? This is a matter of life and death, and seconds count!" His hand holding the scalpel was trembling like a leaf.

"Doctor, how many years has it been since the last time you operated on anyone?"

"Oh, it was probably before you were born."

In one (surprisingly) swift motion I knocked the scalpel from the doctor's hand.

"Listen, Doctor, I think the best thing for you to do right now is to remember where you might have left the bag with the blood. Without it, I'm finished."

I tried to remember all that had transpired from the time we left the house the day before until now.

We left the house in two taxis at ten a.m. the day before. I was the only one with a driver's license, but I hadn't been behind a steering wheel since my accident a decade ago.

"Are you sure you had the blood with you when we left the house?"

"Without a doubt. I had it right in my lap."

Both taxis arrived at the station, and we boarded a train. I could remember how Dr. Omoji looked as he sat in the swaying train, gripping his boxed lunch in both hands.

"In the train, you were holding your lunch in both hands!"

"That's right, that's right. I remember it well. That was a good lunch."

"But what about the bag with the blood?"

"Argh! What an idiot! I must have left it on the train platform!"

What a demented old fool! I wanted to scream, but then I heard a voice behind me.

"That's not it. We picked up the doctor's luggage from the

platform and put it on the train. I myself picked up the black bag with the blood."

It was Tsuguo. At some point he must have returned to the first floor.

"So, Tsuguo, did you take the blood to your room?"

"No. It wasn't in my room." He shook his head. I could feel my shoulders sink in disappointment. I felt as though my body temperature was falling, and my fingers and toes felt cold.

"Dad, you're turning pale."

"No wonder, having lost this much blood. Tsuguo, I want to smoke. Get me a cigarette."

"Cigarettes are bad for you, don't you know that?"

"Is this the time to be having this conversation?"

After we got off the train, we got into some more taxis. We then drove for about forty minutes before arriving at this mountain lodge. Actually, we stopped at a grocery store near the train station first. This was our regular routine. It's hard to shop while carrying a bunch of luggage, so Tsuguo and Dr. Omoji took our bags to the cabin right away.

Unburdened, Nagao, Tsumako, and I took care of the groceries. Nagao, sweating but not complaining, carried the bags of food. As we passed a bakery, Tsumako said she would like to buy something sweet.

"Let's buy some cake, shall we? And we should buy a knife too. If I remember correctly there is not a single knife in the cabin."

I remembered that she was clutching a black bag in her left hand. I was positive that it was Dr. Omoji's.

"Can I just ask one question? Was the black bag with the blood included with the bags that came up to the cabin in the first taxi?"

"I don't think so," Tsuguo said, but he did not seem very confident.

"When Tsuguo and Dr. Omoji got into their taxi, there was a black bag left on the street," Tsumako said from behind me. I turned around. She had come down from the second floor and was now standing behind the chair. "I recognized it as Dr. Omoji's bag, so I carried it while we were shopping."

I glared at the doctor and held up my fists.

"How could you leave something so important lying in the road?"

"Why are you threatening me with your fists? Are you going to hit me? I'm just an old man with not much of a future left to me!"

I was the one with no future!

"That's right, dear. Let's calm down. The old quack is already half-demented, so you should forgive him if he acts a little odd."

Have you no blood, no tears?

"So you were the one who had the bag with the blood. Was it in your room?"

She shook her head. "I'm sure I had it when we got here, but I must have put it down somewhere . . ."

Still not found. My peripheral vision was getting blurry and I was getting sleepy. I was aware that these were bad signs. Like sand in an hourglass, the blood was flowing steadily from my wound. Second by second, I knew my time was growing shorter.

"But you're sure the bag is here in the cabin."

"Yes, just like Tsuguo said."

"But where in this cabin could it be?"

Everybody stood around in silence. Nagao (the hypocrite) spoke from the living room entrance.

"Last night, I saw the bag."

That got everyone's attention.

"What? Really?"

"Yes, I'm sure I saw it. It had fallen over, right near this door."

"So, Nagao, have you found the blood?"

"No, I haven't. But I'm sure that last night, when I was doing my imitation of a platypus, it was lying there on its side."

I remembered last night's dinner. We all ate the meal Tsumako had prepared, and then my wife and two sons put on little performances. Nagao's imitation of a platypus was (by far) the worst of them all.

Tsuguo said, "Nagao, Dad sure made an ass of you last night."

And Tsumako piled on: "The stupid thing is, a platypus can't tell if it's a mammal or a duck, and I don't care if you are my so-called stepson, you're still an ass!"

"Oh, shut up, there's nothing wrong with platypuses. Don't try to make it look like I'm the stupid one. Platypuses are an aboriginal mammal native to Australia. They have short legs and they have bills! It was you, Tsumako, who messed things up last night with your stupid song about the Apple Dumpling Gang. That's what made Dad mad. If it weren't for that, he would have loved my little routine. You didn't know he hates dumplings?"

"I had no idea! How could I have known that his first wife died ten years ago when a dumpling got stuck in her throat? I always thought she died in that traffic accident!"

I closed my eyes and tried to recall the events of last evening. Like a spinning lantern, images of last night seemed to be projected on the back of my eyelids.

Last night, we ate our meal and watched the skits of the three entertainers—Tsumako, Nagao, Tsuguo—in that order. My displeasure reached its peak by the end of Nagao's act, but then Tsuguo did some card tricks that were not bad. He might be a cowardly, worthless, spoiled little brat, but he had some skill at magic. In his room were bookshelves full of mystery novels.

I remember once when he was small, I caught him looking absently up at the stars.

"What are you thinking?" I asked him.

"I'm trying to think of a magic trick for killing people," he said with a twinkle in his eye. I burst out laughing.

"You're such a sissy, why would you be trying to think of something like that? What if you did come up with such a trick, what would you do then, write a story about it? Or use it to kill somebody? You're such a sissy you couldn't do either one. You'll go to college and get good grades and end up spending your days walking the dog."

He just listened, smiling and scratching his head. I could say the most awful things to him and he would just smile. He was pitiful.

Last night, by the time he was through with his magic tricks I noticed it was already ten o'clock. Dr. Omoji started saying he wanted to sing a song by Hikaru Utada, but I cut him off. I decided to go to bed before the others. Even on vacation, I tried to live by my rule of going to sleep at ten p.m. and waking up at five a.m.

Before I went to sleep, Dr. Omoji came to my room to examine me for wounds. I lay down and looked out the window. The window frame was small and practically square, and was set in the wall directly opposite the door. It was right beside the bed and I could look out at the sky full of twinkling stars. Because the window was badly fitted and wouldn't open more than a few centimeters, the ventilation in the room was (very) bad. No one was willing to switch rooms with me, so every time we came to the cabin I always got stuck sleeping in the same room.

The door to my room was open last night, so I could clearly hear the voices of my wife and two sons as they chatted pleasantly in the living room. They were (apparently) in the mood for a piece of cake.

Because my skin lacked all sense of feeling, I could hardly tell what Dr. Omoji was doing with his hands. I worried that he wasn't actually examining me and that he might have nodded off to sleep. I could hear tapping from under the bed, which reassured me that he had not in fact fallen asleep, but when I turned around I could see he was just sitting in a chair next to the bed, visibly drowsy.

Through the open door I could see the table in the living room. I watched Tsumako use the kitchen knife to cut the cake.

"Hey, Doc! They're all digging into their cake in the other room," I muttered to him. He rose from the chair and left the room, yelling, "The chocolate bar on the top is mine!"

I shook my head in disgust as I got up from the bed and approached the door. I wanted to watch the four of them surrounding the cake.

After a while I closed the door, latched it, and was alone in my room. I turned out the light and yawned, and fell asleep on the bed.

"When you went back to your room, we were eating the cake. I have a feeling that the bag with the blood was already missing from the living room."

At the sound of Nagao's voice I opened my eyes and returned to the present discussion. Sitting at the table were four people, and just as before, blood was (still) flowing from my body. Turning to see my flank, I could see the knife still stuck there. At some point it seems, the discussion of platypus imitations had come to an end, and the room was quiet.

"If I am to believe you, Nagao, the bag was gone from the entryway by the time I went to my room at ten."

Tsumako chimed in. She had a peculiar expression on her face. "After that, at eleven or so, we all went to our rooms . . . Come to think of it, there's only one knife in this cabin."

What about it? "A-ha! I get it!" Tsuguo said, failing to fully comprehend her words. "That means the knife in Dad's side must be . . ."

"Yeah, have a look. At the end of the blade, near the handle, there's some whipped cream."

At that, Dr. Omoji laid the bloody knife on the table. It showed clear signs of having been the knife that had cut the cake.

"Hey, hold on a minute! The knife! Somebody must have pulled it from my body!"

I felt my side with my hand and realized the knife was no longer there.

"Heh, heh, heh, who's only half there? I yanked this knife right out of you, and you didn't even notice!"

"You! Are you really a doctor?"

Nagao stood with his arms folded. He looked like a door-to-door salesman trying to intimidate a meek housewife.

"Yeah, and we didn't cut the cake until after Dad had gone to his room."

I nodded. The last thing I had seen as I closed my door was Tsumako using the knife to place a piece of cake on a plate.

"Right after that you latched the door," Nagao said. "So, how did this knife, with the whipped cream still stuck to it, manage to get into your room? I bet you'll want to know the answer to that one, even in the next world . . ."

I'm not dead yet . . .

My head was spinning from loss of blood. I barked at my wife and two sons to check again to see if the bag of blood hadn't fallen behind something. My tongue felt tied, and the words I spoke did not come out quite right.

Nagao, Tsuguo, and Tsumako set about tipping over everything in an intensive search for the blood. I started to believe I was going to die in a (particularly) disagreeable manner. These people were all idiots. I could die peacefully if only I knew that one of my heirs had the mental wherewithal to ensure that my company would not founder.

With Dr. Omoji's help, I made my way to the living room sofa, where I lay down. I no longer had the strength to walk on my own, and my legs were trembling.

"Ah! That's it!" said Tsumako, who was looking for the bag in the kitchen. She approached me on the sofa. Hearing her voice, Nagao and Tsuguo joined us in the living room. "As I was serving the cake, I remember stepping on something near the living room door. I'm such an idiot. Could that have been the bag of blood?"

"What do you mean? What did you do with it after that?" As the strength drained from my body, my voice too was fading.

"It made me angry, so I gave it a good kick."

"My blood . . . !"

"But the bag, where is it now?"

Tsuguo cocked his head. If it wasn't in his room or Tsumako's, or Nagao's or Dr. Omoji's, where could it be?

I was sure I was about to die. At that point, I felt a sense of affection for even my despicable wife and sons. I gave them all one last, long, (loving?) look.

And then, breaking the mood, the half-senile old doctor drew up his chair and sat down right in front of me. He spread out the sports pages and started reading them aloud. A big splashy picture of yesterday's sumo match filled my entire field of vision. That was the last thing I needed to see in my final moments: a photo of a couple of sumo wrestlers smashing into one another. But then I noticed something.

"Dr. Omoji! You're not tapping your foot!"

Beneath the newspaper I could see his feet on the floor. He shot me a look suggesting there must be something wrong with me. "For the past few years now, I've had my restless toe-tapping switch turned to the OFF position," he said and turned the page of the newspaper.

I thought of a possibility, and a mini-lamp of an idea turned on in my head. "Tsuguo, go look in my room!"

My voice was very weak. Tsuguo dashed away in the opposite direction, cutting right between Dr. Omoji and me.

"Huh? No way! I don't even want to think about it. It's too scary. That whole room is covered in blood!"

"All right then, Nagao! Go to my room and have a good look, particularly under the bed!"

My older son did as he was told and entered my room. From where I lay on the sofa, I could see right through the open door. I could see his back as he searched underneath the bed. Finally he said, "I've got it!" When he returned to the living room, in his hands was a black bag.

Just in time . . .

I felt a great sense of relief. I was already little more than half-conscious, but I was confident that I could hang on to life a little while longer.

"But how in the world did it ever get there?" asked Tsumako, tilting her head.

"You may have kicked the bag at the same moment Dr. Omoji was examining me on the bed. You kicked the bag and it came flying into the room. Look, the bed is right across from the door. It just so happened that the bag ended up under the bed."

As Dr. Omoji was examining me, I had (indeed) heard a sound under the bed. I had thought it was the sound of Dr. Omoji tapping his foot, but it must have been the sound of the bag sliding under the bed.

Nagao and Tsumako glanced down at the bag. Their faces suggested disappointment. In high anticipation, I waited for Dr. Omoji to stick the IV needle in my arm.

"Doctor, please. Quickly. I'm at my limit."

"I can't," he said, with a look of regret on his face. He had opened the bag, and looked inside. "This bag, it's empty."

5.

"You old dimwit, you forgot to fill it up," I said with my last gasp of consciousness, one foot (surely) on the threshold of the next world. But my voice sounded like the whimper of a little girl falling asleep. I was aware I was standing immediately before death's door, and I was in shock. My life appeared to have reached its penultimate step.

My entire body went numb, sapped completely of its strength. There seemed to be no way for me to go on living. The only avenue open to me was to close my eyes and sink into that deep ocean of sleep from which one could never resurface.

As my vision began to mist over, I could see Dr. Omoji waving his hand from left to right. He should have been right in front of me, but he seemed far away.

"That's not true, not true. I filled it up. I did, really. Maybe somebody poured it out. To make sure you couldn't get the transfusion. To make sure you would really die.

"I really did put the blood in the bag.

"Really, really. I'm not that far gone. I may be wearing adult diapers, but I'm not that far gone. Bags of type O blood. IV tubing. I did put them in the bag."

"Huh? You wear diapers?" Tsuguo said, surprised.

"Oh, that was just a joke. Just a joke," Dr. Omoji said, chuckling.

Is this any time to be laughing? For an instant I was furious, but then the word "tubing" got me thinking again. Inside my head, everything was turning to white, but that little mini-bulb of thought glowed once more.

But I couldn't believe it. I thought about this idea that had occurred to me, but I just could not believe it was true.

With death itself breathing down the back of my neck, my heart was filled with a single doubt. Could someone really have done this?

"I'm so glad I took out a big insurance policy on you, Dad," said Nagao with a look of relief on his face. I was mad but what could I do? Whatever strength remained had long since dribbled out through my wound. I could no longer summon any voice at all. But my eyes were open, and with them I was able to glare at my older son.

"You, you did leave a proper will, didn't you?" With what little strength I had left I managed to nod. The truth was, I had made arrangements with my lawyer several years before concerning the distribution of my estate. All I owned was to be divided amongst my wife and my sons in roughly equal shares.

A gentle death was coaxing me to close my eyelids. Here, finally, I thought. As if they could sense that this was the moment of my death, the four of them gathered around the sofa and looked down at me. Nagao's and Tsumako's eyes were full of hope and expectation. Dr. Omoji's expression was more complicated, but Tsuguo came to me from his faraway spot in the room, looked at me, and winked. He was smiling. As soon as I saw that, all the unknowing in my heart was cleared.

I would never know exactly how Tsuguo came to plan my murder. I could remember when he was a child, the stiffness of his movements as he showed me his card tricks. I was impressed, and when I praised him, his face was happier than anything in this world. This may have been the final expression of our father-son relationship.

It comforted me to know he at least had enough brains to kill his old man. I always thought of him as weak and cowardly, but now I felt secure leaving the company in his hands.

I think he had it planned even before we set out on this trip. He must have emptied Dr. Omoji's bag on the way up to the mountain lodge—probably when we got on the train.

Early the next morning, I woke at five as usual. Everyone in my family knows my habits. But even earlier than that, Tsuguo had made his preparations for my murder.

Carrying the purloined blood and IV tube, he had gone outside. He walked around to the side of the house where my room was, stuck the tube through the gap in the window, and sprayed my sleeping body with my own type-O blood. Everybody in the family knew about the window lock being broken, and that the window would only open a few centimeters. I groused about it constantly.

Then, he disposed of the empty blood packs and tubing, returned to the living room, and waited for the alarm clock to ring. I will never honestly know why he had to use a knife that still had whipped cream on it, or what he would have done if Tsumako hadn't insisted on buying it. At any rate, at five I woke up.

The sunlight streamed in through the window, and that's when I noticed I was covered in blood. Tsuguo was the first to hear me screaming, and he stuck to his script, pounding on the door for me to unlock it. As he pretended to check my body for wounds, that's when he stabbed me from behind. Because I could feel no pain, strangely enough I didn't notice.

I lay on the sofa looking up at the four people looking down at me. Above their heads, the fluorescent light seemed oddly bright. I smiled, and to Tsuguo, who was standing just one pace apart from the rest, I sent a nonverbal sign that said, "I know."

"Why, why is he smiling I wonder?" I could hear Tsumako's perplexed voice. Blessed with a heart at peace, I lowered my eyelids.

IN A PARK AT TWILIGHT,
A LONG TIME AGO

When I was in elementary school there was a park in my neighborhood. Because it was surrounded by tall buildings, you could visit the park at twilight and the sounds of cars and the hubbub of people would completely disappear. It was the kind of park that offered a small pocket of quiet in the big city.

When dinnertime came, and the friends I was playing with went home, I had to hang around the park waiting until my parents came and got me.

When I grew tired of the swings, I would go to the sandbox in the corner of the park and play. For some reason I always felt drawn to it. Most kids liked the swings and the slide better; the sandbox was often overlooked.

In the late afternoon the sunlight would come streaming silently between the two buildings and dye the world red. With no one to talk to, I was always by myself in the sandbox. I remember there was always a discarded yellow plastic bucket to play with. I took off my shoes and thrust my feet into the cool sand. It felt good to have the tiny grains between my toes.

Sometimes I liked to plunge my hands deep into the sand. I wanted to see how deep into the earth I could reach. With my arms straight down, I would dig as deep as I could until I was up to my shoulders. When I told my father this, he didn't believe me. "Even the sandbox has a bottom, so how could that be?" he would say.

I thought my father was wrong. In reality, it seemed like the sandy pit was bottomless. I was sure of it. I had checked and double-checked numerous times.

I'm no longer sure how many times I had done this, but one day, when the tree in the corner of the park had turned to a black silhouette against the sunset, I was in the sandbox, thrusting my right arm up to the shoulder in the sand, and I felt something odd.

Something seemed to be buried in the sand. It was soft and it was cold. I wanted to find out what it was, so I stretched out my arm as deep as I could. I went so deep the very tip of my middle finger could just barely touch it. I could feel something plump and squishy. I wanted to grab it and bring it to the surface, but it kept slipping out of my grasp.

Pulling my arm out of the sand, I discovered several strands of hair clinging to my fingers. They were dirty and damaged by the sand, but I was sure they belonged to a girl.

Several more times I thrust both my arms into the sand trying to touch whatever it was that was buried there. But I wasn't able to find it again, no matter how deep I reached. I felt sad.

In that twilight time of the day when the world was painted red, I could feel the surrounding buildings looming menacingly above me. It was like I was in a giant cage, just me and the sandbox.

Again I put my arm deep into the sand, and I thought I touched something. It was very faint, much like a small fish nibbling on my finger.

Suddenly something in the sand grabbed me. It fastened tightly around my wrist. I tried to pull my arm out, but I couldn't budge it. It was like I was fastened in place. No one else was around, so even if I called for help, my voice would just echo off the buildings that surrounded the park.

Deep in the sand something opened my clenched fist with an irresistible force. In the palm of my hand, I could feel a very small fingertip. It moved across my palm in a regular pattern, and I was sure it was writing letters. It said:

"Get me out of here."

Someone was writing this message on my palm. I thrust my other arm deep into the sand, and on the back of the hand I wrote: "I can't."

My hand was immediately released. I felt a wave of sadness come back at me. I pulled both my arms out of the sand and went home. After that I steered clear of the sandbox. Later, when the park was torn up to make way for new condominiums, I went to check out the sandbox. My father was right, it was not very deep at all. There was no way anything could have been buried there.

WARDROBE

1.

Ryuji opened the door of his room and called out, "Hey, Miki, you're finally here! As soon as you get a chance, could you come to my room? I'd like to have a word with you about what we talked about on the phone."

Ryuji's room was set apart from the main house, and right outside of his door was a garden. The cold night air flowed in and lowered the temperature perceptibly.

Miki came in through that door. She wore a light coat draped over her shoulders. She had come directly from the train station in the cold November night air. In her right hand she carried a big red suitcase. She set it on the floor.

"I haven't even set foot in the main part of the house yet. I need to rest for a little bit. The house is at the very top of this hill. I got so tired from the walk that my legs can hardly move."

"That's a big suitcase. Are you planning on moving into this old house? I wouldn't have any objection, and I'm sure that would make Mom and Dad happy. How would you feel about living with your in-laws?"

With the tip of her toe, Miki lightly nudged the big bag on the floor.

"I meant to leave this in Ichiro's room before coming here to see you." She glared at Ryuji as if she were looking at a filthy animal. She clenched her left hand in a fist in front of her chest. This was a habit of hers, whenever she felt anxious. Ryuji, smiling, invited her to sit on the sofa.

"This won't take long. It's already nine o'clock." Just as Ryuji said this, his clock chimed nine times. "I still have to go see a friend of mine tonight. This is only the second time you've been to this house, isn't it?"

"Third, if you count the wedding."

"How are things going with my brother? Has he been making your life difficult?"

Ryuji approached the door. He was a tiny man and he walked in small steps.

"Why are you locking the door?"

"It's just a habit of mine. There are a lot of important things in the wardrobe here, so I try to keep the door locked."

"I see you don't bother to keep the room clean though. It looks like a typhoon went through here."

Miki looked around the room. It was a big room, but it was cluttered. It had a wooden floor, and piles of clothes and magazines were everywhere. There was a rusty iron bed in the corner and a wooden desk and chair. On the desk was an old typewriter. Books were stacked in random piles around the typewriter.

"Is this where you work?"

"Yeah, I guess so."

In the middle of the room was a leather sofa set. Strewn across the two-piece sectional was more clothing, dropped right where it had been removed. Between the pair of sofas was a low coffee table, with two half-empty coffee cups. The coffee was cold judging by the lack of steam.

"That door leads out to the shed?" Miki asked, pointing to a door next to the bed.

"That's right. I store things there that I'm not using. Everything. My books. My brother's pictures. Would you like to have a look? That shed is big enough for someone to live in."

Miki shook her head. "Some other time maybe."

The room had just one window, and it was closed. The curtains were wide open, so with the nighttime blackness outdoors, the window was like a big mirror. Miki could see herself.

"And a wooden wardrobe. It seems familiar—it's just like the one in Ichiro's room, isn't it? It has the same bas-relief design on the doors."

"Great-grandma bought one for me and one for my brother. These wardrobes can be locked as well. Sometimes the locks don't work though."

"They're kind of creepy, though, don't you think? Like some giant black box. Is there one in Fuyumi's room too?"

"No. Great-grandma died before Fuyumi was born."

In this family there were two sons and one daughter. Of the three, only the younger son, Ryuji, still lived here with his parents. He was a novelist.

"Where is Ichiro now? He should have arrived yesterday."

"He said he was going to take a walk. Too bad. He was in my room until an hour ago. You two just missed each other. He slipped away while I was in the shed. It's actually tidier than this room, so I find it easier to concentrate if I sit in there and read. I'm not sure exactly when Ichiro left, and I forgot to lock up again until just a few minutes ago."

Biting his nails nervously, Ryuji checked again that the lock was turned in the right direction. He flipped on the stereo and put on a CD. Then he sat down directly in front of Miki. The music was a little too loud, but Ryuji didn't worry about that. His room was far enough away from the main house that the racket wouldn't bother anyone. Miki hesitated before speaking, her gaze not focused on anything in particular.

"So, Ryuji, is it true what you said on the phone? You met Shiori?"

"A month ago. I had an interview about some work with a publishing company. She was the writer who was hired to do it. At first I didn't realize she was your old friend. It was about a week after I first met her that I found out she was in your class in college. You were close back then, right? Anyway, when she figured all this out, she turned very pale."

Ryuji looked intently at Miki's face to see if he could detect any change of color there. She kept silent.

"I wanted to ask her why, but she didn't say anything. One day I found out. We were drinking in a bar."

"She told you something when she was drunk?"

"She was laid out flat on the table in the bar, and she started moaning something about a traffic accident."

Miki let out a big sigh and stood up.

"She said that once, when the two of you were in a car, you hit a junior high student on a bicycle and knocked him down. You told each other not to worry, that you wouldn't tell anyone. And then you drove away."

"We had no idea he would die. We thought he was just slightly injured."

"And when it was in the newspaper the next day, how did you feel? Did you feel guilty? Or afraid? Or perhaps just sorry? And have you spent your whole life since then in fear of the police? What's that been like?"

Ryuji got up from the sofa and looked at Miki. His eyes were like those of a child who has found a treasure. "I want you to tell me, please."

"So that you can tell Ichiro?"

"Don't be stupid! Don't you get it? I'm a writer! I want to take your secrets and your suffering and make them into art!"

He curled his hands like an eagle's talons and yelled in a high, strained voice. His shoulders heaved, and he crumpled back down on the couch exhausted.

"Of course, you don't have to tell me right away."

Miki walked to the stereo and fiddled with the volume control. The music got even louder.

"You haven't told anyone else have you?"

"I'm dying to tell somebody."

"I don't want you to ever say anything to anyone."

Miki picked up a stone ashtray from the shelf. It would be just the right size for bludgeoning the novelist to death.

Ryuji was sitting deep in the sofa with his back to Miki.

"Ichiro doesn't know about this, right?"

"You know, he's the kind of person who wouldn't divorce you even if he knew. What exactly was it about my brother that you fell in love with? He's a little crazy."

Miki set the ashtray down.

"What do you mean, 'crazy'?"

"He's a degenerate. That's why his pictures sell so well. I think they're all scary. Have a look at the one in the shed."

Miki turned toward the door to the shed. Ryuji laughed.

"What a couple! A freak and a murderer! That's so classic!"

"If you say so . . ."

Three minutes later.

The bloody ashtray made a heavy thud as it slipped from Miki's hand to the floor. Ryuji, who had been struck from behind, was still seated on the sofa, the upper half of his body slumped forward. From behind, Miki reached out and grabbed him by the shoulder, pulling him back so that his weight rested against the back of the sofa. Miki made certain that he had no chance left. She managed to control her breathing and take a deep breath. She spread both her hands in front of her face and stared at them. Her ten fingers trembled uncontrollably.

There was a sudden knock at the door. It was an insignificant sound, like when a chef cracks an eggshell on the lip of a saucepan. Miki stiffened and stared at the door.

"Ryuji, are you there?" It was Ryuji's mother. "You're there, aren't you? I can hear your music all the way out here. You have a phone call from your editor." Miki said nothing and turned back to face the speakers. The music was still blaring.

"Is it all right? I'm coming in."

The doorknob turned and the door shook. But the now-dead master of this chamber had locked the door, and so it remained, and it did not open. Ryuji's mother gave up and went away. Miki let out a long sigh. But her expression remained hard. She turned off the stereo, put both hands to her forehead, and shook her head.

"How could this have happened?"

She looked at the body.

"What happened here?"

She kept her voice low. It wouldn't do to raise a big fuss.

"I have to get him out of here."

But where could she take the body?

"Where the hell can I hide this?"

She looked around the messy room. Clothing lay everywhere so there was hardly a place to step. She quickly gathered the clothes and piled them in a corner.

Her gaze fell on the wardrobe.

"A black wooden wardrobe . . . Just the perfect size for the body of a novelist."

She decided to check the wardrobe and open the door. But it wouldn't open. Ryuji had said he locked the wardrobe as well as the room door. There was a golden keyhole just below the knob of the wardrobe door.

She searched his pockets and found several keys. One in particular was quite old-fashioned: gold with no spine.

"I bet this is the one," she said and inserted it in the lock and turned it.

Ten minutes later.

Miki had finished hiding Ryuji's body. He was a small man so it wasn't hard work. But there was too much clothing. In order to fit Ryuji, she had to make more room. She removed an armful of clothes and piled them with the rest in the corner of the room.

Turning to leave, Miki glanced one last time at the pile of clothes. She bit her lower lip and clenched her left hand into a fist.

She closed the door. The sound of the key in the lock made an unexpected loud clicking noise. Miki took all the keys she had found in Ryuji's pockets, including the bedroom key. All that was left in the room was a wardrobe with a person in it.

2.

Breakfast the next morning.

Miki arrived at the table. The sky outside the window was gloomy and covered with thick clouds. Perhaps for that reason, it seemed that day had not yet properly dawned. Even with the lights turned on, the corners of the room seemed bereft of light; darkness cloaked the room like a swarm of flying insects that refused to be shooed away.

The temperature was noticeably colder than the day before. Miki scrunched her shoulders and shivered. Maybe because it was an older house, it seemed there were cracks and gaps everywhere that let in a draft. Whenever anybody walked around, the floorboards scraped against one another, raising a sound that was painful to the ears.

"Mom, what can I do to help?"

"Oh, don't you mind, Miki. Just have a seat."

Miki did as she was told and sat down in a chair. She watched as the food was brought to her.

"Miki!"

Miki turned her head. Fuyumi sat down next to her.

"What time did you get here last night? I didn't even notice you had arrived. The streets are so dark at night. You didn't get lost, did you? The forest is big and there are no decent streetlights. Didn't you feel like Little Red Riding Hood?"

Fuyumi smiled as she said this. Her skin was an unhealthy-looking bluish white, but her lips were deep red.

"Yeah, I was afraid the wolf might jump out and attack me at any moment."

"Gosh, Miki, the wolf attacks Little Red Riding Hood while she's visiting Grandma's house! So the place to be scared is not the forest, it's the house!"

"You may be onto something there."

Fuyumi poked at her food with the tip of her finger, a finger so sickly white it was hard to believe blood actually flowed through it.

"Miki, would you like a cardigan or something? You look awfully cold."

Miki was wearing only light clothing.

"No, that's okay. I have warmer clothes with me. I just wasn't thinking."

"Who would have expected it to get so cold overnight?"

Fuyumi turned to look at the turn-of-the-century stove. It was gigantic, much too big for one person to lift, and it was rusty. Atop the stove was a battered teakettle which was slowly puffing out steam. The window was covered with drops of water. Fuyumi let out a sigh.

"Ryuji is late for breakfast. Everybody else is here. I'll go wake him up."

She started to get up, but Miki stopped her.

"On my way down here I knocked on his door, but it was locked. He must still be sleeping. Maybe we should just leave him alone. I bet he was up late last night."

One lie after another.

"That's right. He did say he was going to see a friend last night. That must be why he's sleeping late. Or maybe he isn't even back yet. I never know when he's in his room and when he isn't, since he keeps his door locked all the time."

Breakfast proceeded without Ryuji. From the quiet breakfast table, everyone could hear the ringing of the telephone in the living room. Mother got up from the table and came back a few moments later.

"Who was on the phone, Mom?" Fuyumi asked.

"Ryuji's friend. He wanted to know why Ryuji didn't show up last night. He was worried. I told him Ryuji was still asleep, and he said that he would call back."

"So, it seems Ryuji didn't go out last night after all. I wonder if he had an accident," Fuyumi said, continuing to eat her breakfast. She didn't seem particularly interested in the idea. "Maybe he's dead. In a traffic accident or something like that."

"Why would you say something like that?" Miki said, her chopsticks held motionless in midair. Fuyumi tilted her head and looked at Miki.

"Is something wrong?"

"No . . ."

"I'll go check his room."

"Dad, there's no need to keep after every little thing like that," Fuyumi said, trying to hold her father back, but now there was another empty seat at the breakfast table.

"He says he's going to have a look, but what's he going to do about the lock?" Miki asked, and Fuyumi responded, "Dad should have a spare key. He keeps spares of all the keys in the house."

"Really?"

"Oh look, here he comes. How's Ryuji? Was he there?"

"No. I even checked the shed but it was completely empty. But of course that room is still a total mess, as ever. The clothes were all piled up in the corner. What does he have that wardrobe for anyway? If he's not going to use it, he should just get rid of it."

Two hours later.

Miki entered Ryuji's room and locked the door behind her. She looked around. She could detect no change from the previous night. The room was still a complete mess.

She approached the sofa where Ryuji had been sitting when he died. She clamped her eyes shut and pressed her fingers to her forehead, telling herself this must all be a bad dream. Taking a deep breath, she opened her eyes and looked carefully all around the sofa for clues.

On the table she found a few drops of dried blood. Ryuji's father hadn't noticed this when he came into the room apparently. She found no other traces of blood. Ryuji had bled surprisingly little. She managed to remove one of the dried flecks of blood by scraping it with her fingernail. Just as she was about to remove the next fleck, there was a knock at the door.

"Miki, are you there? I saw you as you went in. Let me in too." It was Fuyumi. Miki hesitated for a moment and then picked up one of Ryuji's shirts and tossed it over the red spot on the table to cover it up. She unlocked the door and let Fuyumi in. Fuyumi looked around the room.

"You're by yourself. I thought maybe Ryuji would be back by now. Miki, what are you doing in here?"

"Ichiro wanted one of Ryuji's books so I came to get it."

"Huh? Where is Ichiro anyway?"

"He went out for a walk. He said he'd be back by lunchtime."

Miki started to head toward the door of the shed where Ryuji kept his books. Fuyumi showed no sign of knowing that Miki was lying.

"Ichiro has told me a lot about you. So much that by the time I finally met you, just before the wedding, I felt like I already knew you well."

"That's kind of embarrassing."

"He told me that your family is really rich. I wish my dad was a doctor."

"Don't be silly. My dad is just an ordinary village doctor. Our house is pretty ordinary too."

"Ichiro always likes things to be so tidy, it must be hard to keep up with the housework. Ryuji is so different. Just look at this room! He'll never be able to get married. As long as we're here, we might as well tidy up a bit."

Fuyumi went directly to the pile of clothes in the corner, picked up a bundle as big as she could carry, and started to walk toward the wardrobe.

"Fuyumi, wait!" Miki said, emerging from the shed. She ran up to Fuyumi and took the clothes out of her arms.

"Miki, what are you doing? If we put these things in the wardrobe, everything will look so much nicer . . ."

"But, it won't open. The lock on the wardrobe is broken. Actually, it's just locked and won't open, I think." Miki's voice rose. Fuyumi frowned almost imperceptibly and touched the knob of the wardrobe with her raw white finger.

"You're right. It won't open. Ryuji must have taken the key with him when he went out. I just thought he might appreciate it if we cleaned up a little bit."

As she spoke, Fuyumi balled up Ryuji's shirt that was lying on the table and tossed it into the corner of the room.

"He just drops his dirty clothes wherever he pleases! What a jerk!"

The red flecks on the table were exposed.

"Miki, what's wrong? You look terrible!"

Fuyumi had not noticed the dried blood. Miki was carrying the clothes she had taken from Fuyumi to the corner.

"Nothing at all. Shall we go?"

The two of them left the room before Fuyumi had a chance to notice the blood on the table. Miki came back ten minutes later to take care of the bloodstains. She also went back into the shed and took out one book.

Just as the clock struck noon, Miki returned to the dining table. All the others except Ryuji were already there.

Miki stopped in her tracks. Fuyumi and her mother were talking with their faces close together.

"Is everything okay?"

"Miki, look! This weird letter was in the mailbox."

Miki stepped up to the table and took the white paper that Fuyumi held out to her. Miki read the paper and went pale.

"It's typed: RYUJI OGISHIMA WAS MURDERED. HE WAS BEATEN TO DEATH IN HIS OWN ROOM. "

Fuyumi stood up and crossed her arms across her chest.

"Who could have written something like this? Mom, did you tell anyone outside the house that Ryuji is missing? The person who left this letter in the mailbox must be watching our house. And what's this about 'murdered'? Why would he say that?"

Miki felt sick as she returned the paper to the table.

"I don't feel very well."

Fuyumi placed her wraithlike white hand on Miki's shoulder. Miki shuddered as if someone had held ice to her neck.

"The letter isn't stamped. Someone must have hand-delivered it. Ryuji murdered in his room . . . His room *is* on the first floor and set apart from the rest of the house. It's possible some criminal could have crept into his room and we wouldn't be aware of it. Miki, I'd like to talk with you after lunch. Alone. Anywhere you like. Perhaps your room would be best. I mean, Ichiro's room. Say, in an hour?"

3.

One hour later.

Fuyumi entered the room and looked around.

"It's been a long time since I've been in Ichiro's room. This wardrobe is just like the one in Ryuji's room. When I was little, I used to wonder why I didn't have one. I was jealous."

"Sorry it's such a mess in here."

Clothing and luggage were piled in the corner of the room.

"Compared with Ryuji's room, this place is neat. Don't worry about it."

For a while Fuyumi looked at the pictures hanging on the walls, but finally she pulled the chair back from the desk and sat down. From her pocket she pulled out the white piece of paper from lunchtime.

"Could this person be telling the truth? Ryuji, murdered . . . ?"

"That letter . . . it was really in the mailbox?"

"Are you implying that I wrote it?"

"No, not at all."

"It was really in the mailbox. I found it there. But I have something more interesting to tell you. Last night Ryuji had a phone call from his editor, and Mom says she knocked on his door at about nine o'clock. The door was locked, but there was music playing inside. What do you think?"

"What do you mean, what do I think . . ."

"The letter says, 'WAS MURDERED IN HIS OWN ROOM.' Here's what I think. I think when Mom went to his room, Ryuji was there. I can't be sure of course. But I don't think he would go out and leave the music playing."

Fuyumi got up from the chair and paced around the room.

"If what this letter says is true, maybe after the killer murdered Ryuji he carried the body out of the room and left the music on. Ichiro says he was in Ryuji's room until about eight last night. They talked for a while and then Ichiro left. As far as I can tell, he was the last person to see Ryuji."

"Are you suggesting Ichiro is the criminal?"

"Not at all. But I know that Ryuji has a habit of locking his door, and that's what bothers me. It would not be easy for someone to simply walk into his room and kill him. First, he would have to break the lock or smash in the door. But Ichiro says he let himself out while Ryuji wasn't paying attention. He's not sure if Ryuji locked the door after him. So the room may have been unlocked for some part of the time between eight when Ichiro left the room and after nine when Mom knocked on the door. That would make it easy for someone to get in and out. Miki, you were in Ryuji's room this morning. You said Ichiro wanted to borrow a book and you went to get it. You came out at the same time as I did. Ten minutes later you remembered the book and went back to get it, didn't you."

Miki nodded. That's when she was dealing with the blood on the table.

"The book that you got from the shed, where is it now? What

book did you pick? Ryuji's library is very interesting, but some of the books are not . . ."

"Oh yeah, the book . . . where did I put it?"

"What's wrong? Did you misplace it?"

"No, I'm sure I brought it up here. I'm pretty sure I put it in the wardrobe . . ."

Miki checked her pockets as she approached the cabinet. Ichiro's wardrobe was just like Ryuji's, and it also had a lock. Miki plucked out an old-fashioned gold key, put it in the keyhole, and turned it.

"Is something wrong?" Fuyumi asked. Miki seemed to be taking forever to open the wardrobe door.

"It's nothing. This lock seems to be broken. It should be unlocked, but the door won't open."

She put her fingers on the knob and pulled but nothing happened.

"Maybe . . ." Fuyumi started to speak, but then she shut her mouth. Her eyes were wide open and her facial expression suggested she was witnessing a horrific murder scene.

"What's wrong?"

"Nothing." Fuyumi got up and avoided Miki as she left the room. That night again, Miki would not have the time she needed to dispose of Ryuji's body.

On the morning of the second day after Ryuji died, nearly everyone in the household gathered at breakfast. Miki heard Fuyumi explain that she had found a second letter in the mailbox. Just like the first letter, this one had been placed directly in the mailbox with no sender's name.

The typewritten text said, "RYUJI WAS KILLED WITH AN ASHTRAY."

After breakfast Miki went back to her room so she and Ichiro could walk around the halls. They found Fuyumi standing in the second-floor hallway with a pair of binoculars. She seemed to be observing something through the window.

"What do you see?" Miki asked. Fuyumi gestured for quiet, putting her index finger to her lips.

"I am trying to figure out who sent those letters. I'm sure the sender is watching this house from somewhere close by."

Her face was dead serious as she said this, still holding the binoculars to her eyes.

Outside the window was an expanse of dull-colored trees. The clouds threatened rain at any moment. A cold wind prickled Miki's skin and ruffled her long hair. The skin right below her nose was red from the cold and her eyes looked like she was about to burst into tears.

"You're taking those letters seriously, I see."

"It's not that I believe them completely. If I were to express my curiosity as a pie chart, I would probably give it about 120 degrees."

"But the person who wrote those letters, why would he think Ryuji was murdered in his room? How would he know an ashtray was used as the weapon?"

"Ryuji's room has a window, right? Anybody could look in from outside. If the person who wrote the letters had been out in the dark woods, he would see a bright window standing apart from the old house on top of the hill. It wouldn't be difficult to see a man being killed with an ashtray. I don't find this scenario hard to picture at all. By the way, Miki, don't you sometimes have a strange feeling that someone is looking at you funny? Like you're being watched or something?"

"Watched?" Miki said, shaking her head.

"Is that so? I guess it's just my nerves."

"Fuyumi, here's what I think. I think whoever wrote those letters is someone right here in this house."

"Someone in this house?"

"That's right. And on top of that, I think whoever wrote the letters is the person who killed Ryuji. That is, of course, assuming Ryuji has actually been killed."

Fuyumi laughed. "I think I could really get along with you,

Miki. But why in the world would a criminal send letters exposing his own crime? And do you really think someone in this family could have killed Ryuji?"

Miki was silent. From whatever angle, any explanation seemed hopelessly confused. The apparent facts just didn't add up. On her white forehead, one drop of sweat appeared.

"Miki, I have no idea who sent those letters, but I do have an idea who might have killed Ryuji," Fuyumi said, smiling and bringing her face close to Miki's. "And I think you do too, don't you?"

Lunchtime.

Once everyone was gathered at the dining table, the subject of the letters came up.

"I have a bad feeling about this. Maybe we should call the police."

"But who could believe Ryuji has been murdered . . . Tomorrow morning, let's see if another letter arrives, and then we can call the police."

"Dad, you have all the spare keys for this house, right? Do you have the key for the wardrobe in Ryuji's room?"

As Fuyumi uttered these words, she glanced sidelong at Miki and raised the corners of her lips.

"No, I don't think there *is* a spare key for the wardrobe. Oh and by the way, I meant to tell you, Fuyumi, but since you moved out I haven't had a chance. I lost all the spare keys about six months ago."

Miki's expression suggested secret surprise. "You mean the key for Ryuji's room too?"

"That's right. There is no spare key. It was carelessness on my part, but I lost them."

"So, if you didn't have a spare key, how did you know yesterday morning that Ryuji wasn't in his room?"

"It wasn't locked. I let myself in and had a look around."

For a while Miki continued eating in silence. When she was

finished she said to Fuyumi, "I have something I have to tell you later. Meet me at Ryuji's room at two, just the two of us. Okay?"

As she had hoped, Fuyumi nodded.

"Perfect. I have something important I need to talk to you about too."

4.

1:58 p.m.

Two minutes before the appointed time, Miki entered Ryuji's room, which stood apart from the main house. She sat on the sofa just as she had on the night of the murder. From time to time she cast a glance at the wardrobe. It was November, so it was cold. The heat was not on, and her breath came out in white puffs.

Fuyumi showed up at two. Behind her were a pair of men in green uniforms. Miki winced when she saw them.

"Who are these people?"

"They are some colleagues of mine who do a little part-time work for a moving company. I told them we had to get rid of some oversize garbage, so they came right over to help out."

"Oversize garbage?"

As Fuyumi nodded, one of the two men approached the cabinet. He spread his arms and started to measure its width. The other man pointed his finger at the wardrobe and asked Fuyumi a question.

"Yes, this is it. This thing. Could you take this out to the truck?"

"What are you doing?"

Fuyumi's pale face had a faint smile that seemed out of place.

"Right in front of the house is a small truck that I've borrowed. These two men are going to carry the wardrobe out there for me."

The two men grabbed the wardrobe at each end and lifted it.

One of them said something to Fuyumi.

"What's that? It's surprisingly heavy? As if there was a human body in it? Yeah, right. I'm sure you're right. Be very careful with it. Don't shake it up. And by all means, don't let it fall over or turn it upside-down."

The men took the wardrobe away. The two women followed behind.

"So this is what I have to say to you, Miki. You did it. I think you know exactly what I'm talking about."

"You're mistaken."

"Come off it. Tell me the whole truth."

Ryuji's room stood apart from the rest of the house, so once the wardrobe was through the door they could see out into the garden. The truck was parked just outside.

"After you put it in the truck, what are you going to do with it?"

"I was thinking I might drop it off in front of the police station. What do you think of that idea?"

The wardrobe lurched once.

"Be careful there!" Miki burst out abruptly.

"Miki, do you remember last night when we were talking in Ichiro's room? You went to open the wardrobe, and it wouldn't open. Do you know why?"

"You seem to think you know."

"Last night, you said the lock was broken and wouldn't open."

"Yes, I checked this morning and it was broken. All the screws from the fastener were missing," Miki said, as if making excuses. Fuyumi just laughed.

"But I bet it wasn't really broken at all. It just means you woke up and realized your own mistake, and then to bring the facts into line with the things you said you had to break it."

"My mistake?"

"Oh come on, don't pretend you don't know what I'm talking about. Last night, the key you put into the lock in Ichiro's wardrobe was the wrong key. It was the key to Ryuji's wardrobe, wasn't it? The two wardrobes are identical to one another, and the keys to each look the same: gold and old-fashioned. I know this because my brothers showed them to me when I was a child. But just because they look similar doesn't mean they are the same. Only the handles are identical. Each of the keys can open only one of the wardrobes."

The two men were about to put the wardrobe onto the truck. Miki and Fuyumi stood to the side, facing each other.

"Last night you didn't notice that you had mixed up the two keys. You were trying to open Ichiro's wardrobe using Ryuji's key. When you couldn't open it, that's when I figured out what was going on. I think reading those letters put me onto the idea. After that I wondered to myself how it came to be that you had the key to Ryuji's wardrobe. And that's what led me to the horrifying conclusion."

The two men were using a rope to secure the wardrobe to the truck.

"Whatever's hidden in this wardrobe, you're the one who put it there. And then you locked it so that no one would find out. You took the key to the wardrobe and the key to Ryuji's room and you put them in your pocket."

Fuyumi turned to the two men. "Thanks, that was a big help. I'll take care of the rest."

As Fuyumi thanked them, the two men bowed their heads and silently left. Only Miki and Fuyumi were left standing in front of the wardrobe.

"Now it's just you and me, Miki," Fuyumi said, her arms crossed in front of her. Miki shook her head.

"Nope. The three of us."

Fuyumi faltered for a moment, as if she had broken through to a void. Soon, however, that sly smile was right back on her face. "I knew it. I knew it was you who killed Ryuji. And you hid the body in here. You decided to leave the body in the room until you had time to dispose of it."

"You're wrong! You've misunderstood! I admit I went to Ryuji's room two nights ago. But I didn't kill him."

"I don't believe you."

"How can I even try to explain? How did things come to this? That night, the criminal got away unseen! And there I was, the one most likely to be suspected. That's why I hid Ryuji's body. I had no choice!" At this point, Miki was yelling.

"That night, Ryuji called me to his room to talk about some ancient history. He was playing loud music, and for about three minutes I was in the shed. He told me he had a few of Ichiro's paintings in there. When I emerged from the shed and came back into the room, he was lying there with his head bashed in, dead."

"With an ashtray, like it said in the letters?"

"That's right. The bloody ashtray was left on the table. I picked it up—that's why my fingerprints are on it. The ashtray slipped from my hands and fell to the floor."

"You're saying you were in the shed when he was killed?"

"I couldn't hear anything because the music was so loud. So I didn't notice what was going on. I was standing there in front of his dead body, wondering what to do, when your mother knocked on the door and tried to open it. As you know, the door was locked and she couldn't open it."

"Nobody could get in or out of the room? If what you say is true—and I'm not saying I believe you yet at all—for your story to be true, the criminal would have to be someone who had a key to Ryuji's room. While you were in the shed, that person would have to have quietly unlocked the door, entered the room, struck Ryuji in the head with the ashtray, and left the room again. Then he would've had to lock the door again from the outside. The criminal would have to have been able to do all that."

"But the key to the room was in Ryuji's pocket. At first, I thought the criminal must have the spare key. Left alone with the corpse I cursed whoever had done this. But I didn't want to go to the police . . ."

Miki stopped speaking. Fuyumi tilted her head slightly.

"Why ever not? If what you say is true, you should have just told the police the honest truth."

Miki covered her face with her hands.

"That is my punishment. Now I can never tell the police. I will have to live with this pain . . . This is the punishment God has meted out for me. God killed Ryuji, and then to make me suffer, he sent those awful letters . . ."

"Miki, are you all right?"

"I'm sorry. It's nothing . . . Someday, I'll be able to tell you the real reason," Miki said, her words mixed with sobs. Her eyes were all red. Even so she looked unflinchingly at Fuyumi.

"Let's get back to the matter at hand. At first, when I thought about the spare key, I suspected your father."

"My dad? Yes, I guess I can see that. I told you he had all the spare keys. But he says he lost them half a year ago. Of course it's possible he created that story to deflect suspicion from himself. Regardless, the murderer must have had access to a spare key somehow."

"But by that line of reasoning, there's still one thing I can't understand. Yesterday morning, when Ryuji failed to appear at breakfast, your dad went to his room to get him. The night before, when I left Ryuji's room, I used the key from his pocket to lock the door. So, there's no way your dad could have opened the door and looked around unless he still had a spare key. Naturally that's what I thought until this morning. But he doesn't have the spare keys anymore. Yesterday morning he said the door to Ryuji's room wasn't locked. I'm certain I locked the door when I left his room, but the next morning it was unlocked."

"If we assume that Dad actually still has the spare keys . . . Actually, whether it was Dad or anyone else for that matter, why would they need to unlock the door in the middle of the night? Maybe someone went into the room at night to do away with the murder evidence? And then forgot to lock the door when they left . . ."

"There's an even simpler answer. Maybe there never was any

spare key. Your father lost it after all. Maybe the murderer didn't need a spare key."

"Huh?"

"When Ryuji called me into his room, maybe the murderer was already there. In the room. He waited for me to go into the shed, and he chose that moment to kill Ryuji. And he stayed right there in the room holding his breath and hiding. That's all. It's that simple."

"So, you're saying the criminal might have stayed in the room and waited for you to leave?"

"That's right. When I left the room, I used Ryuji's key to lock up. So, when the murderer left after me, he had no way to lock the door again. And that's why the door was left unlocked."

"But where in Ryuji's room could the murderer hide?"

Miki stared silently at the wardrobe. At first, Fuyumi's facial expression suggested she didn't understand, but then she got it, and burst out, "Huh? You mean . . . ?!"

"That's the only place in that room where someone could have hidden. He could have been hiding in there and jumped out when I went into the shed. Then he could have grabbed the ashtray and hit Ryuji with it. And then he could have gotten back into the wardrobe. That's what must have happened."

"I thought Ryuji's body had to be hidden in the wardrobe."

"That's what I thought I had to do at first. But I couldn't get the door open no matter what I tried. I put the key in the lock and tried to turn it, but it seemed to be stuck on something and wouldn't open. I thought the lock must be broken. Ryuji said the lock would get a little fussy sometimes. I mistakenly believed he meant that even if he twisted the key a little the lock wouldn't open. But what he really must have meant was that even if he twisted the key, the lock wouldn't lock. Probably, on that night, someone did something to the wardrobe from the inside so it wouldn't open. Because I couldn't get the door open, I gave up on trying to hide the body in there. I looked around and noticed the suitcase I brought with me. Ryuji was a small man so my impulse was just to put him in that."

"So you put him in the suitcase with the weapon?"

"Because my fingerprints were on it. But of course the suitcase was filled with my clothes, so there was no room to fit a body. I decided to take out the clothes, put in the body, and leave the clothes in the room."

"So, those clothes are your clothes? The women's clothes?"

"That's right. So, I couldn't let anyone find them. It would be suspicious. There was already a pile of clothes in the corner of the room. I thought that was perfect, and I just added my clothes to the pile to hide them. I meant to come back when everyone else was asleep. But in the end I wasn't able to follow through with that plan."

"That's why you were wearing only light clothing the next morning. You had nothing to change into. And after that, you were in Ryuji's room not to borrow a book but to collect your clothes. When I tried to gather up the scattered clothing and put it in the wardrobe, you got anxious and took the clothes away from me. Just before that, I was wondering about your behavior. You were anxious because I might notice there was women's clothing in the pile I was carrying. In other words, yours."

"That's right. My bra was hanging down from the pile of clothes in your arms."

"So, where does that leave us? Who did this?"

"I don't know. On that night, between the time when Ichiro left Ryuji's room and the time when I entered it, it seems that for at least a little while the door was not locked. During that interval anybody in the world could have gotten in."

"Wait. Hang on a minute. When you and I were talking in Ichiro's room, didn't you get the two wardrobe keys mixed up?"

Miki nodded. "That's why I thought the lock was broken. Really, it wasn't. On the night of the murder, the killer was hiding in the wardrobe and keeping the door closed. I put the right key in the keyhole that night and turned it. Of course I was trying to open it, but I think I actually locked it. So the person inside was trapped. He had to break the lock to get out. And when the lock on Ichiro's wardrobe broke as well, it was probably for the same reason. The murderer was hiding in the wardrobe the whole time, and he overheard our conversation. Look, there's a small gap between the two doors. He might have pressed his eye to that gap and watched everything."

Fuyumi got an idea. "That's right! That's right . . . That person had no way of knowing you were onto him. And then today, in front of everybody, you said you had to talk to me, and you specified the time and place."

"I thought the person in question would sneak into the wardrobe."

Miki pounded on the door of the wardrobe with the flat of her hand.

"So, what's in here right now is not a corpse but a criminal, someone who wanted to hear what you and I had to say to one another."

Fuyumi thumped on the wardrobe. "Is anybody in there? If so, answer me. Just knock on the door."

Fuyumi and Miki stood with their arms crossed, looking up at the wardrobe standing on the truck bed. For several long seconds everything was quiet.

And then came a knock from inside the cabinet. The two women looked at each other.

"Somebody is in there!" Fuyumi said in complete surprise.

"Did you kill Ryuji? If so, knock twice. If no, knock once," Miki said.

Two knocks. Yes.

"Did you send the letters?" Fuyumi asked.

Yes.

"Did you write those letters so that the body would be found and make me look like the murderer?" Miki asked.

No.

"Was it premeditated?" Fuyumi asked.

No.

". . . because of my past?" Miki asked with a pained expression.

Yes.

"Did Ryuji tell you?" Miki asked.

Yes.

"You wanted to kill Ryuji because he knew my secret, and then you wanted to punish me more?" Miki asked.

Yes.

"Let's see who's in there."

As she said this, Fuyumi slowly opened the door. Her eyes met mine, peering out through the gap in the wardrobe door. The faces of my wife and my sister were completely drained of blood, and they were the ones who were as pale as corpses.

SONG OF THE SUNNY SPOT

1.

I opened my eyes to discover that I was lying on a slab. I sat up and looked around and saw that I was in a big room filled with a jumble of odd things. I could also see a man sitting quietly in a chair against the far wall. He seemed to be deep in thought, but when he noticed me looking at him, a smile came to his face.

"Good morning," he said without getting out of his chair. He was dressed in white from top to bottom.

"Who are you?" I asked. Before answering he stood up and walked to a nearby locker and retrieved some clothes and shoes.

"I am the person who created you," he said, approaching me. The white light from the ceiling shone down on both of us. As he came closer I could see how pale his skin was. In sharp contrast, his hair was deep black. He placed the clothes in my lap and told me to get dressed. I glanced down at the shirt and trousers; they were exactly the same style and color as his. I had nothing on.

"Happy Birthday," he said. Looking around the room again, I noticed that we were surrounded by various tools and building materials. I could also see a big thick book set next to the platform I was sitting on. It looked well read and seemed to contain a series of complicated schematic notations.

I put on the clothes and followed him out of the room. We

went down a long hallway with a succession of doors and shutters. Eventually we came to a stairway leading up. At the top of the stairs we came to another door. When he opened it, a burst of bright light hit me in the face and momentarily blinded me. It was the light of the sun. That's when I realized that the room where I first opened my eyes was below ground. My skin quickly began to absorb the warm sunlight.

As we passed through the doorway I could see that we were surrounded by a hillside covered with grass. Atop this broad, gentle green slope, we had a commanding view of the land before us. The door from our subterranean chamber let us out near the very top of the hill. The structure was a very simple, concrete, rectangular construction no taller than I. There was only one door leading in or out. The roof was merely a flat concrete surface partly covered by a patch of turf. A bird had built a nest on top of it.

I gazed around the landscape getting my bearings. All around our little hill were mountains. The hill was shaped like the upper third of a sphere one kilometer in diameter. The mountains were covered with trees, and I could see no other broad expanse of grass like the one we were standing on. Based on the contrast with the surrounding landscape, I surmised that the hill we were standing on was manmade.

"The house is in those woods down there," he said, gesturing with his outstretched arm. At the bottom of the hill was a clear boundary, and from there to the top of the mountain seemed to be nothing but trees. Through a gap in the foliage I spotted the top of a roof.

"In that house you will look after me," he said, and we headed down the hill.

At a spot near the woods, two white wooden poles were lashed together to form a cross. The incline was very smooth, but that particular spot was noticeably elevated.

"A grave," he explained.

From up close I could see that the house was large and very

old. It was clear to me that the building was in the process of surrendering itself to nature's will. Plants had rooted in the walls and green leaves sprouted from between the roof tiles. In front of the house was a big yard with a meadow and a well, and a rusty old truck.

The door was wooden with peeling white paint. I followed him inside. The floorboards squeaked under our feet.

The house had two stories and an attic. I was given a room beside the kitchen on the first floor. It was a small room with just a bed and a window.

He waved me into the kitchen.

"First, I'd like you to make some coffee."

"I know what coffee is, but I don't know how to make it."

"That's right."

He took a small canister of coffee beans down from a shelf and boiled some water. As I watched, he prepared two cups of fresh coffee. He gave one of them to me.

"Thank you," I said, bringing the dark liquid to my lips. "I have now seen how you make coffee. The next time I'll make it." Tipping the cup, I allowed the hot liquid to flow into my mouth.

"However," I said, "I do not like the way it tastes."

"Yes," he nodded. "You should probably add some sugar."

I did as he suggested and drank the newly sweetened coffee. This was the first sustenance I had introduced into my body since my awakening. The mechanisms in my stomach absorbed the nutrients properly.

Being a little tired from the walk, I sat down and set the cup on the kitchen table. A metallic decoration was hanging in the window. Rods of metal, each one a different length, blew in the breeze, making a not-unpleasant sound. Silently, we both listened to the irregular clanging.

A small mirror hung on the wall. I stood in front of it and looked at my face. I knew beforehand what people looked like, so I was not surprised to see that my profile faithfully reproduced that of a human female. I was aware that my entire makeup—my white skin, my red hair, and every last detail—was designed to resemble that of a human.

In the kitchen cupboard I found some old photographs. They showed two people posing in front of the house. Him, and a white-haired old man. "Where are the others besides you?" I asked.

He was seated in his chair, and I could see only his back. He answered without turning to me. "Nowhere."

"What do you mean by 'nowhere'?"

He told me that humans were mostly extinct. The germs, he explained, had spread through the sky and within two months had eradicated the planet's entire population. No exceptions. He was lucky, however. Before he became infected, he was able to retreat to his uncle's house in the countryside. His uncle eventually died and he was buried on the hillside. The cross we had seen earlier marked his grave.

"I tested myself two days ago," he said. "I have learned that I am now infected."

"So you too shall die."

"Yes, but I have been lucky. For decades the germs were unable to find me."

I asked his age and he told me he was nearly fifty.

"You don't look it. From what I can tell, I would say you appear to be closer to twenty."

"I have taken measures."

It seems that with surgery humans can live for 120 years.

"But in the end I couldn't outrun the germs."

I got up and inspected the various appliances in the kitchen. In the refrigerator there were vegetables, seasonings, and various other foodstuffs that could be eaten once thawed. On top of the electric range was an unwashed frying pan. I turned the switch and the coil on the stovetop slowly grew hot.

"Please give me a name," I said.

He was looking out the window at a rabble of butterflies fluttering across the lawn. He was clearly distracted.

"What's the use?"

The outdoor breeze came in through the window. The metal chimes hanging in the window made their soothing sound.

"When I die," he said, "I want you to bury me up there on the hillside. I want to be put to rest by my uncle's grave. That is what I made you for."

He looked me in the face.

"I understand. I was made to do housework and to bury you."

He nodded.

"Those are the reasons for your existence."

I began cleaning the house. I swept the floor with a broom and washed the windows with a rag. While I was busy doing my chores, he sat in the chair looking out the window.

As I wiped the dust from the window, I noticed a small bird lying still on the ground. I assumed it was dead so I went outside and picked it up. The bird's body was cold, thus confirming my suspicions.

At some point he stood up by the window. From inside the house he looked at the dead bird in my hand.

"What will you do with it?" he eventually asked me.

In response, I flung the dead bird into the woods. My muscles were no more developed than any random adult female, but I was able to throw it a long way. The bird skittered through the branches of a few trees and disappeared from sight.

"Why did you do that?" he asked me, tilting his head.

"Because it will decompose and become compost," I answered.

He nodded.

"When the time comes, I want you to bury me correctly. You need to learn something about death," he said.

He was right. I did not understand death. I was perplexed.

2.

And so began our life together.

In the morning I would wake up and take the bucket from the kitchen to the well to draw water. All of the water we used for cooking and washing came from this single well. We had a small electric generator in the cellar, but we had no pump to retrieve water.

A twisty stone path led from the house to the well. Every morning I would disregard the path and walk in a straight line. Not only did I ignore the walkway, I also stomped on the blooming flowers on my way to get water.

The well had its own bucket with a rope, and I let it drop down deep to the bottom of the well. It made a splash when it hit the water. Pulling up the bucket I was continually surprised at how heavy water was.

After drawing water I would brush my teeth right away. The inside of my mouth was covered with an unpleasant film every morning. During sleep the digestive powers of saliva are suppressed, and I used my toothbrush to clear it away.

Necessities and basic food items were kept together in an underground storage room. I noticed right away that this room was next door to the room where I was born. I would go there to get food for the day, which, together with some vegetables from the garden, I would cook in a frying pan on the electric range. While I cooked he would come down from his room on the second floor and sit down at the table. He always drank coffee with his meals.

"Don't you have any photographs or any other recorded images of the past?" I asked one day at breakfast. After we were done eating, and after I finished cleaning up, he showed me some photos. Like all old photographs, their colors were faded. The pictures showed a town where lots of people lived. I studied the tall buildings, the cars, and all the people.

I spied him in one photograph standing in front of some sort of building. I asked him what it was, and he told me it was where he used to work.

In another photograph there was a woman. Her face and hair looked just like mine.

"You were very popular," he said.

The house we lived in was at the place where the mountain met the hill. At the rear of the house was a road that led to the foot of the mountain. The road was overgrown with weeds and showed no signs of anyone ever using it. The road came right up to the house—it was truly the end of the line.

"If you take this road to the foot of the mountain, what's there?" I asked him another day after breakfast.

"That is where the ruins begin," he replied, tilting his coffee cup to his lips. Through the trees in the yard I had a good view of the base of the mountain. As he indicated, I could see what once was a town. I saw buildings in shambles, creeping vegetation, and absolutely no sign that anyone lived there anymore.

Yet another day during breakfast, he speared some of his salad on a fork and showed it to me. There were tiny teeth marks on the edge of the lettuce leaf as if something had nibbled on it. It was lettuce from our own garden.

"Rabbits," he said. He and I even ate the leaves the rabbits had nibbled on with little concern for hygiene. All things considered, I would have preferred lettuce without teeth marks.

After breakfast I walked around the house in thought. I was thinking about what would happen when his life activities ceased. At some point I too would cease to move. An existence like mine has an active period that is predetermined from the start. It would be some time before I ceased to function, but I had the ability to know how much time remained in my life span. I held my wrists up to my ears and I could hear the sound of tiny motors whirring. This is what will stop, I told myself.

I returned to the underground storeroom and verified there was a shovel available. Since he wanted to be buried on the hillside,

I decided I needed to practice digging.

I still could not imagine what it would be like to die. That must have been why, no matter how many holes I dug, all I could think was, "So what?"

Next to every window in the house there was a chair, and during the day he would choose one of them to sit in. Most were wooden chairs made for one person, but the seat by the window with a view of the well was a longer bench.

I approached him and asked if there were anything he would like me to do. He just smiled and said, "Nothing." Sometimes when I brought him a cup of coffee he would say, "Thank you." Then he would turn back to the window, squinting as if looking at something very bright.

Several times I was unable to find him anywhere in the house. I would eventually see him outside, standing alongside his uncle's grave, his white clothing matching the white of the cross.

I had some knowledge of graves. They were places where corpses were buried. But I could not understand his attachment to this one particular grave. By now his uncle had probably decomposed and become plant food.

The green vegetables in the yard had been there since before I was created. He had cultivated them. Now I was tending them.

From time to time rabbits would come and nibble on the vegetables. With all the plants in the forest available to them, they seemed to prefer the selection we supplied in our garden.

Sometimes when I had nothing in particular to do I would stand watch over the hedge. When I spotted something small and white approaching the vegetables I would spring forward and try to nab it. Unfortunately I had only the same functional abilities as any adult female human, so I was never able to catch a rabbit. They would just laugh at me as they scurried through the garden and disappeared into the forest.

Often when I would chase rabbits I would stumble on something and fall. Then from behind the window I would hear a chuckle.

I would look back toward the house and see him smiling at me. Shaking my head in defeat, I would stand up and beat the mud from my white clothes.

"As your life goes on you're becoming more and more like a human," he told me with a smile when I returned to the house. I had trouble understanding what he was trying to say. When he laughed at me it just made me mad. My body temperature rose and I fumbled for a way to respond. More often than not I would just scratch my head and exclaim, "A-ha!!" Was this how it felt to be embarrassed? I didn't know. All I knew was that I resented him for laughing at me.

At lunch he rapped on the table twice to get my attention. I was eating a bowl of soup and he was eating salad. The lettuce, as usual, had plenty of little rabbit nibble marks.

"Why is it that the vegetables in my salad have been chewed by rabbits and the ones in your soup have not?"

"Coincidence, don't you think? This is a matter of sheer probability," I said and resumed eating.

On the second floor there was a room with no bookshelves, desks, or chairs. There were only some plastic toy blocks scattered about, the kind that would amuse a toddler. I had never seen an actual child, but I had some awareness of what they were.

The first time I peeked into this room the entire space was bathed in a reddish light from the western sun. In the intense light, the blocks took on an even deeper shade of red.

The interconnected blocks had been partially assembled into the shape of a sailboat. Completed it would have been so big I would have needed both arms to surround it. The bow of the boat had fallen apart, and stray blocks lay helter-skelter across the floor.

"I kicked it once and it collapsed," he said from right behind me. He gave me permission to play with the blocks, but I wasn't sure where to begin. I felt as though my brain had frozen suddenly.

"Building things may be hard for your sort," he said. I would only be able to do things with the help of detailed directions. He said I could never create music or art. So I just sat there, unable to do anything.

The sun went down. Outside it got dark and the lights in the yard came on automatically. The white lights shone through the window.

He sat down and started stacking one block on top of another. He was building a sailboat. From all angles, he examined the newly reassembled red boat. I wished I could play with blocks the way he could.

There were always moths flying around the lamp by the well. When we brushed our teeth in the evening the shadows of the moths would flit across the ground. We rinsed our mouths and spit the water in the gutter. The gutter ran under the thicket at the edge of the woods, and from there it ran to the river at the foot of the mountain.

From the time we brushed our teeth until the time we went to bed, we listened to records in the living room. Neither of us liked to go to sleep until late in the evening. Sometimes we listened to quiet music and played chess. We each won about half the time. The mental capacity I had been given was no more than that of an average human being.

Screens covered the windows to keep bugs out. When the evening breeze came in through the kitchen window, the metal chimes would swing and make their familiar sound. They had a clear and beautiful tone.

"The sound of those chimes in the window is the music of the wind. I like it . . . that sound," I said to him as he contemplated his next move on the chessboard. He listened, furrowed his brow, and nodded.

I was relaxed. When I first came into this house the wind chimes just sounded like irregular clanking. At some point, though, I realized it had become more than that. A whole month had passed. During that time, without my being aware of it, my heart had changed.

That night after he had gone to his bedroom, I took a walk outside alone. The night was inky black, but by standing beneath a lamp I was showered in light. I stood there thinking about the changes that had taken place in me.

One day, I can't remember when, I stopped walking from the kitchen to the well via the shortest distance. I now walked on the twisting pebble path and made sure that I wouldn't trample the windflowers. Once upon a time I would have thought that to be a waste of time and energy. Now, I took pleasure in looking around me as I walked.

When I emerged from that underground chamber for the first time, I could only appreciate the sun for its bright white light and the warmth on my skin. Now, though, I understood it in a more personal way—in a way that perhaps could only be expressed in poetic terms. Now the sun was something that had an intimate connection with the deepest interior of my heart.

Many things were now precious to me: the house with the plants growing from its walls, the grassy field on the hillside, the door to the underground storeroom, the bird's nest on top of it. I treasured the blue sky high above and the cumulonimbus clouds that climbed up to it. Bitter coffee was something I didn't like, but coffee with plenty of sugar was good. Drinking it while it was still hot, its sweetness spreading across my tongue, made me happy.

I prepared the meals and continued to keep the house clean. I washed the white clothes and mended any rips with a needle and thread. A butterfly came in through the window and alighted on the record player. I listened to the sound of the breeze and closed my eyes.

I looked up at the night sky and contemplated the moon. The trees swayed in the breeze and the leaves rustled. I loved it all, including him.

Through the trees I could see the ruins of the town in the distance. There wasn't a single light. All was darkness.

"In one more week, I will be dead," he said the next morning when he woke up. A medical test had told him exactly when he would die. I still did not fully understand what "death" meant, but I told him I understood.

∃.

His body had weakened, and it took him longer to get up and down the stairs. We decided he would sleep in my bed on the first floor. I, in turn, would sleep upstairs on the second floor.

I tried to help him get out of bed and walk to a chair by the window. He said that wouldn't be necessary and kept me at a distance. Nothing I did could be described as nursing. He never complained of pain or had a fever. According to him the germs didn't work like that; they didn't bring pain, only death.

To minimize his need to move around, we got into the habit of eating wherever he was sitting. If he were sitting on the bench, I would bring our meal to him there on a tray. If he were sitting in some other chair, I would sit cross-legged at his feet and eat some bread.

He talked about his uncle and how the two of them would drive to the ruins in a truck. They would scavenge for anything useful and return home at the end of the day. The truck they used was now a rusted heap, immovable for lack of fuel.

"Do you ever wish you were a human?" he asked abruptly in the midst of a conversation.

"I do," I said. "Whenever I hear the chimes hanging in the kitchen window I think it would be nice to be human."

Even the wind is able to create music, I thought to myself. I am unable to create anything at all. That makes me sad. In conversation, I was able to use poetic expressions, and even to lie. That was about the extent of my creative powers.

"I see . . ." he said. Then he turned the conversation back to his uncle. Together they had spent weeks exploring the ruins of the town.

I understood that he loved his uncle deeply. That is why he

wished to be buried beside him. That's why I was created—to care for the sick until death came.

A half-eaten piece of bread fell to the floor next to where I was sitting cross-legged. He had dropped it. It made a faint sound no louder than a puff of wind.

His right hand was trembling slightly. He tried to control it, but he couldn't. Gazing calmly at his unsteady hand, he asked me, "So, now do you understand about death?"

"Not yet. What is it like?"

"It is frightening."

I picked up the fallen piece of bread and put it back on the tray. I decided not to eat it for hygienic reasons. I did not yet understand death very well. I knew that at some point I too would die. But I was not afraid. Is there anything frightening about simply stopping? Somewhere between cessation and fear I could sense there was something missing. And that would be something I would have to learn.

I tilted my head and looked at him. He was probably unaware that his hands were still trembling. His eyes were now staring fixedly outside the window. I looked outside too.

The yard was full of light, and the brightness made me squint. I looked beyond the forest that surrounded the house and saw the decrepit mailbox, the abandoned truck, and the garden beside it. Tiny butterflies fluttered above the rows of vegetables.

A small white fuzzball was half-hidden in the shadows of the green leaves. A rabbit. I stood up and went out through the window. I knew this was not proper behavior, but the instant I saw the rabbit I knew this would give me a bit of a starting advantage in hunting it.

Five days before he died it was a cloudy day. I went walking in the forest to gather wild vegetables. There was plenty of food in the storeroom, but he believed that fresh garden vegetables and natural foods were better.

From time to time his hands and feet would spontaneously start to shake. These episodes wouldn't last long, but they became a regular occurrence. He was quickly losing control of his motor functions. For example, he would reach for a cup of coffee and spill it all over the table. Despite his deteriorating physical condition he did his best to retain his composure. He was never vexed, and he would gaze cool-headedly at his unresponsive body.

After I had been walking in the woods for a while I came to a cliff. He had told me once to stay away from the cliff because it was dangerous and I might fall, but I could see there were a lot of wild vegetables near the edge. And I could not resist the wonderful view.

It seemed to me that the ground just suddenly ended and became sky. I kept picking vegetables and putting them in the basket I held in my hand. All the while I continued looking up at the range of mountains beyond the cliff. The mountains faded and melted into the clouds that covered the sky. They seemed like giant shadows amid the gray.

My gaze fell on the edge of the bluff. One spot was crumbling as if someone had kicked it to pieces.

I stuck my head over the edge and looked down from the cliff. Thirty meters below flowed a stream that looked like a piece of twine. Twenty meters down there was a stone outcropping about the size of a tabletop. It was adorned with a patch of grass on top.

I could see something white. A rabbit. It must have lost its footing and fallen from the edge of the cliff, but the outcropping had broken its fall. There was no way for it climb up or down.

From far away came the heavy sound of thunder. On my arm I felt a drop of rain.

Setting my basket of wild vegetables on the ground, I grasped the edge of the cliff with both hands and slowly lowered myself down the precipice. One step at a time I climbed down until I was standing on the stone ledge next to the rabbit.

A cold wind blew through my hair. Until now I had always thought of rabbits as annoyances, but now, seeing this one unable to move from this spot, I felt compelled to save it.

I reached out my hand to the rabbit. At first it took a defensive stance, but then the furry white animal allowed me to pick it up. In my hands I could feel its smallness, its warmth. It felt just like a little ball of heat.

The rain started to really come down. In the next instant I heard the sound of something crumbling, and an alarming tremor shook my body. The cliff suddenly thrust upward. For an instant I was floating in air as the ground fell from beneath my feet. The cliff where I had just set down my basket of vegetables grew taller, smaller, and further away. I hugged the rabbit securely to my chest.

I felt a strong jolt at the moment of impact. A cloud of dust hung in the air for a brief second, but the rain soon washed it away. We had fallen to a spot beside the stream at the base of the cliff.

Half my body was damaged. One leg was dangling and unresponsive, and a big gash ran from my abdomen to my chest. My inner mechanisms were spilling out, but I was sure I would be able to get back to the house under my own power.

I looked down at the rabbit I was clutching. Its white fur was stained with red. I realized it was blood. The rabbit's body was cold. I could feel the body heat drain from between my arms.

All the way back to the house I held the rabbit in both arms. I was hopping on one foot and this forced odd bits of my body to fall loose upon the earth. There was nothing I could do. The rain was pounding on my back.

I entered the house and immediately started looking for him. Water poured from my body and spread across the floor. My hair was soaked and plastered to my skin. Much of my synthetic skin had been peeled away by the violent storm. He was sitting by the window where he could see out into the garden. He was visibly shocked when he saw me.

"Please fix me," I said, explaining what had happened.

"All right," he said. "Let's go to the storeroom."

"And can you fix this little one too?" I pleaded, thrusting the rabbit at him with both my hands.

He shook his head. The rabbit was already dead. That's what he told me. The rabbit had been unable to survive the shock of the fall. It had fallen to its death in my arms.

I thought back to the rabbit that had run among the vegetables in the garden and how agile it was. And then I looked at the lifeless creature in my arms. Its white fur was stained red and its eyes were shuttered forever. His voice sounded strangely distant as he told me to hurry toward the storeroom. He wanted to examine and repair me quickly.

"Ah . . . Ah . . ." I opened my mouth, trying to say something, but no words would come. Deep in my chest there was an incomprehensible pain. It seemed to have nothing to do with my actual physical pain, but for some reason I could think of no other word for it. My body was sapped of strength and I fell to my knees.

"I . . ." I discovered I had the ability to shed tears. "I've grown enormously attached to this little one," I said.

He looked at me, his eyes full of pity. "This is what death is," he said, placing his hand on my head. Then I knew. Death was the awareness of loss.

4.

He and I walked together to the underground storeroom. It was raining hard and visibility in the storm was limited. I was still hopping on one foot, clutching the rabbit to my chest. When we left the house he told me to leave the rabbit behind, but I was unable to bring myself to do this. In the end, while I was undergoing emergency procedures on the operating table, the rabbit was lying on the desk beside me.

I lay on my back directly beneath the ceiling light. Nearly two months ago I had been lying here just like this. I had opened my eyes and he had greeted me with a "Good morning!" It was my very first memory.

He examined the insides of my body but was unable to stand for long periods without taking a break. From time to time he grew tired and rested in a chair.

During the examination, I turned my head to one side so I could keep an eye on the rabbit lying on the desk. Before long, he too would be as motionless as the rabbit. And not just him—at some point death comes to everything, even to me. Even before, I knew this. Never before, however, had this knowledge been accompanied by fear as it was now.

I thought about my own death. It was not just a matter of stopping. It would be a parting from all there was in this world, even a parting from myself. And this would still be true no matter how much I loved something. This is what made death so terribly sad.

The more one loves, the heavier the meaning of death becomes, and the deeper the sense of loss. Love and death are not different things, they are the front and back of the same thing.

I sobbed quietly the entire time he was replacing all the things from my body that had fallen out. When he got about halfway through the repairs he sat down for a break.

"The emergency procedures will be finished by tomorrow. But then I will need another three days or so before I will be completely finished."

His body was reaching its limits. This meant that I myself would have to take care of everything after the initial procedures were completed. I was familiar with the basic inner workings of my body. I had no experience, but if I perused the plans, I was confident I could take care of the necessary operations.

"I understand," I said, my voice choking with tears. "I feel sorry for you."

Why did he make me? If I had never been born into this world I would never have had to love anything or feel any other emotion. Nor would I ever have known the fear of death.

Still lying on the operating table, I pushed these words from my mouth in a voice halting with sobs.

"I love you. It pains me that I will have to bury your body. If my heart has to feel so much pain, I wish I never needed one. I hate you for ever having given me this heart."

His face was so sad.

With my torso wrapped in bandages, I took the cold, stiff rabbit and left the underground storeroom. Outside, the rain had stopped and the air hung damp above the meadow covering the hillside. It was dark, but I could tell the dawn would arrive soon. Clouds were drifting across the sky. Behind me, he opened the door and emerged.

With the emergency procedures finished, I was able to walk normally. But my repairs were not fully complete, so I was forbidden to make any sudden movements. For the time being I had no intention of undertaking the repair operations on my own. I still had to take care of the house and fix meals for him.

As we slowly made our way back home, the sky began to grow brighter in the east. We stopped and stood in front of the cross at his uncle's grave.

"Four more days," he said.

That morning I buried the rabbit. In one corner of the green lawn was a spot where lots of birds always gathered. That's where I decided to bury the rabbit. I thought maybe the birds would keep the rabbit company. While I was refilling the grave with dirt, my chest felt as if there were a great weight pressing down upon it. I would have to do the same thing for him. Thinking this, I began to doubt whether I had the strength.

A few days later he lay in the bed on the first floor and could not get up. All he could do was lie at the edge of the bed, staring out the window. I made breakfast and brought it to him. I could no longer smile at all. It was hard for me to remain beside him.

Finally I understood why he liked to stare out the window all the time. Like me, he still loved the world. So until death came to take him away, he wanted to get a good look and burn the image of the world into his mind. I wanted to spend as much time as I could with a man like that. One second at a time I could sense his death approaching. I could feel it no matter where in the house I was.

Ever since the storm the sky had been cloudy. There was no wind and the chimes in the kitchen window were silent. We had no energy for listening to records. The house was quiet. The only sound was the squeak of the floorboards beneath my feet.

"That light bulb is starting to burn out," he said one evening, staring out the window as usual. One of the lamps in the yard was growing dim. It would stay lit for a while, and then it would flicker and go dark.

"By tomorrow noon I will be dead," he said, gazing at the sputtering lamp.

When he fell asleep, I climbed the stairs to the second floor. I went to room where I could once again see the red-block sailboat. I looked at it and became lost in thought.

I loved him. But at the same time, something else was still tugging at my heart. And that was the resentment I still felt for him for having brought me into this world. A black cloud covered my heart.

My relationship with him was defined by these complex emotions, this mixture of gratitude and resentment. But externally I revealed none of this.

There was no need for him to know anything about the turbulence in my heart. Tomorrow at noon all I would say and express to him would be my thanks for his having created me. Doubtless that would be the best way for him to die, free of any regrets.

I picked up the red sailboat made of interconnecting blocks. I decided to bury all my resentments and dark emotions deep within my heart. But every time I thought about this, I found it hard to breathe. I was afraid. And I felt like I was lying to him.

Unexpectedly, the boat snapped apart at the place where I was gripping it. The hull of the boat crashed to the floor and smashed to pieces. As I gathered up the scattered blocks I wondered what I would do. Someone like me, not a human, could never paint a picture or create a sculpture or make music. Once he died, these blocks would remain separate forever.

That is when I realized there was one thing I knew how to make out of blocks. I could remember how to make the sailboat. I had watched him as he created it and I had memorized it. One by one I pieced the blocks together as I saw him do. In this way I too was able to create a sailboat.

As I did, I cried. Perhaps. Perhaps. Deep within my heart, that is what I thought, over and over.

The next morning the whole sky was blue—nothing but blue, from one end to the other, without a single cloud. While he was still sleeping I stood by the well, brushed my teeth and rinsed my mouth. When I drew water from the well into the bucket, some of it splashed onto the nearby wildflowers. The tips of the flowers were bent over with dew. As I watched, the drops of dew fell to the ground, reflecting the brilliance of the sun in the morning sky.

Because of the long string of cloudy days, the laundry had piled up. I decided to wash several days' worth of clothing. As I hung the wet laundry up outside, the bandages came loose from around my body. I had to pause more than once to adjust everything.

Just as I was finishing the laundry, I realized he was looking out the window at me. Not from his bedroom window, but from the sunny seat in the hallway. Surprised, I ran to him.

"Are you all right, getting up like that?"

"I would like to die on this seat."

It seems he had summoned his last strength to reach this spot.

I entered the house and sat down beside him. I could see the washing I had just hung up. I noticed how strikingly white it all was. It was a fine morning, without the faintest whiff of death.

"How many hours left?" I asked, still gazing outside. He was silent for a while and then told how long he had left, in seconds.

"Does the death these germs bring have such a rigid concept of time?"

"I wonder."

His voice was detached. I asked him, "Did you fail to give me a name because you could not, just as I cannot draw a picture or make music?"

Finally, he turned his gaze away from the window and looked at me.

"I know the time of my death to the second. For somebody like me, the term of life is predetermined. And you too . . ."

In truth, the germs had never infected him. In all likelihood, he had once seen a human build a sailboat from blocks. That is why he knew how to build a sailboat. He was the only survivor in a world from which all the humans had disappeared. He looked at my face for a moment, then hung his head. A shadow had fallen across his pale face.

"I am sorry I deceived you . . ."

I hugged him and pressed my ear to his chest. I could hear the faint sound of tiny motors.

"Why did you pretend to be human?"

In a low voice he explained to me that he had idolized his uncle, from the very bottom of his heart. His uncle was the one who had created him. From time to time I thought it might be nice to be human. It seems he had felt the same way.

"At first I thought you would never see things that way."

He thought my pain would be lessened if I believed myself to have been created by a human instead of by another being just like myself.

"You are a fool."

"I understand that now." As he said this, he placed his hand softly on my head. At least for me, it made no difference at all whether he was a human or not. I embraced him tightly. The time remaining was ticking away.

"I wanted to be buried beside my uncle. I needed to have someone to shovel the earth over me. And that is the selfish reason for which I made you."

"How many years were you alone in this house?"

"Two hundred years have passed since my uncle died."

I fully understood the emotions that compelled him to make me. At the instant when death comes to call, how good it is to have someone to hold your hand. And so until that moment when death hovered over him, I wanted to hold him tight. That is how he would know he was not alone.

There was a chance that when the time came for me to die, I would do the same thing he had done. All the tools, plans, and parts I would need were in the underground storeroom. When I could no longer stand my own solitude, I might create a new life to hold close to me. And so I forgave him.

Together on the long bench, he and I spent a quiet morning. The whole time I pressed my ear to his chest. He said nothing and just looked through the window at the laundry blowing in the breeze.

Since my emergency procedures, my body was covered with bandages. He adjusted the bandages around my neck. The sunlight streaming in through the window struck my lap. It was warm. Everything was warm. It was kind and soft. As I sensed these things, I could feel the negative emotions in my heart breaking up and floating away.

"I am grateful to you for having created me." My thoughts slipped naturally from my lips. "But I also hated you."

With my ear against his chest, I could not see his face. But I could tell he was nodding.

"If you had not made me to bury you, to nurse you through your sickness, I would never have known what it is to fear death and to be plagued by a sense of loss at someone else's death."

His weakened fingers touched my hair.

"The more I love something, when I lose it, the more my heart cries out. And as I live through the time remaining to me, I will have to put up with this pain repeatedly. That is so cruel. If that is the way it's going to be, I would rather never love. I wish to be a person with no heart at all . . ."

From outside I could hear a bird calling. I closed my eyes

and imagined several birds flying across the sky. Tears streamed down my cheek.

"Right now, though, I am grateful. If I had never been born into this world, I would never have seen this grassy hillside. If I didn't have a heart, I could never have taken pleasure in the sight of a bird's nest, never grimaced at the bitterness of a cup of coffee. How lucky I have been to be able to experience each of these glittering gems. If I think about it that way, even if the pains in my heart seem to make me bleed, that too is just irrefutable proof that I am alive."

Strange combination, isn't it—gratitude and resentment? But this is the way I think. Actually, I think everybody thinks that way. Even the children of the humans who died long ago, I think they lived their lives holding similar contradictory thoughts about their parents. They were raised to learn about love and death, and they lived out their lives passing from the sunny spots to the shady spots of this world.

And those children grew up, and they in turn took on the burden of bringing new lives into this world.

I will dig a hole in that hillside, beside the place where your uncle sleeps. And I will lay you down there, and as with a blanket I will cover you with earth. I will erect a cross of wood, and I will plant wildflowers from beside the well. And every morning I will go to greet you. And every evening I will report to you the events of the day.

And so the time passed quietly as we sat together on that long bench. It was nearly noon, and the sounds of the motors in his body grew more faint. At some point I could no longer hear them at all. Deep in my heart, I whispered, "Good night."

KAZARI AND YOKO

1.

If Mom ever decided to kill me, how would she do it? She might just hit me over the head with something hard the way she always does. Or she might strangle me the way she sometimes likes to do. Or she might push me from the veranda of the apartment building to make it look like a suicide.

That was it. The best thing for her to do would be to make it look like I committed suicide. When someone asked my classmates and teachers about me, this is what they'd say:

"Yoko Endo was always troubled about something. Her troubles must have finally gotten to her, and she killed herself."

No one would doubt that I killed myself.

Lately, Mom had gotten more direct about the way she abused me, and lots of times she caused me physical pain. When I was just a kid her torment was more roundabout. There would be cake for my younger sister, but none for me. She would buy new clothes for my sister, but none for me. Mom really went to work on my psyche.

"Yoko, you're the older one, right? Learn to deal with it" is what she'd say.

Kazari and I were identical twins. Kazari was beautiful and active, and she smiled like a flower in bloom. At school, all the teachers and all the other kids loved her. I loved her too because sometimes she gave me the leftovers from her supper.

Mom never made supper for me, so I was always hungry. If I ever dared open the refrigerator, Mom would come running at me with an ashtray in her hand. I was so afraid of her I could hardly even eat snacks. Sometimes I was so hungry I thought I'd die. I'd be gasping, and Kazari would come to me with a plate full of her leftovers. Honestly, to me she looked like an angel. With a half-eaten plate of macaroni and cheese or some cut-up carrots, she was an angel with white wings.

Mom could see that Kazari gave me food, but she didn't get angry. She never scolded Kazari. She treated Kazari very well.

I thanked Kazari as I ate her leftovers and thought to myself how valuable my sister was to me. I would even kill someone, if I had to, to protect her.

In our family there was no dad. By the time I realized this there was just the three of us—Mom and Kazari and me. That was the way we lived, right up to the time I was in my second year of junior high.

I didn't know what effect this had on my life, living without a dad. If I had a father, Mom might not break my teeth or stub out her cigarettes on me. Or maybe she would anyway. I didn't know. Maybe I would have been bright and cheerful like Kazari. In the morning, when I saw Mom smiling, with a plate of toast and fried eggs, that was what I thought about. She put the plate in front of Kazari, of course. Never anything for me. I knew I would be better off not looking, but I was awake, and I was right there in the kitchen, so how could I not look?

Mom and Kazari each had their own room. I didn't. My things were stuffed in the closet with the vacuum cleaner and junk like that. Thank goodness I didn't have much stuff. I never needed much space for living. I hardly had anything besides my schoolbooks and school clothes. My only other clothes were a few of Kazari's hand-me-downs. Once in a while I had a book or a magazine to read, but Mom would just take it away. The only thing that was really mine was a beat-up old *zabuton* cushion. I put it on the kitchen floor next to the trashcan and sat and studied, or just thought, or hummed a song. I had to be careful not to stare at Mom or Kazari. If I made eye contact with Mom, she might throw a knife at me. My zabuton was also my futon. I curled up on it to sleep, just like a cat, and I knew no pain.

Every morning I left the house without breakfast. I could never get out of the house fast enough because as long as I was there Mom watched me with frightful eyes that said, "What is a child like this doing in this house?" If I was even a few seconds late getting out the door there was a good chance I'd end up with a bruise. I could be doing nothing at all, and Mom would find fault and look as though she wanted to beat me.

I walked to school, and often Kazari passed me and I gawked at her. When she walked, her hair swung back and forth. When we were with Mom, Kazari and I hardly ever spoke to one another. Even when Mom wasn't with us, we didn't chat away like two close sisters.

At school, Kazari was very popular. She had lots of friends, and they were always having a good time together. I was jealous, but I never had the courage to join that circle.

I didn't know anything about TV programs or popular singers. If I watched TV Mom got mad at me, so I knew nothing about life with television. For this reason, I lacked confidence about keeping up with the topics of conversation that interested everyone else. I had no friends. During break I put my head down on the desk and pretended to be sleeping.

Kazari's presence was a great comfort to me. Everybody loved Kazari, and I was proud to be her sister, to share the same blood.

I looked a lot like Kazari. Of course, someone might say, you're identical twins, so naturally you look alike. But no one would ever confuse one of us for the other. Kazari was lively, cheerful. I was dark and moody. Even when we wore our matching school uniforms, mine was dirty, stained, and smelly.

One day, on the way to school, I saw a poster for a lost dog on a telephone pole. A female terrier named Aso. There was a simple drawing and below that, in beautiful handwriting, "If you find my dog, please contact me. Suzuki."

I read the poster and didn't think much about it. The truth is my arm, still bruised from the day before, hurt like hell. In class that day it hurt so much I wasn't able to concentrate. I decided to see the school nurse. She was shocked by the bruises on my arm.

"What did you do to yourself?" she asked.

"I fell down the stairs."

That was a lie, of course. The truth was, Mom came home late, got into the bath, and found a long hair in the tub and got mad and hit me, and that was how I got my bruises. I fell and hit the corner of a table, and in my own head I chewed myself out for being such a klutz.

"It was your hair that fell out in the tub and stuck to me and made me feel all creepy. Why do you hate your mother? I come home and I'm so tired. Why are you doing this to me?"

This had happened before, and I had resolved never to take a bath before Mom took hers. So I knew that the hair Mom was complaining about wasn't mine but Kazari's. But my hair and Kazari's were about the same length, and I knew I would not be able to explain this to my angry mother no matter what I said, so I said nothing.

"There don't seem to be any broken bones, but if you're still in pain you should go to the hospital," the nurse said. "Miss Endo, are you sure you fell down a stairway? You've been here before saying you fell down the stairs, haven't you?"

The nurse asked me these questions while she wrapped my wounds in a bandage. I said nothing. Just hung my head and left. I could see that next time I would have to think of something else besides the old stairway excuse.

I was dead serious about covering up my mother's abuse. Mom had told me to keep it a secret, and if I ever told anybody, I was sure she would kill me.

"Don't you get it? I hit you because you're bad, and there's nothing I can do about it. But don't you dare ever tell anybody. You understand? As long as you get it, I'll do you the favor of not pushing the switch on this blender."

I was in elementary school at the time. All I could do was nod through my tears. Mom removed her finger from the switch and let go of my arm. Quickly I removed my hand from the blender.

"Just a little push and your hand would have been juice."

Mom smiled, and on her breath I could smell the chocolate ice cream she lifted to her lips, so sweet it almost made me puke.

Mom was not good with people. With me she was the devil incarnate, but outside the house she had much less to say. She had to work to raise her two children, but to other people she could never express her own opinions. Deep down, Mom and I were probably a lot alike. One thing we had in common was our admiration of the ever-cheerful Kazari. When personal relationships at work did not go well for Mom she came home in a terrible mood. And then she would find me and punch and kick me.

"I gave birth to you. Your life and death are in my hands, and nobody can do anything about it!"

Better than being told I wasn't her kid. That was what I thought whenever Mom had me by the hair.

2.

It was clean-up time, and a classmate spoke to me. It was the first time in three days and six hours that a classmate had spoken to me. The truth was, the conversation of three days before had gone something like this: "Hey Endo, lend me an eraser." "Sorry, I don't have one." "*Tsk.*" That was it. This day's conversation was longer.

"Yoko Endo, you know you're the exact copy of Kazari Endo in Class 1, don't you? But somehow you don't even look like sisters."

That was what my classmate, a girl holding a broom, said to

me. All the other girls around us laughed. What she said was nothing new to me, so I didn't react much, but all the other girls' laughter made me feel strange.

"Don't. You'll hurt her feelings."

"I'm sorry. I didn't mean to be mean."

"All right."

At least, that was what I meant to say, but my voice let me down because I hadn't spoken a word in so long. I kept sweeping the floor, wishing they would all just go away. It was everybody's responsibility to keep the classroom clean, but in reality it was always only me who swept the floor.

"Say, Endo. You went to the nurse's office today, didn't you? Did you get another bruise? Isn't your whole body just one big bruise by now? I know all about it. In gym, when we had swimming, I saw you getting into your bathing suit. But nobody would believe me. Take off your clothes and show us."

I stood there, not knowing what to do, when the door opened and the teacher walked in. The girls who had been clustered around me all scattered and pretended to clean. Thank goodness, I thought to myself, with a sigh of relief.

On the way home from school, I sat on a bench in a park and remembered the other girls' laughter. People shouldn't say things that hurt other people's feelings, I thought, and felt nauseous. All over again, I felt their ridicule. What would I have to do so that everyone would talk to me like they did to Kazari? I just wanted to be like everybody else. I wanted to skip my cleaning duties, roll up some paper into a puck, and play a game of hockey with my broom.

When I looked up there was a dog beside me. It had a collar, so at first I assumed its owner would be nearby looking after it.

After about five minutes I realized that was not the case. The dog was sniffing my shoes, so I cautiously tried scratching its back. The dog was not startled. I could tell it was used to being around people. I noticed then that it was a female terrier, and I thought it might be Aso, the dog I saw on the poster that morning.

I picked up the dog and went to the Suzuki address written on the poster. It was a small house. The sky glowed with the reddish light of sunset. It was seven in the evening. I rang the bell, and a white-haired old lady, not very tall, came to the door.

"Oh, Aso! My Aso! It's really my Aso!"

She hugged the dog tight, her eyes popping with delight. There was no doubt in my mind this was the Suzuki who had written that poster.

"Thank you so much. I was so worried about this puppy. I want to thank you. Won't you come in for a minute?"

I nodded and went in. I was ashamed to admit it, but I was hoping for some sort of reward. Some sweets, a little money, anything would have been okay. I was always hungry, so it didn't matter what. I just wanted something.

We went into the living room and sat on two zabuton.

"So, your name is Yoko. I am Mrs. Suzuki. I just put up the posters yesterday, and already my Aso is back with me. I can hardly believe it."

Mrs. Suzuki snuggled Aso's cheek to her own and got up and left the living room. It seemed she lived alone in this house.

She came back with coffee and some cookies on a tray. Aso tagged along behind her. She set the tray on the low table and sat down again across from me. She wanted to know exactly where I had found her dog. There was nothing very interesting or dramatic to the story, but as I talked she kept asking questions, smiling.

I opened some little straws of sugar and individual containers of milk, dumped them in my coffee, and gulped it down. The cookies were gone in two bites. Both the coffee and the cookies were good. My usual diet did not include a lot of sweet foods, just the occasional dessert that came with school lunch. At home of course I seldom got anything to eat besides what Kazari didn't want. If I were to go to a high school that didn't serve lunch, I wondered if I would survive. Yes, my head was already preoccupied with worry about that.

With a kind expression on her face, Mrs. Suzuki poured another cup of coffee for me. This time I tried to savor the coffee as I drank it. "I would love it if you would stay for dinner," she said. For a second I thought, I would love to. But somewhere in the back of my mind, a tiny, grumbling voice of reason said I had never met this person before, and I shouldn't be pushy.

"Truth be told, I haven't done a thing to get dinner ready. I was so worried about Aso."

She hugged the dog tight. I was jealous of the dog's happiness.

"Oh, I should give you some sort of a reward. What should it be? I'll go and have a look for something. Just wait here a moment."

Mrs. Suzuki left the dog behind and walked out of the living room. Wondering what she would bring me, I experienced an unaccustomed feeling of excitement. I was often jumpy, but rarely excited. I thought I might just get a few more cookies and munch them on the way home. If I took them home they would only be taken away.

Aso was sniffing me. I remembered that I hadn't taken a bath the night before, so I bet I was smelly. I looked around the room. There was a TV. No VCR though. An older lady like Mrs. Suzuki probably wouldn't know how to use one. I had heard rumors that VCRs were difficult to operate. I myself had never laid a finger on either a television or a VCR.

In the living room a large bookcase filled an entire wall. I was examining the spines of the many books when Mrs. Suzuki came back with a troubled look on her face.

"I'm so sorry. I wanted to give you my most precious possession, but I've forgotten where I put it. I'll have to keep looking. Won't you come back tomorrow? I'll have supper ready for you."

After promising, with great enthusiasm, to come back again, I decided to go home. Outside it was dark. Mrs. Suzuki saw me to the door. I had a refreshing thought: Ah, this is what it's like when someone sees you off. Not once before in my life had anyone ever seen me to the door.

The next day, on the way home from school, I stopped off at Mrs. Suzuki's house. Even before ringing the bell, I could smell a delicious aroma coming from the house. Mrs. Suzuki was happy to see me, and I was glad I had come. Just like the day before, she led me into the living room, and I sat on a zabuton. Aso remembered me. It was just like the day before all over again.

"Yoko, I'm so sorry. My treasured possession, the one I want to give you—I still haven't been able to find it. I looked all over for it, but I can't imagine where it has gone. I hope you won't mind, though, if we still have dinner together? Do you like hamburgers?"

Was she kidding? I was crazy about hamburgers, no two ways about it. I would sell one of my kidneys for a hamburger. I said as much, and she smiled so hard her face filled with wrinkles of kindness.

While eating I wondered, why hamburgers? Did Mrs. Suzuki really like hamburgers so much? I couldn't imagine. She probably just guessed that I would like them. I could understand someone wanting to make hamburgers to make a child happy.

"So, Yoko, tell me something about yourself," she said as we ate.

Geez, what should I tell her?

"Well, tell me about your family."

"I have a mother and a younger twin sister."

"Really. A twin?"

I could tell by her face that Mrs. Suzuki wanted to ask more about Kazari, but the truth was so dark and gruesome I couldn't look her in the eye, and I lied to her.

I told her that even though I had no father, the three of us lived happily together. I told her my mother was very nice, and that every year for our birthday she bought new clothes for my sister and me, always the same color, never too showy, but nice, quiet colors, like the kind grown-ups wear. On days off the three of us liked to go to the zoo to see the penguins up close. I told her that my sister and I had always shared a room, but that I was starting to really want a room of my own. I told her that when Kazari and I were younger and watched a TV show that was too scary and we couldn't sleep, Mom would hold our hands. I couldn't stop talking, and I told her all kinds of things that never could have been.

"Your mother sounds lovely," she said.

Mrs. Suzuki mumbled a bit, visibly moved. I listened to what she said and wished that all my lies were the truth.

She asked me to tell her about school, so I lied some more and told her I had gone to the beach with some of my school friends. Looking at her smiling at me, I thought to myself that she must never discover the truth. But the part of my brain that was thinking up all these lies was getting tired, and my voice was becoming a bit shrill. I knew I had to change the subject.

"Uh, you sure have a lot of books!"

I swallowed the bite of hamburger I had been chewing and looked toward the bookcase against the wall. Mrs. Suzuki looked very happy.

"I really like books. These are just part of my collection. There are lots in other rooms too. I also like to read comic books. Yoko, what kind of manga do you like?"

"Well, actually . . . You see . . . I don't know, really . . ."

"Oh?"

Mrs. Suzuki looked sorry for me, so I had to do something. I don't know why, but I didn't want this old lady to dislike me.

"Well, if you know an interesting book, would you tell me about it?"

"Sure, anything you like. I would love to have you borrow some books to take home. That's it. Let's do that. You can return them when you come back again."

Mrs. Suzuki piled up lots of interesting-looking novels and

manga in front of me. I selected just one comic book and left. I picked only one because I wanted to finish it quickly and maybe come back even the very next day. If I did that, I speculated like a greedy princess, maybe she'd give me something scrumptious to eat again. I would be able to see Mrs. Suzuki and Aso again. There were a lot of things I wanted to talk to her about. I could picture myself hanging out with Mrs. Suzuki and Aso so long that my rear would become permanently attached to the zabuton on the floor.

I kept going back to Mrs. Suzuki's house, even though a lot of painful things happened. Each time, when it was time to leave, I would borrow another book, so I would have to come back again to return it. And no matter how much she looked, Mrs. Suzuki never seemed to be able to find the precious possession she wanted to give me.

Of course, returning the books was just an excuse to visit her again, but without an excuse like that I would have felt like a perfect stranger with no real reason to stop by. Mrs. Suzuki was the first person in my life I felt I could really be myself around. I didn't want her to dislike me because I kept coming back and hanging around without a reason.

Whenever I went, Mrs. Suzuki was always waiting for me with dinner ready. Every day I would read the book or manga I had borrowed and tell her what I thought of it. She and Aso and I became quite close. When school ended early I would take Aso for a walk. I helped peel potatoes, and if a light bulb burned out I would be the one to replace it, and other things like that.

"The next time you have a school holiday, shall we go to a movie?"

When I heard this, I nearly jumped for joy.

"But I wonder if it'll be okay with your mom. I seem to be keeping you all to myself lately. Next time, why don't you bring Kazari along with you?"

Hmmm. I nodded, but in my own mind I didn't know what

to do. Mrs. Suzuki had believed all of my lies.

After the movie, Mrs. Suzuki and I went to one of those conveyor-belt sushi places. I tried to make some excuse not to go, but she was insistent. I had hardly ever eaten sushi in my life. I didn't even know the names of the different kinds of fish. I was familiar with the basic rules of how a conveyor-belt sushi place works, and I tried to pick things that would be inexpensive, but the truth is I didn't know what was expensive and what wasn't. While the plates of food moved past us, Mrs. Suzuki talked about family.

"You know, I have a grandchild who's just about the same age as you."

Mrs. Suzuki looked lonely.

"Maybe one year younger than you. A girl. She doesn't live very far away, but I haven't seen her in three years or so."

"Couldn't you live together with your family?"

Mrs. Suzuki didn't answer. There must have been some reason.

"What if you sent her a letter? 'I want to see you. I want to cook for you. I'll make you whatever you want to eat.' You could write something like that. I'm sure she'd come see you."

At that point I gave some serious thought to how I would respond if someone wrote to me, "You can eat whatever you want." I mean, that could be a once-in-a-lifetime question. It might come up, so I needed to start thinking about it now. As I thought, the sushi continued to stream past before my eyes.

"You are a very sweet child, aren't you," Mrs. Suzuki said under her breath. "Actually, there is something I must tell you. It's about the thing I wanted to give you as a reward for bringing Aso back to me. The truth is there never was any such thing. I made it up. I wanted to see you again, so I made up an excuse. Please forgive me. And to make it up to you, I want you to have this."

She handed me a key and closed my hand around it.

"This is the key to my house. We don't need any excuses anymore. You can come over whenever you feel like it. Because

I enjoy your company very much."

I nodded, over and over. I had a wonderful thought. How many times had I regretted ever being born and wondered if I should climb to the top of a tall building, climb the fence at the edge of the roof, and, with the wind whirling all around me and my nose dripping like a faucet, jump. But no matter how many times, I could still have a day like this.

Ever since that day, whenever something painful happened to me, I gripped in my hand the key Mrs. Suzuki gave me, and somehow it helped me regain my footing. Like some kind of double-A alkaline battery, the key gave me a jolt of energy, and it helped me feel up to taking on the world again.

I kept the key hidden in whatever book I had borrowed, like a bookmark.

3.

On a Friday, two weeks after Mrs. Suzuki gave me the key, something happened at school. Kazari came to my classroom during recess. She said she had forgotten to bring her math textbook, and she wanted to borrow mine.

"Please. I'll do something nice for you."

It had been a long time since Kazari had said a thing to me, so I was happy. I had math that afternoon too, but she promised she would bring the book back to me in time for my class, so I gave it to her.

At lunchtime, though, I went to Kazari's classroom and she wasn't there. I had to sit through my own math class with no textbook.

The math teacher was a very nice man. I had hardly ever spoken to him, but sometimes I had seen him in the corridor, talking and laughing with Kazari in a familiar way. So I was sure if I just explained to him why I didn't have my textbook, everything would be okay.

At the very beginning of the class, though, he asked me, "Why don't you have your textbook with you?" And he made me stand up beside my desk.

"I . . . I lent it to my sister."

"I don't believe my ears! Blaming your problems on somebody else! Could you really be the twin sister of Kazari in Class 1? And don't you think you should pay a little more attention to your appearance?"

As the teacher was saying this I heard giggles from here and there around the classroom. My face grew hot and I wanted to run away. I knew my hair was mussy and my clothes were dirty. But what was I, who slept in the kitchen, supposed to do about it?

When school was over for the day and I left the classroom, Kazari caught up with me.

"I'm sorry I was late giving you back your textbook. I want to make it up to you. My friends and I are going to McDonald's. Won't you come too? I'll treat you to a hamburger."

Kazari gave me a beautiful smile. She had never before invited me to do anything like this. It made me very happy, and of course I said yes. Going somewhere with Kazari and her friends was like a dream for me. I stepped on my own left foot so hard it hurt.

So four of us went to McDonald's: Kazari, two of her friends, and me. Kazari ordered for everyone together. I didn't know Kazari's friends, and they didn't say much to me, but they talked to Kazari a lot and laughed.

"Say, is it true you never have any money? I don't believe it. How come Kazari gets an allowance and you don't?" One of Kazari's friends asked me this as we stood in line in front of the cash register. Kazari answered for me.

"That's what our mom decided. If she gives my sister money, she just spends it all right away."

When our order was ready, we took it up to the second floor and sat down at a table. Kazari had bought enough juice and French fries and hamburgers for three. Kazari and her friends started eating, and I just stared at them. I couldn't bring myself to ask, "Where's mine?" It was unthinkable that I should ever speak directly to either Mom or Kazari.

"Here. I'm done with this."

One of Kazari's friends thrust her half-eaten hamburger in front of me.

"Yoko, I've heard you eat things other people leave behind. Is that true?"

Kazari was delighted to answer her friend's question.

"It's true. Yoko always gobbles up my leftovers." Kazari turned back to me. "Isn't that right, Yoko? These two don't believe what I tell them. So let's just show them. Here, eat this."

Kazari took her half-eaten hamburger and pushed it in front of me. She and her friends stared at me, their eyes filled with curiosity. I gobbled up the food greedily, just like a pig would do. And when I was done, the three of them applauded.

When we left the place, the three of them clasped my hands and said goodbye, and then disappeared in the direction of the nearby train station. Left by myself, I suddenly had difficulty breathing. In my heart I cried out, "Oh, God!"

By the time I got to Mrs. Suzuki's house my head was in a panic. Why in the world had Kazari gotten her friends together just to treat me like that? But actually, Kazari had treated me the way she always did. The only thing different was that usually we were at home, and this was outside. I tried to calm myself down with that thought, but my breathing difficulty persisted. Maybe I had scarfed down a bit too much.

Mrs. Suzuki coughed a little as she poured me a cup of coffee.

"I seem to be catching a bit of a cold," she said, coughing some more. "Yoko, what's wrong? Your face is an odd color. Is everything all right?"

"Well, actually, I think I overate . . ."

"Overate? Really?"

As she said this, she peered deep into my eyes. Why are old people's eyes always so clear? I remember thinking to myself as I pressed my hand to my heart.

"I'm having trouble breathing. It hurts . . . here."

I could barely get those words out of my mouth. My head filled again with thoughts of Kazari and her friends. Mrs. Suzuki stroked my head, saying nothing.

"Something bad must have happened to you." She led me to the bedroom and sat me down in front of the vanity.

"Smile for me. You know, you're really very beautiful." She stroked my cheeks and pinched them lightly. She was trying hard to make me smile.

"Stop it," I said. "Stop it! All I see in the mirror is a little clown. My chest is feeling a little better, though, so you can stop pulling at my cheeks."

"Better? Well, that's good," she said, coughing again. And it was not just a little throat-clearing cough. It was more of a nasty, raspy kind of cough that made me worry.

"Are you all right?"

"I'm fine. That's right. I've been thinking. We should go on a trip somewhere. You know, Yoko, you are just like family to me, closer than anyone else."

"Could we go somewhere and never come back?"

"Sure, we could venture out into the world and stay there forever. We could pretend you're my real granddaughter."

I knew Mrs. Suzuki was just making up something she thought would make me feel better. But I thought it was a wonderful idea. All I could think was, wouldn't it be wonderful if she *were* my real grandmother.

Mrs. Suzuki pointed at the mirror. Reflected in it was me, smiling. I looked just like Kazari.

On my way home, I tried walking like Kazari. I raised my head and put on a happy face, and zoomed right along. I realized then that normally I walked all slouched over.

I stood next to the trashcan in the kitchen, studying, and remembered the things that happened at Mrs. Suzuki's house. Mom came home, carrying her laptop computer.

Mom needed her laptop to do her work, and she always took good care of it. Once she had left it out on the kitchen table and I tapped on it a little.

"Keep your filthy hands off that!" she yelled, and hit me in the face with a casserole dish. I learned that the laptop was more important than I was.

Mom looked tired. She took one look at me and turned away in disgust. Kazari called out to her from the living room, and Mom's face relaxed. Kazari had gotten home before me and was watching TV in the living room. I was not allowed to go into the living room, so we hadn't spoken. If I had broken Mom's rule and gone into the living room to watch TV without permission, I think she would have marched me naked around town.

Mom went into the living room, and I smoothed my blouse and thought happily to myself that maybe today might go by without a bruise. I could hear Mom and Kazari talking in the living room, and I paid attention with half an ear while I solved my math problems.

"Say, Mom, have you noticed how late Yoko's been coming home lately?" When I heard Kazari say that, I put down my pencil. "She seems to have made a friend. She's hiding a lot of books in her closet. I wonder where she gets the money to buy them."

I could feel my blood turning cold. Mom came flying out of the living room, right past me, and flung open the kitchen closet door. She didn't even look back at me, as if I didn't exist. She took my textbooks from the closet and threw them around, until deep in the closet she discovered three books I had borrowed from Mrs. Suzuki.

"Where did you get these books?" she demanded, in a low voice. I was quaking with fright, but I managed to find my voice. If I didn't answer her she would hit me for sure.

"I borrowed them . . ."

She was beating the books against the floor.

"You have no friends who would lend you books like this. I've had it with you. You stole them, didn't you? Every day I have to work for you, and these are the kinds of problems you make for me!" she said quietly as she made me sit in a chair. "You've always been this way. You've always been a good-for-nothing. You do nothing but cause trouble for Kazari and me."

Kazari stood in the doorway of the living room looking at me. Her face filled with compassion as she said, "Mom, forgive her. I bet it was just an impulse."

Mom smiled at Kazari. "You're a good girl, Kazari," she said, and turned back to me. "This one, on the other hand, is rotten to the core. I don't know what else to think. Kazari, go back in the living room."

To me, Kazari mouthed the words, "Hang in there," and stuck up her thumb. She went back into the room and closed the door. I could hear the sounds of the TV.

Mom stood behind me and put her hands on my shoulders. I sat still because I knew if I moved she would hit me.

"Have I ever made problems for you? I may have slapped you now and then, but only for your own good."

She tenderly stroked the tendons of my neck, and then she closed her hands around my neck.

"Sto—op!" I moaned as I struggled with her.

"When I hear you talk like that I get so irritated. I'm the one who's been raising you. Don't you think I deserve a little more respect?"

I could feel Mom tighten her grip. I could no longer make a sound. I couldn't breathe. I could not say, "Just stop, Mom, please, forgive me, I'll do anything, I beg you."

I think I was out for only a second. When I came to I was lying on the floor, drooling. Mom stood over me, glaring down like some ancient temple guardian.

"You'd be better off dead. One of these days I'm going to kill you. It is simply beyond me how twins could be so different from one another. Everything about you just makes me so mad, from the way you talk to the way you walk."

Mom took the three books and disappeared into her room. My heart was racing to pump oxygenated blood to my head.

As I lay there on the floor I decided I had no choice but to leave this house. If I stayed, my life would be in danger. The littlest thing could cause Mom to explode with rage, and I was sure she would kill me.

I wanted to see Mrs. Suzuki. I wanted the three of us—Mrs. Suzuki and Aso and me—to go somewhere far away.

Lying there on the floor, I remembered something important. The precious key to Mrs. Suzuki's house, which she had given to me, was hidden in one of the books Mom had taken with her into her room.

4.

The next day was Saturday. No school. Mom went out, saying she had things to do and wouldn't be home until six. Around midday Kazari left to hang out with her friends. Left all alone in the house, I went into Mom's room.

I had rarely ever been in Mom's room. Ordinarily I would absolutely never dare to step foot in it. I knew that if she found me I would get a terrible beating. Worst case: death. Even knowing the danger, I just had to get back one thing; I had to retrieve the key to Mrs. Suzuki's house. The key was very important to me because it represented the bond between Mrs. Suzuki and me. If the books were gone I was sure Mrs. Suzuki would forgive me. But I had to have the key. If it was gone, I could never forgive myself.

Mom's room was as neat as a pin, not a speck of dust anywhere. On her desk was a vase of flowers, and beside that was her laptop. There was a biggish bed, and for a minute I had the strange sensation that Mom was there, just getting out of bed. Next to the bed was a portable CD/radio/cassette player and in the bookcase was a row of CD cases. I was not in the habit of listening to music, but Mom and Kazari often talked about music I knew nothing about.

Mrs. Suzuki's books were stacked carelessly in the corner. I took just the key and gripped it firmly in my hand. All I had to do was get out of the room as fast as I could. I decided to leave the books right where they were. If I took them, Mom would figure out I had been in her room.

Just as I squeezed the doorknob, I heard the sound of the front door opening. I stood absolutely still, afraid to make a sound. If I left the room I would be found out. I pressed my ear to the door. I could hear whomever it was coming toward me.

I looked around for a place to hide. The bed was against the wall, but there was a gap just big enough for me to slip into. I made a quick decision and wedged myself into that space. I must have looked like I had slept badly and fallen out of bed. But the width of the gap was a perfect fit, as if someone had planned for me to squeeze myself in there.

I heard the door open and my whole body stiffened. My heart was pounding so loud I prayed for it to stop and be silent. The sound of footsteps moved about the room. I turned my head so I could see out from under the bed. On the other side of the room was a full-length mirror. Reflected in the mirror I could see Kazari's face. It was Kazari. I didn't know what she was doing here in Mom's room, but I wished she would get out fast. Kazari stood before the bookcase and looked at the CD cases. She hummed to herself as she picked out a few albums. I realized she had come into Mom's room to borrow some music. She took the CD cases, stacked them carelessly on the desk, and looked back at the bookcase. She took out a few more discs and again piled them on the desk.

From under the bed I could see her hand in the mirror as it struck the vase. In that instant I cried out, "Ah!" The vase tipped over and the water spilled across Mom's laptop computer. Kazari showed no sign of having heard my voice, because she herself was crying out "Ah!" at the same time. Quickly she set the vase upright again, but it was too late. She looked at the drenched laptop and in the mirror I could see her turn white as a ghost.

She looked frantically around the room, but before long she

was smiling again. She had pulled back to a spot I couldn't see in the mirror. From under the bed, though, I could see her socks and her ankles. Her feet moved around the room, stopping in front of the three books stacked in the corner. The books I had borrowed from Mrs. Suzuki, the books Mom had taken away from me. Kazari's hands reached out to grab them.

Then Kazari picked up the CDs from the desk and put them back in the bookcase. It seemed she had decided not to borrow them after all. Instead she took Mrs. Suzuki's books to her room. After she had been in her room for a while I could hear her footsteps moving to the living room. In a few minutes she returned to her room and settled down, and I couldn't hear her footsteps anymore.

It didn't take long for me to understand why Kazari had taken the books. When Mom came home she would find her drenched computer and wonder who was responsible, Kazari or I. But if the books she had taken from me were missing from her room, Mom would come to the conclusion that I had gone into her room to take the books back, and that I was the one who had knocked over the vase.

I could picture Mom getting angrier than I had ever seen her. Nothing this terrible had ever happened before. There was no doubt in my mind that I would pay for this with my life. I remembered Mom's face from the night before. She was standing over me, arms akimbo, gazing down like a *Nio* statue at the temple gate. Her face was stern and unforgiving.

Carefully I extracted myself from between the bed and the wall and left the room quietly so that Kazari would not hear the sound of my footsteps. I left by the front door and ran to Mrs. Suzuki's house. The only way for me to stay alive would be for Mrs. Suzuki to shelter me. But when I rang the bell, it was not Mrs. Suzuki who came to the door, but a young girl wearing makeup.

The girl looked me over from top to toe and said, "Who're you?"

I sensed immediately that this was Mrs. Suzuki's granddaughter.

"Well, I . . . Where is Mrs. Suzuki?"

"You mean my grandmother, right? She's dead. This morning her neighbor came to tell us the dog was making an awful racket, and that he had found her dead, collapsed in the front doorway. Complications of a bad cold, apparently. And this was my day off from school, too, and now we have to take care of this. Nothing but trouble."

I remembered that Mrs. Suzuki had said just the day before she seemed to be catching a cold. Behind the girl in the doorway I could dimly see a few other people milling around.

"Eri! Who's at the door?" a woman's voice called from somewhere in the house.

The girl turned around and said, "I dunno. Some kid I've never seen before." She turned back to me. "I can't believe she up and died on us. What a pain. What're we supposed to do with the dog? I wonder if we should take it to the animal shelter?"

For an instant I thought to myself, Lord, would it be okay for me to strangle this kid? But in the end all I could bring myself to do was hang my head and leave Mrs. Suzuki's house.

I sat down on a bench in the park. It was the same bench where I had found Aso. There were a lot of kids playing in the park, sliding down the slides, swinging on the swings, laughing with all their might. I curled myself up in a ball and closed my eyes. I could not bring myself to believe Mrs. Suzuki was no longer in this world. This is too much to bear! I thought to myself.

The clock in the park pointed to six. Soon Mom would be home. I figured I had been sitting on the bench for about three hours. It was then that I noticed a puddle at my feet. At first I thought it was from all the tears I'd been crying, but then I noticed it had flowed from a nearby water fountain.

I stood up. I decided I would run off to the ends of the earth. But then from the corner of my eye I spotted Kazari. I thought I was mistaken at first, but no, it really was Kazari walking along the sidewalk by the park. From her hand hung a bag from a local convenience store. She had left her room to do some shopping. I ran after her.

"Kazari! Wait!"

She stopped in her tracks and saw me running up to her. Her eyes were two round circles.

"Kazari, I want you to tell Mom the truth about what you did in her room and apologize!"

"You know about that?"

"I know all about it. So you better tell Mom the truth, that you were the one who did it."

"No way. I don't want Mom to be angry with me!" Kazari was shaking her head vehemently. "Why don't you take the blame? You're used to it. I couldn't stand it if she got angry at me. It's shameful. I couldn't take it."

Again my chest felt constricted. If I had a knife I would happily have pierced a hole through my own heart. Then I could have been at peace.

". . . But you, you're the one who spilled the water, aren't you?" I pleaded with her.

"Are you dense or something? Didn't I just say you should be the one to say you did it? When Mom comes home, you better apologize, get it?"

"But I . . ." I shoved my hands in my pockets.

"Well?" she said, rebuking me.

I squeezed the key in my pocket so hard I thought it would bleed.

"I . . ."

From the bottom of my heart, I loved her. But that was ten seconds ago. And then the pressure in my chest loosened. My breath flowed easily in and out once again.

"All right. It's okay. Forget it. Kazari, listen to me . . ." I had made up my mind. "I'm sorry to tell you this, but Mom already knows it was you who did it. It's the truth. She knows you took the books to make it look like it was my fault. She came home right after you went out to the store. I was standing at the front door, and I could hear her screaming in her room. I ran to the park, but Mom had already figured out it was you who knocked over the vase."

Kazari turned white again.

"There's no way she could have known!"

"But she did. I could hear her from the front door. She was yelling that the CDs were out of order, and that you must have done it. That's what she was screaming. So she's waiting for you to come home and apologize. I'm begging you, please just go do what she wants."

Kazari looked at me, confused.

"She already knows everything?"

I nodded.

"I couldn't bear it if she got mad at me and hit me the way she hits you!"

I pretended to be confused too, and I pushed the conversation ahead.

"Okay, I know what to do. I'll take your place and apologize."

"What are you going to say?"

"Just for tonight, let's switch clothes, and I'll pretend I'm you. I'll wear your clothes, and you'll wear mine. Until tomorrow morning I'll pretend to be you, and you can be me, slouching around."

"You think she won't be able to tell?"

"Don't worry. We look completely alike. But you have to remember to act a little sad like I always do. As long as you do that, no problem. She'll yell and scream and hit me. You have nothing to worry about."

We switched clothes in the park restroom. I put on everything of Kazari's and puffed my hair up. When Kazari put on my dirty things, she made a face.

"Your clothes smell weird!"

Kazari's clothes were clean and beautiful. I put on her socks, her watch, and I combed through my hair with my fingers to put it in order. I don't know how well I did, but I smiled as I looked in the restroom mirror. I looked more or less like Kazari. Seeing that smile made me think about Mrs. Suzuki. I pressed my hands to my mouth. Something like water was coming out of my eyes, tears or something like that. I did my best to wash my face with water from the sink to hide my tears from Kazari.

"What are you doing?" Kazari had been waiting outside, and now she stood in the doorway of the restroom looking upset. We left the park and headed toward our apartment. It was sunset and the whole building towering above us was bathed in red light. Looking up, I saw the windows of our apartment on the tenth floor. A few moments ago, I had lied to Kazari when I told her Mom was home already. She had not doubted me.

Although I had no confirmation, I believed that Mom would be home by now. Mom was pretty precise about things like that. If she said she would be home by six, she always was.

"Kazari, when you go into the house, pretend you're me."

Kazari did not look happy about that plan. She whined, "I know. So, who's going to go in first? We haven't arrived home together since we were in second grade. It won't seem right."

We played rock, paper, scissors to decide. We matched perfectly, thirty times in a row. Maybe because we are twins, we always guessed in the same direction. On the thirty-first try, I won, so Kazari, disguised as me, had to go in first. I saw her to the entrance of the apartment building. I pressed my back against a tree growing in front of the building and gazed out at the town, bathed in the light of the sunset. In my hand I had Kazari's bag from the convenience store. The plastic rustled as it brushed against my knee.

A boy pedaled past on a bicycle, casting a long shadow. The clouds in the sky were red, as if glowing from the inside out. Someone called out, "Kazari!" and I turned to see a lady from our building, looking at me. "How's school?" she asked. "Are you doing well?" "So-so," I replied. Right after that, something fell from above with a thud, and the lady cried out in surprise. On the ground, in dirty clothes, lay a girl who looked just like me.

5.

When I went up to our apartment, I had to write a note from the dead Kazari. Mom made me do it. She said I had five minutes or less to write it before the police arrived. When I agreed, she told me what a good girl I was, and how much she loved me. Those were words I only ever heard in the middle of the night, in my dreams.

This was to be a note the dead Yoko would have written before dying, so it was easy for me. All I had to do was write down what I thought about when I wanted to die.

No one expressed any doubts about Yoko Endo's suicide. About the time the sun went down and the sky grew dim, obscuring the crowd that had gathered in the darkness, the police were in our apartment, asking us questions, and Mom and I told them our story. Mom had not discovered my true identity, but I was sure it would not be long before she did, and she would be horrified. I decided I would pack my bags that night and hit the road for somewhere far, far away.

The talks with the police went on until late into the night, and Mom and I looked haggard. I was truly exhausted, but for Mom it seemed to be an act. Once the police were gone she massaged my shoulders and gave me words of encouragement. If I were to die, I don't think Mom would even be sad. What a sorry excuse for a human being I turned out to be. Deep in my heart, I was truly sorry about Kazari, who was no longer with us.

Mom went to her room, and I went to Kazari's room, which was filled with so many cute things I couldn't calm down. I knew I would have been much more comfortable in the kitchen next to the trashcan. Once I was sure Mom had settled down for the night, I packed a bunch of stuff in a bag. I tried to squeeze in my beat-up old zabuton, which I used in place of a futon, but it wouldn't fit. I took some of Kazari's clothes out of the bag to make room for the cushion.

I left the apartment and ran to Mrs. Suzuki's house to get Aso. I remembered someone saying something about taking the dog, which had been abandoned through no fault of its own, to the animal shelter. I was worried whether Aso would still be at the house. But when I got there, Aso was very conveniently tied up right at the front door. Inside the house, it appeared, Mrs. Suzuki's children and grandchildren were staying, so they could prepare for the funeral. Aso had been driven out. What the hell, I thought, same as me.

Seeing me, Aso wagged her tail so hard I thought it would start a tornado. I undid the rope and kidnapped the dog.

Dog in tow, I headed off in the direction of the train station. I was very sorry to miss the funerals of both Mrs. Suzuki and Yoko Endo. I did not have a clear idea of how I would be able to live. I had no money at all, and for all I knew I would starve to death. But I was used to being hungry, and I had confidence in my iron stomach, which would allow me to get by on the kinds of things restaurants threw away, like carrot peelings. In my pocket I kept a firm grip on the key, which gave me the strength I knew I would need to carry on, and in my head I shouted out, "Yes!!"

SO-far

SO (significant other)
1 (Soc.): a person of importance (parent, friend, etc.)
2 (U.S., informal): spouse, lover (abbreviation: SO)

far (distance)
1: at a great distance

1.

By now I have grown up a little. I've made my way through elementary school, and soon I'll be in junior high. So now I have a bit of perspective on those strange events that happened a long time ago. At that time I was just a kid in kindergarten. I was jittery and easily upset by any little thing. Everyone was bigger than me, and I had to look up to talk to them. Whenever an adult put their hands on their hips and made a grumpy face I worried that I must have done something wrong. So even if I had tried to explain my story to a grown-up, I just knew it wouldn't have come out right.

A long time ago I thought something must be living under my bed where the light couldn't reach. I thought I could make a pencil fall over without touching it just by thinking real hard, *Fall over!* In the end most things like that proved to be false, but they didn't seem impossible, if you know what I mean. I have always believed in science, but I still think there are things in the world that science just can't explain.

This is something that happened when I was in kindergarten. I think my own direct memory of the event must have faded considerably, but later I was able to recall one detail after another, and heard more about it from other people. Putting all the pieces together, I now remember it very well.

I lived with my father and mother; it was just the three of us. We rented an apartment on the second floor of a large complex. The building was on a little hill, and from our windows we could look down on the lights of the town. Train tracks ran from one end of our neighborhood to the other, stitching together all the nearby buildings. This was the view from our place and I liked looking out at it.

We had a living room and a kitchen, and maybe two more rooms. I remember a floor-to-ceiling post near the front door. It was there that I tacked a picture I drew of my dad. That's also where I hung up my school cap and backpack.

I loved my parents. The only card game I knew how to play was Old Maid, and we liked to play it all the time. We also liked to play hide-and-seek in the house. We would eat dinner at the kitchen table, and then we would sit on the living room sofa and talk.

The sofa was gray. I think it was the most important piece of furniture we owned. We would sit on it and watch TV or read books or take a nap. The fact that we had this soft but sturdy sofa was the real secret of why we were such a happy family. The sofa was important, as were the coffee table and the TV.

While watching TV I always sat right between my parents.

Mom's seat was to my left and closest to the kitchen. That made it easier for her to pad to the kitchen in her slippers and bring back drinks for my dad and me whenever we requested them. I drank juice and Dad drank beer.

Dad sat to my right. That was the best place for watching the

TV. It was also the seat nearest to the air-conditioning unit. My dad, who always said he was uncomfortably warm, would sit there and cool off. I would sit in the middle of the sofa, dangling my feet, and tell them what happened in school that day. My parents would sit on either side of me with smiles on their faces.

At first I didn't realize what was happening. By the time I figured it out it was already too late.

My dad and I were sitting on the sofa watching TV. Dad sat there bent forward with his jaw propped on his hands. He had a dark look on his face. We were watching a show about miracles—a ghost story. I knew it would be scary, but for some reason I couldn't stop watching. The story was about someone who died in a traffic accident and turned into a ghost. But there was a twist. The ghost didn't realize he was dead and just went home like nothing tragic had happened.

Mom opened the door and came into the living room. Like my father, she did not look very cheerful.

"What are you doing watching TV by yourself?" she asked me. She said it in a completely normal voice, and I almost didn't hear her. But thinking back, I'm sure she said, "by yourself."

I felt uncomfortable and turned to my father. I thought he would be angry about being ignored, but he seemed not to have noticed that my mother had entered the room.

"What are you doing?" asked my mom. "Why did you turn and look to your right? There's nobody sitting there."

My mom had a really odd look on her face, and that made me kind of nervous.

After a while, my dad got up quietly from the sofa and left the room. He did not turn even once to look at my mom or me. I was confused. Something strange was going on, but I didn't know what. I'm sure I looked like I was about to cry. My mom got out a deck of cards and said, smiling, "Let's play Old Maid!" I started to squirm. But Mom's smile was friendly and reassuring, so after a while I calmed down.

After my mom and I had been playing for a while, my dad

came back into the living room.

"What are you doing playing solitaire?" he asked me.

He held out his hand to me.

"Let's eat out tonight," he said.

I got down off the sofa and ran over to my dad. I looked back and saw my mom holding the deck of cards. She was looking at me as if to say, "Where are you going?"

I thought she would be going out to eat with us, but she didn't. As soon as I was out of the living room, my dad turned out the lights and closed the door. Mom didn't come with us.

Dad and I went to a family restaurant, and the whole time we were there I was worried about Mom.

"From now on, life is going to be tough . . ." said my dad to himself.

Dinner the next day was also strange. Mom made just enough dinner for her and me. On the kitchen table she set out plates and chopsticks for two.

Then my father came home and acted as if he couldn't even see the food my mom had made. From a bag he took some boxed meals he had bought at a convenience store and laid them out on the low table in the living room. There was one for him and one for me.

In the kitchen I asked my mother, "Where's Dad's dinner?"

"Huh?" she asked, gulping as she looked at me. She appeared to be struck speechless, and I was left wondering if I had said something I shouldn't have. I got scared. I didn't want to ask again.

Then from the living room I heard, "Hey, what are you do-ing in there? Which of these meals do you want?" It was my father. When he was talking to Mom, the pitch of his voice was different from when he was talking to me, so I could tell he was talking to me.

I left the kitchen and went into the living room. Dad was in the process of loosening his tie.

"None for Mom?" I asked. Dad looked at me oddly and his hands stopped moving. I was right. This was a question I just couldn't ask.

I felt I had to pay attention to both of them, so I went back and forth between the kitchen and the living room several times. I ate a little bit of the meal Mom had prepared, and then I went back to the living room and ate some of the takeout meal. I did this several times.

In the end I could only finish about half of each meal, but nobody got mad at me. When dinner was over I did what I usually do: I went and sat in the middle of the sofa. Mom sat to my left, and Dad sat to my right. We all sat there quietly watching the TV. There was a report on the news about a train accident that had happened a few days before.

Ordinarily this would be a fun time of day for us and I would be rolling around laughing. On that day, though, my parents were completely silent. Something terrible had happened and caused a strange rift between the three of us. As I was thinking about that, Mom turned to look at me. The expression on her face was very serious.

"Listen. Your father has died, and now our life will be just the two of us. It'll be hard but we'll manage somehow."

I had trouble understanding this. But my mom's tone of voice was so serious, I got really scared. As I sat there confused, Mom said, "Don't worry, we'll be fine." She gave me a nod and a little smile.

Next, my father turned to look at me. He looked straight into my eyes as if my mother did not exist.

"We have to be strong. That's what your mother would have wanted."

That's when I realized they could no longer see each other. My father couldn't see my mother. My mother couldn't see my father. Each of them thought there was no one else sitting next to me.

From what each had said I understood that one of them must have died. My father thought my mother had died and that he and I would have to learn to get along without her. My mother, on the other hand, thought my father had died.

Neither of them could see the other, and they couldn't hear each other either. I was the only one who could see both of them.

2.

At that time, my vocabulary was more limited, so I was unable to express myself clearly to my parents. I did try to explain to each of them that I could see the other, but they didn't take me seriously.

"Dad is right over there in the other room," I told Mom, tugging on her apron as she stood in the kitchen washing the dishes. Dad was sitting on the sofa in the living room reading his newspaper.

"Yeah, uh-huh . . ." At first, Mom just nodded her head lightly, but when I repeated myself she crouched down in front of me so she could look into my eyes.

"I know this is hard for you," she said, very sincere and truly worried. And that made me think there must be something wrong with my head, and that this was a matter I was not allowed to even mention.

Even so, I tried several more times to explain the situation I found myself in.

One evening the three of us were sitting on the sofa. Of course, by "the three of us," I mean from my own point of view. My father and mother each seemed to think they were sitting alone with me on the sofa.

"Mom is wearing a blue sweater," I said to my father on my right. They both looked straight at me.

"What?" my father said, furrowing his brow. I could tell by the look on his face that he was concerned about me. He obviously thought I was making things up.

"She is! She's wearing a blue sweater!"

My mother, meanwhile, was also looking at me strangely.

"I can see you both. Mom, Dad, we're all here in this room."

And each of them gave me a cross, perplexed look.

This happened many times. At first my parents only pretended to be listening to what I had to say.

Once, though, when I couldn't open a bag of snacks, my mother went searching for a pair of scissors.

"Where did your father leave the scissors?" she asked herself distractedly as she fumbled around in the junk drawer. "I wish he'd left them someplace I could find them."

Dad was sitting right there on the sofa with his legs crossed. It seemed he couldn't see my mother even though they were in the same room. So I asked him where the scissors were.

"I'm pretty sure I put them in the drawer in the kitchen cabinet," he said to me. I repeated these words to my mother even though she was right there.

"He says they're in the drawer in the kitchen cabinet. That's what Dad just told me."

And that's where they were. Things like that happened all the time, and that's how my mom and dad each came to believe me.

"I can see Dad. And I can hear him too."

My mother still seemed confused, but she nodded at my words.

"Mom is right here. So you and I are not alone. If there's anything you want to say to her, just let me know and I'll tell her." When I said this to my father, he nodded with a happy smile on his face. He patted my head and said, "Yeah. It really seems to be so."

That's when I started passing along bits of conversation to both of them. And that was a lot of fun.

Just like before, the three of us would sit on the sofa and watch the same TV programs.

"I like travel shows," my mom would say, and I would relay

this message immediately to my dad.

"Mom wants to change the channel. She wants to watch a travel show."

"Tell her she'll just have to put up with this cop show," Dad said, his eyes never leaving the screen.

"Dad says he doesn't want to change the channel." Hearing that, Mom would get up and go into the kitchen.

I would giggle. It was funny because our life had returned to the way it had been long before. The only thing that was different was that I had to be in the middle if my mom and dad wanted to talk to each other. Once again I really felt like we were a family of three. And that made the whole room feel warm, and I was happy.

At that time I thought a lot about the worlds my mom and dad were living in. From what each of them told me, I think one of them was in that train accident I heard about on the news. Actually, and this gets a little complicated, I have to admit I was certain they were both in that train accident and died.

It seems that somebody had to bring something to some relative. So they decided to play rock, paper, scissors, and the loser would have to get on the train and go to the relative's house.

After that, however, their stories diverged. In Mom's universe, Dad lost and had to take the train. In Dad's universe, it was Mom who went to the relative's house.

Then, of course, came the train wreck. Each of my parents thought they had been left behind to live with me.

My mom's universe and my dad's universe were interlinked, like overlapping semi-transparent photos with me as the common point. I was able to see into both of these worlds at the same time. I was kind of proud of this. I felt like I had been promoted to a special position, like I was now the liaison officer between my dad and mom.

Let's say Dad had just opened the door and entered the room. For Mom, who was unable to see Dad, it might seem that the door had opened and closed all by itself. What actually happened, though, was that she would never notice the door moving at all. Only if I mentioned it would she say, "Oh, yeah, you're right, I just noticed." And then she would understand.

Let's say Mom was in the kitchen washing the dishes. Dad would be unable to see her or see what she was doing. For each of them, things that could not be explained in terms of their own world would simply not be visible.

At mealtime, as always, they ate separately. Mom would cook, Dad would buy something from outside, and that's what they would eat.

"Dad, can't you see this curry rice?" I would ask, setting a plate down in front of him. But it seemed he really couldn't see it. He would just look back at me confused.

Sometimes Dad would turn to a random corner of the room and start talking as if Mom were right in front of him. She would be behind him, but he was unaware of that. Mom was unable to hear his voice anyway, so I would have to tell her what he was saying. I told them both how strange I thought all of this was.

When it occurred to me that one of them was actually dead, it made me very sad. I understood that I existed at the seam where my parents' worlds intersected.

At first I was scared when they could no longer talk to one another, but after a while it didn't bother me. I could sit on the sofa between the two of them and feel comfortable and safe.

But even I, child that I was, understood that we could not go on like this forever. I knew that at some point I would have to choose one world or another. At the bottom of my heart I knew this.

3.

As it was in the beginning, so it was again. But at some point Mom and Dad started fighting. And I don't mean the kind of scuffles you see on kindergarten playgrounds.

After dinner one evening the three of us were sitting on the sofa. We were watching TV, and I was automatically repeating what each of them said to the other. This had been going on for some time, so I was mostly just repeating things like a parrot without thinking about them.

One of my favorite cartoons was on TV, and it had my whole attention. I was lying stretched out on the sofa with my chin cupped in my hands. Mom didn't like it when I took up the whole sofa like that, and she would tell me it was rude, but I liked to do it anyway.

Suddenly Dad slapped his newspaper down on the table. That was the first time I noticed my parents were in a bad mood. They had been saying hurtful things to one another, and I wasn't paying attention at all.

Mom got up and walked into the bedroom.

"Mom went to her room," I said.

"What about it?" Dad spat back.

I got scared and forgot all about my cartoon show. I wanted them to make up. Without the two of them sitting on either side of me I wasn't happy.

"Hey," Dad said to me after a little while. "Go tell your mother."

"What should I tell her?"

"Tell her I'm glad she's dead."

My Dad had a frightening look on his face. I didn't want to do it, but I was afraid that if I didn't tell Mom his message, he would be mad at me. So I got up and ran after Mom.

She was in the bedroom lying on the futon mattress. She was already lost in thought. As I entered the room, she propped herself up.

"Dad says he's glad you're dead. He told me to tell you," I said, suppressing the urge to cry. Mom didn't say a thing, but she started weeping, the tears freely flowing down her cheeks. I had never seen a grown-up cry before, and I was afraid. I stood rooted where I was; I didn't know what to do.

"Well then, you can tell your father . . ." and she said a few bad things for me to tell my dad. There were some words I didn't understand, and she had me practice them. I was just a child, but somehow I knew these were terrible things to say.

"I won't! Stop it!" I clung to her but it was no use.

"You go tell him! Understand?"

So, like a dutiful mailman, I went back and forth from the bedroom where my mother was to the living room where my father was. I was forced to repeat, memorize, and transmit words I hated.

My mother and father glared at me with each new comment. I could tell they hated me for taking part in their war of words. They weren't shouting at each other, they were shouting at me. I felt like I was the one being cursed out.

At first it took a massive amount of energy to talk to my parents in such a way. As their argument continued, however, I eventually went numb and felt nothing. I couldn't hear their voices at all.

My mouth was like a tape recorder. I would record and replay, record and replay. I couldn't stop crying; I loved my parents and I hated myself for saying such awful things.

After about an hour, the fight was over.

I wanted all of us to sit back down on the living room sofa again, but I was afraid to suggest it. I waited by myself on the sofa, my heart pounding. My father left the living room and went to the bathroom to wash his face. This helped settle him down, but he still looked a little upset.

While he was gone, Mom had come back into the living room. I was afraid of what I would do if they started fighting again. Mom sat down beside me, looking a little distraught. Her weight on the sofa cushion forced my body to lean slightly into hers.

"I'm sorry," she said, stroking my head. After that, I stared at the door expecting my father to return at any moment. I was watching carefully so I could tell my mother promptly when my father returned. But he didn't come in.

Mom got up to go to the kitchen. As she walked away, I heard the rustle of a magazine beside me.

At some point, my father had taken his usual seat on the sofa. I was staring at the door, but I had failed to notice him entering the room. He was even smoking a cigarette. I hated cigarette smoke, and I got queasy whenever I would get a whiff of it. But until that very moment, I hadn't noticed any smoke at all.

My father had a stern look on his face.

"I've been talking to you this whole time, but you didn't look at me," he said, stroking my hair just as my mother had been doing. I was certain his hand existed, and it was warm. I felt strange, wondering why I hadn't noticed him before.

I waited for Mom to come back. I waited and waited, but she never returned. My father and I continued to sit on the sofa watching a variety show on TV.

"Would you ask your mother what's on the schedule for tomorrow?" my father asked. He formulated his question carefully so that he wouldn't say anything upsetting. I got up to go to the kitchen.

I opened the door and looked for my mom. But no one was there, just water dripping from the tap. In order to go from the kitchen to anywhere else in the apartment, she would have to go through the living room. It was actually quite strange that she wasn't there.

As I was trying to figure this out, I returned to the living room, and there she was sitting on the sofa. How she had gotten past me I have no idea. But there, where no one had been just a moment before, she sat sipping from a coffee cup as if she had been sitting there for a long time already.

My father was nowhere to be seen. No ashtray, no half-smoked cigarette, no smoke hanging in the air.

I just stared at my mother, forgetting even to ask the questions in my mind.

"Is anything the matter?" she asked me, tilting her head to one side.

I realized then my mother had been there all along. And not just my mother, the two of them had been there, on either side of me. But now I could only see one of them at a time.

I got up and left the living room again. Then I immediately came back in. This time there was no one where my mother had been sitting. Not even a dimple in the sofa. But I saw my father in the other spot. That is when I understood everything.

I sat on the sofa and closed my eyes for a while. The half-smoked cigarette to my right disappeared, and the coffee cup appeared on my left.

Now I couldn't hear them both speak at once. My father's universe and my mother's universe were starting to split apart from one another.

When I was in one, the other completely ceased to exist.

I wasn't standing in the overlap between their two worlds anymore. I was merely moving back and forth between them—and those two worlds had begun to separate from one another.

I was so sad I could barely speak to either of them for the rest of the night. No longer would the three of us be able to share the same sofa.

It took me some time to process this new information. My mom was worried by my silence, and she gave me a big hug. I could see that inevitably we would be ripped apart, and I would have to choose one or the other.

4.

The next day was Saturday as I recall. The sky was cloudy, and it looked like it would rain. Mom was out somewhere, and Dad sat on the sofa staring at the newspaper. I could not believe my mother was gone, and I searched the whole apartment for her. But I knew that if I was in the same room as my father I would not be able to see her. For all I knew she might have been sitting right next to me.

I walked in and out of various rooms until I was convinced she wasn't around. Defeated, I sat down on the sofa next to my dad.

For a while I was at a loss how to break the silence. One of my favorite superhero programs was on TV, but I was too fidgety to watch it. My father ran his weathered right hand across his stubbly jaw and carefully turned the pages of the newspaper.

"We won't be able to see her together anymore . . ." I finally said hesitantly. Dad slowly leaned his head toward me, causing his shoulders to tense up.

"What's that you say?"

"I can only see one of you at a time now, you and Mom . . ."

He stopped reading and set the newspaper down on the coffee table. "What do you mean?" he asked carefully.

His eyes suggested I was just a child who had done something wrong; I was afraid he was mad at me, and I wanted to run away. My stomach was tied up in knots and I knew I should have kept this a secret. My father's hard gaze made me want to crouch down with my hands on top of my head.

"When I'm with you I can't see Mom anymore."

I repeated myself desperately, fitfully, but finally he seemed to understand what I was trying to say. His face turned pale and he grabbed me by the shoulder. He looked straight into my face as if he wanted to ask me something.

"It . . . it's true." I was crying from fear. I could sense that my father truly loved my mother. I had been the thread holding their worlds together. And that's what made me sad. It was my fault I could no longer see them both at the same time. If I had really been a good boy, we would have been able to live together forever—that's what I thought.

My father was angry, but I couldn't say anything more. I was crying and that seemed to make him angrier. He raised his hand and struck me on the cheek. I fell to the floor. I told him over and over how sorry I was. I knew I was a bad son. All I wanted was to disappear. Everything was my fault. And my father hated me.

I got to my feet and ran from the room. My father called my name, but he didn't run after me. I dashed out the front door without putting my shoes on. I went down the stairs of the apartment building, down the asphalt street, and toward the neighborhood park. I couldn't stay in that apartment. I loved my father and the living room with the sofa so much I couldn't stand it. My father's slap told me he didn't need me anymore. The soles of my feet stung as I ran, but I hardly felt it.

No one was in the park. The other kids were probably staying home because it looked like it was about to rain. Ordinarily the park would be filled with laughter, but today the slide and the swings were empty. I didn't feel like playing anyway, but being in the big park all by myself just underscored my loneliness.

I sat in the sandbox and dug my feet deep into the sand. All I could think about was my dad. How could he love a kid like me? Last night's fight was entirely my fault. If I were a good boy, the kind of kid who could eat a meal without spilling food on his clothes, who picked up his toys when he was done with them, they would never have fought in the first place.

The sand was black and warm and stuck doggedly to my hands and feet. From behind I heard someone call my name. My mother was looking at me, surprised. A shopping bag swung from her bent arm.

"Did you come here with Dad?"

Smiling slightly, she looked around the park. I shook my head. Mom came up beside me, a concerned expression on her face.

"Where have you left your shoes? And why is your cheek so red?"

I covered my injured cheek with my hand. I didn't want her to know that Dad had gotten mad at me. I thought she would scold me too. My mother seemed to understand how I felt. She set her bag down on the ground and reached out both arms. She gave me a great big squeeze.

"What happened?" she asked. Her familiar smell comforted me, and I immediately felt better.

"Dad got mad at me."

Mom asked me what had happened. She listened silently and softly stroked the top of my head. I couldn't stop sobbing. There in the quiet park, with no one around, my mother performed a small miracle. She made me, her little crybaby, feel safe and loved.

"Mom, do you remember what you said a long time ago?"

"What was that?"

"You told me it would be just the two of us from now on. You told me that it would be hard but that we would manage somehow."

"Yes, I remember," she said, nodding. At some point a fine misty rain had started to fall. My mother brushed my wet bangs back from my forehead.

"I want to live in your world," I said. I had made my decision. She looked at me intently. She carried me in her arms as we made our way back to the apartment. I cried the whole way.

I never saw my father again.

Even now as a junior high student, I can still clearly remember the events of that time. I have told many people about my unusual experience. At times I have sought counsel from others.

I remember the day—the day after I saw my father for the last time. The sky was blue and without a single cloud. Every leaf on every tree made its own distinct shadow on the ground. Mom and I held hands as we walked around the neighborhood. It was warm out and I was extremely happy. I turned my face to the sky and closed my eyes. The backs of my eyelids glowed red from the sunlight. Mom took me to a place where there were lots of toys and picture books. There were also lots of other kids my age. After we all played for a while, someone took my hand and led me to a room. Inside this room was a man sitting at a table. I was told to sit in the chair across from him.

The man asked me about my father, and I explained that Dad had died in a train accident. The man seemed troubled. He crossed his arms. Then he smiled a little bit and asked me a question. "Who is the gentleman standing behind you?"

I looked behind me, but there was no one there. My mother was standing beside me. I told the man that I didn't see anyone.

"He seems to have lost the ability to see his father," my mother said. She was crying. "He can hear my voice, but he can't seem to hear his father's. When his father squeezes his hand, or strokes his head, he doesn't seem to feel a thing. If he picks him up or tugs at his arm, he goes limp and expressionless just like a doll."

"I see," the man said. He continued talking to my mother. "In other words, you and your husband had a quarrel, after which you each acted as if the other were dead. You spoke to your child in the same way and made him play along with the story. And after a while this is what happened."

The man looked behind me. He seemed to be talking to someone and nodding frequently. I followed his gaze with my own eyes, but there was nothing there except an empty space.

Now that I have grown up, I understand what my mother and the doctor were talking about that day. I think I also understand how it came about. My mom told me that my dad was there, so I reached out my hands to touch him. Unsure about what I was doing, I asked her where he was.

"Why can't you feel him?" she asked. "You're touching him right now!" Frustrated, she burst out in tears. After a moment, she looked over my shoulder and started talking. I couldn't figure out whom she was talking to.

Now that I'm like this, my parents never fight anymore. I still can't see my father, but when my mother cries, I can sense that he is somehow comforting her. Nobody can deny that we are a happy family. Everyone says that I was permanently traumatized as a young child. But I don't see it that way. I've come to realize that this is exactly what I wanted all along: to keep my mother and father together.

WORDS OF GOD

1.

My mother was smart. When she was little, she used to read really difficult books and eventually went to a famous university. She was very personable and she participated enthusiastically in volunteer activities. She was dearly loved by everyone who lived in the area. When she stretched her spine out straight, she looked just like an elegant crane standing quietly on a winter lake. She had intelligent eyes and looked at the world through clear, dust-free eyeglasses.

If my mother had one failing, it was that she couldn't tell her pet cat from a cactus. For this reason, some time ago, she once grabbed our housecat in both hands, stuck it in a planter, piled dirt on top of it, and watered it. And then there was the time she mistook a cactus for a cat, rubbed her face against it, and ended up with a cheek full of scratches, all bloody.

My father and brother would frown at my mother's mysterious behavior and ask her why she did the things she did. My otherwise smart mother would ignore them as she opened a can of cat food and put it in front of the motionless cactus plant.

All of this was my fault. I did something wrong and I am so sorry.

When I was very small, I was often told that my voice was very beautiful. At New Year's and in summer during the Buddhist

Festival of Souls, we would go to my mother's family home, and all my relatives whom we only saw on special occasions would fuss over me. I was not the most socially adept person, but they would have a few drinks, and I would laugh at their jokes and say enough to show I was paying attention, and I would pretend to understand even when their country accents made it hard for me.

"You really are a good kid," my aunt would say to me, and I would show her a faint smile. The truth was, though, that I was not a good kid. My heart was all shriveled up and rotten. I was just faking it.

I was unmoved by what my relatives said about me, and I was never happy. I was always bored, and all I ever wanted to do was run away. But I was always afraid that if I ever were to run away from my relatives, my stock with them would drop like a rock. Even if I wasn't really interested in what they were talking about, I would pretend to be listening, and I had no choice but to continue mouthing the affectionate responses they expected to hear.

At times like that, in my heart of hearts, I loathed myself. Just because I wanted people to think of me as a good boy I would put a meaningless smile on my face. But really I was miserable.

"Your voice is like music, so crystal clear," one young female relative told me. To my own ears, though, my voice sounded ugly and distorted, like an animal trying vainly to imitate a human being.

My earliest memory of using the power of my voice was when I was in first grade. As a class activity we were growing morning glories, and our potted plants stood in a row on the concrete along the outside wall of the school. My morning glory was big—its green tendrils wrapped firmly around their supporting stick, reaching for the sky. The dew clinging to the down of its broad leaves caught the morning sun, and its soft, thin, semi-transparent petals were dyed a reddish purple.

But my morning glory was not the best in the class. There was another that was bigger and more beautiful. Three seats in front of me sat a boy who was a fast runner named Yuichi. He was very lively, and he never seemed to stop talking. I talked with him often, but what interested me was not so much what he said as how his expression changed. He was very popular in class, and I thought the secret lay in his expression. Whenever I stood facing him, I would observe his face closely. I wanted to be able to master the same kinds of ever-changing expressions that seemed to come bursting and bubbling out of him.

It seemed, however, that his expressions were not deliberate, and did not emanate from a desire like my wish to be seen as a charming child. To me this was proof of the dark and small nature of all human beings. I didn't realize it at the time, but I secretly felt inferior to Yuichi.

Yuichi and I could always get a laugh from our classmates. He would strike up a friendly conversation, and I would come up with some witty response. He enjoyed our little game, and he would respond with a hearty "Hey, hey!" each time we did it. But I never felt he was really my friend. I just smiled my fake smiles and responded to his greetings with something witty and unexpected.

It was Yuichi's morning glory that was the biggest and most beautiful in the class. Whenever the teacher praised his flower, I felt miserable. I felt like a filthy little animal living inside me was trying to break through my skin and scream. Needless to say, that filthy little animal was my own true self.

One morning I arrived at school earlier than usual. No one else was in the classroom, and it was quiet. It was easy for me to set aside the mask that usually covered my face.

I knew right away which was Yuichi's pot. It was a head taller than any of the other morning glories. I leaned over his pot and stared at the blossom, just beginning to open. I focused my powers on the darkness in the pit of my stomach.

"You will wi-i-i-ither . . . You will die and ro-o-o-o-t-t . . ."

I clenched my hands tight together and squeezed all the strength of all the muscles in my body into my voice. I felt a strange sensation deep in my sinuses and realized my nose was bleeding. The dripping blood made red circles like drops of paint on the concrete.

Just like that, like a head being chopped off, the stem bent and the blossom drooped. A few short hours later, Yuichi's morning glory shriveled up and started to turn a dirty brown. But he didn't get rid of it. He just left it there. Pretty soon it started to smell bad, and it attracted some nasty bugs, and a lot of maggots started to crawl around in the dirt in the pot. The teacher decided he had to throw the dead plant away, and Yuichi started to cry. And that's how my morning glory came to be the best one in the class.

My good mood lasted for about thirty minutes. After that, though, I couldn't take it anymore. If anyone said anything good about my flower, I felt like I wanted to cover my ears.

From the moment I had incanted over Yuichi's flowerpot, my own morning glory had become a mirror reflecting the terrible animal that was hidden within me, which I could not bear to see.

I was unable to explain very clearly just why Yuichi's flower had obeyed my wishes and died. At the time I was in first grade, but vaguely I could sense the terrible power contained within my voice. If another child was terribly angry with me, I had the power to calm them down. Something disagreeable might happen, but even though I was a mere child, I could make my case to others as if apologizing. Even adults would bow their heads before me.

Let's say there was a dragonfly, resting on a guardrail half-buried in a hedge. Ordinarily, if you reached out your hand to grab it, the dragonfly would quickly take flight on its translucent wings. But if I commanded it not to move, the dragonfly would completely freeze—even if I plucked off its legs or wings.

That time back in first grade was the first time I remember consciously using the power of my words. Since then I have used this power again and again, against people I didn't even know.

In my last years in elementary school there was a giant dog that terrorized my entire neighborhood. He would hide just inside the gate of his house and bark whenever people passed by. Often he would lunge at his intended prey until he was jerked back by his heavy chain. His collar would dig deeply into his neck. The beast desperately wanted to sink his fangs into any poor passerby. He seemed to have some skin condition that left his mud-smeared coat patchy in places, and his eyes were so full of anger they seemed to be on fire. This dog was well known in the neighborhood, and we used to test each other's courage by seeing how close we dared get to him.

One day, I stood outside the gate staring at the dog. Seeing me, he started a menacing growl that sounded like a rolling quake beneath the earth's surface. That day I decided to use my power.

"You will not ba-a-ark at me . . ."

The dog's ears twitched in surprise, and he opened his rheumy eyes wide and shut his mouth.

"You will obe-e-ey. You will obey me-e-e . . . Obe-e-edience . . ."

I felt like fireworks were going off in my head. At the same time, blood dripped from my nose and stained the sidewalk. I have to admit I was showing off to my friends. I wanted to prove to them that I could transform this scary dog into a docile plaything.

This was a stupid plan, but it worked beautifully. The dog did whatever I wanted it to, giving me his paw, rolling over, anything. And among my classmates, I became the leader of the pack.

At first, this made me feel really good. Before long, little by little, I started feeling guilty. What did I think I was doing, acting like some kind of superhero? In reality I wasn't brave enough to tame a goldfish. I was consumed with guilt for deceiving other people.

The dog's eyes were the worst thing of all. Before I used the words on him, the dog had eyes that were seething with anger. Now he looked meek. I had stripped that dog of his fighting spirit.

Seeing his eyes, once so ferocious, now the eyes of a whimpering little animal, I felt nothing but self-reproach.

The power of my voice was virtually limitless, but there were a few rules I had to observe. For one thing, the voice only worked on living things. Plants and bugs, fine. But I could incant all I wanted with all the power I could muster at rocks or plastic, and I couldn't bend them to my will.

Also, once I used the voice, I couldn't undo whatever I had done. One day I had a little disagreement with Mom. Without thinking I whispered, "You-u-u will no longer be able to te-e-ell the difference betwe-e-e-en cats and cactuses!"

It was an emotional moment, and I did not immediately grasp the significance of what I had done. My mother had entered my room without my permission, and while she was tidying up, she knocked over my favorite cactus. I wanted to impress upon her just how much I treasured that cactus, and so I was telling her it was as important to me as her pet cat was to her. Later, when I saw my mother plant her cat like a cactus, I was tormented with regret. I should have known better. Even if something happened that was not to my liking, I should have known that using the power of the voice to mess with people's heads was a seriously sinful act.

So I tried to use the power of words on my mother again so that she could once more tell the difference between a cat and a cactus. Never again, though, would she be able to separate the two.

2.

The power of my voice was capable of stirring not just people's minds, it could also cause physical reactions. I was able to manipulate animals in the same way I had that morning glory so many years ago.

Even after I became a high school student I continued my pitiful habit of always sucking up to adults. I was simply unable to control this bad habit of mine, and to me it was proof of my own cowardice. I was always so afraid of the ripples that naturally emanated from normal human interactions that I was always walking on eggshells, and still I was afraid of doing something that would diminish my worth in the eyes of others. Whenever I had a conversation with someone, I always felt that person was scrutinizing me. I could always picture them going off furtively somewhere and laughing as they discussed my shortcomings. I was so frightened of the world I could hardly stand it. For this reason, I had a fake smile I always wore to disguise my true feelings. The effort this required also made me miserable.

My father was a university professor, cold and strict. He was the kind of person with a face like a craggy cliff where no vegetation could take root. He gazed down upon his two sons from a great height and made grand, fatherly pronouncements. I looked up to him as if to a heavenly being. He took a stern view of all things and had absolutely no patience for things he didn't like. Once he determined that something was of no value, he lost interest in it completely. He paid it no more mind than he would some random flying insect.

Unbeknownst to my father, I bought a handheld electronic game. It was a cheap little thing, the kind of toy any elementary school kid might have. It was only about the size of the palm of my hand. My father did not have a high opinion of computer games, and if he found it, he might be very disappointed in me. I got frightened just imagining it.

My younger brother did as he pleased. When he wanted to play a game, he went to a game center. If he wanted to study, he was the kind of person who could grind pencils down to stumps. This was his recompense for being the sort of person who could stand up to a parent's disappointment, not that Kazuya had ever had to face disappointment of any kind. I was not like that. I studied my little heart out just trying to get a little love and attention from my father. Depending on whom you asked, some people said this made me seem like a refreshingly cheerful young man. Of course, that was just a façade. Underneath that mien was a dark red, gooey glob.

One day as I was secretly playing my game in my own room, my father unexpectedly opened the door. He entered without knocking like a police officer bursting onto a crime scene. He took the game from my hands and looked down on me with cold eyes.

"So this is what you're doing!" he spat at me.

If Kazuya played a game, father would look the other way. My father was never committed to the idea of raising his second son to be a healthy, upstanding child in line with his own ideals. For this reason, it seemed, his expectations were that much higher for me, his older son, and his anger all the greater.

Ordinarily I might have cried and begged him for forgiveness. In that instant, though, perhaps because I accepted his reaction, or because I felt myself to be under attack, I became acutely aware of the injustice that my brother was free to do whatever he wanted, while I was forbidden to do anything. I had a great sense of indignation that I was being censored simply because I wanted to play a game. Without really thinking, I grabbed my father's left hand. I desperately wanted my game back. Ordinarily I kept my mask of obedience firmly in place, and this was the first time in my life I had ever fought back against my father. He held tight to the game in his left hand and did not let go. I put the power into my voice and intoned: "The-e-ese fingers! Will fall o-o-off!"

For a brief instant the space between us quivered with my voice. I felt a tugging at the blood vessels deep in my sinuses. The game fell to the floor with a crack. And then, one by one, the fingers fell from my father's hand to floor, and they rolled to my feet. All five, fallen cleanly off, right where they joined his hand. Blood from his fingerless hand spewed everywhere, staining the floor bright red. Blood dripped from my nose as well.

My father started screaming. That is, until I told him that

was enough, and commanded him to shut his mouth. And he did. For all that his voice was stilled, his eyes grew wide with pain and fear, and he stared unbelievingly at his left hand with its missing fingers.

I felt nauseated, and I ended up gulping down a lot of the blood from my nose. I felt faint and couldn't figure out what to do. There was no way I could reattach my father's fingers back where they belonged. Once the words were spoken, the changes they wrought could not be undone.

I had no choice but to render my father unconscious until I could come up with a plan. "Sleep!" I ordered him. I knew based on past experience that the power of the voice would be fully effective on people even if they were unconscious. Being observed while I invoked my powers made me nervous, so it would be easier if I put him to sleep.

As my father lay on the floor, I whispered in his ear, "The wounds on your left hand are healed," and "When you wake up, you will have forgotten everything that happened in my room." Almost immediately, a thin layer of skin had grown over the wounds on his left hand where the fingers had been. The bleeding stopped immediately.

I had to make my father believe it was completely natural that he no longer had any fingers on his left hand. I had to go beyond that, so that anyone else seeing my father's left hand would find nothing unnatural about it.

I had to think hard about how to accomplish this. I knew how to invoke changes in someone I was speaking directly to, but how could I convince the rest of the world to turn a blind eye to my father's damaged hand?

I had an idea, and I spoke the following words:

"When next you open your eyes, you will look at your hand and you will believe it has always been this way. And you will be able to convince everyone else that this disability is completely normal."

In this way I was able to anticipate people's reactions to my father's left hand. I simply commanded the hand to "give a natural impression."

I cleaned up my blood-spattered room, wrapped the fallen fingers in tissue paper, and stuffed them in my desk drawer. My father's clothes were also bloody, but I spoke a command for all my family members not to notice.

I helped my father out of the room. Out in the hallway we passed my brother Kazuya. For a second I thought I saw a look of surprise on his face. It was unusual for me to be helping my father this way. Through the open door, Kazuya looked into my room. My game lay on the floor. Kazuya suppressed a laugh and smiled at me.

At dinner, my father seemed to be having some trouble eating. He was unable to hold his rice bowl in his fingerless left hand. But I have to say he looked very natural doing it. Without his fingers, his hand was remarkably smooth and round. I bet no one else in my family was even aware of my father's deformity.

I noticed that my brother Kazuya was looking at me scornfully. He was the sort of person who realized that the world was filled with spoiled kids. He and I went to the same high school, where I was one year ahead of him. I could not live my life the way he lived his.

At school my brother would joke around with his pals as they walked down the corridors. That was the way real friends got along with one another, and it just made me feel all the more left behind and lonely. My teachers always thought of me as the kind of cheerful person who could make any class fun. But in truth, there was no one whom I could think of as a really close friend. Lots of people liked me, I guess. Some may even have thought of me as their close friend. To my thinking, though, there was no one with whom I could really be myself. Of my acquaintances, even those who said they really knew me would look at me with faces that suggested they were seeing something truly strange.

My brother was a good kid. He was not like me, always trying to hide and cover up with a fake smile. He was comfortable in his own skin, able to relax around his friends. In that sense, he was a much healthier and more complete person than I would ever be.

Strangely enough, it seemed that everyone saw me as the more capable child. Most likely this was because of the stupid mask of obsequiousness I persisted in wearing. If this made my brother feel inferior to me, that meant I had treated him badly. I wanted to apologize to him. But the relationship between him and me was not one that allowed us to talk easily about anything. If by chance at school we were to make eye contact, we would divert our gaze and pretend not to see each other. It was sad.

This was my fault. That is to say, I think he was somehow aware of my ugly inner self. He knew all about me, just how pathetic I was, that all I was interested in was listening to my parents and doing what my teachers told me to do, earning points so that those around me would accept me as one of them. Talking about this would be repulsive. All he could do was look at me scornfully, wordlessly.

Whenever I ingratiated myself with someone and felt I had created a safe comfort zone, that was when I would usually encounter his condescending gaze. He found me ludicrous, laughable. It was as if my world had developed a crack in it, and a Band-Aid was muffling all sound.

A group of students were all gathered around the vending machines at school, chatting amiably. None of them had any intention of buying any drinks; they were just goofing off. I wanted to buy something from the machine, but I didn't feel like pushing my way through the crowd, so I stood nearby waiting for them to be on their way. I suppose I could have just asked them to move a little bit, and that would have been the end of it, but something in my brain was afraid they would say no and look at me strangely. I had difficulty approaching people I didn't know. So instead, I stood just a little ways away from the vending machines and pretended to be engaged by some poster that was actually of no interest to me at all.

That was when Kazuya showed up. Without a moment's hesitation, he worked his way through the crowd and put his coins in the machine. Only when he had his can of soda snugly in his hand did he notice I was there too. His smile suggested he had grasped the entire situation in a wink, right down to why I was staring at the poster.

Kazuya knew. He knew that his big brother, whom everyone thought of as popular and friendly, and studious, was really a fabricated illusion. Kazuya knew everything about me, about my pathetic little heart with its fake smile, which had only one preoccupation: to be liked by somebody. And he knew all about my pathological cowardice, that I couldn't even muster up the courage to say "Excuse me" to a bunch of kids clustered in front of a vending machine.

At some point, it came to be that even passing by my younger brother, whether at home or at school, I would break into a sweat. I became afraid of Kazuya because he knew all about the real me. In his eyes, I was sure, I appeared not as his older brother, but as some ugly mud doll fit only to be scorned and spat upon.

I had few opportunities to speak with Kazuya, but whenever we found ourselves at the breakfast table together it made my stomach queasy. I felt like I was burning under his disdainful gaze, and my hands got all sweaty, leaving me unable to grip my chopsticks properly. Even so, as if I were an actor in some comedy movie, I smiled and greeted my parents, and dug into my breakfast with great enthusiasm. This had been our pattern for a very long time, and even now I nearly always threw up everything I ate.

I spent my nights in sleepless convulsions. I had no peaceful dreams. I saw the faces of many people on the backs of my closed eyelids. Just like my brother, all of them stared at me with disdain. I cried and chanted Buddhist prayers to expiate my sins. Sometimes when I opened my eyes and daydreamed, my room filled up with floating eyeballs that all accused me. When that happened, I felt like I wanted to die.

Or better yet, I wished I was the only person in the world, and then I would not have to endure this suffering. Other people had always been terrible to me. That was the cause of all the filthy things I ever did, just trying to get people to like me. Having people hate me, or look down on me or disdain me was all a bitter pain, and to escape this pain I had to keep this ugly little beast locked up in my heart. If there were no other people in the world, if I were the only one, how much easier life would be for me.

I must never let anyone else see me ever again. No one must ever look at me with a pained smile or with disappointment. So I spent some time thinking about how I could erase my image from the minds of all the people of the world.

How about this idea?

"One minute from now, I will no longer be reflected in your eyes!" I would say this phrase of power to someone, anyone. And then, after that, I would say this: "Your eyes, which can no longer see me, will transmit these words you have heard to everyone with whom you make eye contact."

In other words, the first person to lose sight of me through the power of my voice would at some point make eye contact with someone else, and my existence would vanish from the perception of that second person as well. And if that second person should make eye contact with someone else, then that third person's retinas would no longer be able to form an image of me. Through the repetition of this process, people in whom this change of visual perception had occurred would exchange glances with other people, enhancing my invisibility. Once all the people of the world could no longer see me, I would be completely invisible, and I would be able to enjoy eternal peace.

Before I would be able to put this plan into action, though, I would have to think of a way of excluding myself from the shackles of this command. Otherwise, I might look in the mirror and not be able to see myself.

When I realized what kind of appalling things were making me feel so happy, I got disgusted with myself.

3.

Then one night, the dog died. I mean, the dog on which, back in elementary school, I had used my magic voice simply to make myself look good in the eyes of my schoolmates. I had never forgotten about that dog, whose eyes would fill with fear at the sight of me.

When my parents told me the dog had died, I went to the house where the dog had lived. The owner knew me and showed me the dog's body. Once so big and ferocious, the dead animal now lay motionless on the pavement. I hugged the dog and cried. I was filled with a mysterious sadness that I couldn't figure out. Sensitive to my needs, the dog's owner left me alone for a moment.

With all my body's strength, in a voice that came trembling from deep within me, I commanded the dog to rise up and live. But the dog did not come back to life. Here and there, I noticed the hairs on his back stirring in the night breeze. But nothing else happened. Even if my words were successful in satisfying my base desire for some sort of a sign, they were not able to bring the dog back to life.

And that was not the only thing. This attempt of mine to bring the dog back to life did not stem from some heartfelt sadness on my part. I could only guess that I was subconsciously trying to lighten my burden of sin, at least a little.

Now with a tranquil expression on my face, I closed my eyes. I felt as if the dog had been liberated by death, and I envied him.

One night I stood in the middle of my bedroom holding a chisel and crying. My body was dripping with sweat, and I was mumbling repeatedly, "I'm so sorry. I'm so sorry." I probably intended to cut my wrists with the chisel, but I was able to control my emotions just in time. I looked down at my wooden desk and noticed a single gouge made with the chisel. I also noticed a spot on the desk wet from my tears. When I leaned closer, I noticed an ugly smell of decay like rotting flesh.

Opening the desk drawer, I found the half-forgotten fingers wrapped in a wad of tissue. They were starting to turn black, and I could tell they had been left in the desk for a long time. Seeing the dark hairs on the knuckles, I remembered that they belonged to my father. I had completely forgotten that I had shoved them into the desk drawer. The power of my words helped erase the memory of what I did.

I took the decaying fingers outside and buried them deep in the yard. But even after that, the smell of decay that wafted up from the desk did not disappear. With each passing day it seemed to grow stronger. It almost seemed as if somewhere deep in the drawer was a link to another world, and the smell of rotting flesh emanated unceasingly from the depths of that darkness.

Over time the number of gouges in the desk increased, without my awareness. Within a few weeks there were nearly ten chisel marks. I had no memory of these hackings.

Morning. I opened my eyes to the usual pain and suffering.

The person making breakfast for the family and the cactus, the person holding down the newspaper with his fingerless left hand so it wouldn't rustle in the breeze, I didn't think of them as people, I thought of them as dolls that could move. The person who checked my ticket on the train on my way to school, the person sitting in the seat beside me, the people who passed me by in the school hallway, I didn't think of them as living things. They were just objects, incapable of thought, like billiard balls crashing into each other. Only their skins were elaborately crafted, and everything inside was really just a collection of manufactured components.

Even so, the only thing for me to do was to keep on smiling and playing my part so they wouldn't get rid of me. For the person who made me breakfast, I had to demonstrate that I sincerely understood all the trouble she went to on my behalf by eating all my food, telling her how delicious it was, and speaking in a voice that conveyed my satisfaction. When riding a train, I must vow never to ride without a proper ticket covering my entire journey, and I must show the conductor my commuter pass when requested like a model passenger. In the classroom too I would have to change, no longer pleading that I was a necessary member of the class, so people should please, please, please not pick me last, and instead I would be the one to gently replace the flowers in the vase. And I would decorate with flowers so cleverly people would think it was just a natural part of my personality, and no one would realize it was all part of a plan.

My heart turned so bleak it was actually easy for me to wear a bright shiny smile all the time. And all along I was growing ever more afraid of my brother. Even if I no longer imagined that people from all over the world were living in his little skull, thinking all kinds of thoughts, still I was afraid of Kazuya, and of him alone. I could no longer hear the breathing of other humans, but his shadow grew ever darker.

Kazuya never said anything pointed, but there was not a doubt in my mind that the chilly smile that spread across his face was meant as a comment on my ridiculous self. That was what terrified me more than anything else in the world. This followed me around like a ghost and tormented me. At times like that, even if I was climbing the stairs at school, I would check that there was no one around. And then to still my heart I would tear at my hair and kick the wall again and again. But despite hating my brother so much, I couldn't stand myself even more.

Even now I felt that Kazuya was at the root of my sufferings. From these feelings arose my desire to kill him.

I pressed the stop button on the cassette deck and rewound the tape to the beginning. Listening to this story and ruminating about it, I could barely contain my trembling. My field of vision blurred with tears, and I put all my strength into the chisel and cut another gouge. There it was: another notch in the desk.

I was sweating and I frowned. I imagined the silent world stretching out from my window without end. I was aware of a fetid smell in the raging wind. Bacteria causing flesh to rot, spreading that evil odor.

Unable to stop the emotions roiling up inside of me, I perched myself on the edge of the bed, gripped the chisel tightly in my hands, buried my face in my arms, and cried.

When I finally cleared my head, I found I was still perched on the edge of the bed with the chisel in my lap. I swept it to the floor like I was brushing a caterpillar off my jeans. Looking over at my desk I noticed that the number of gouges had increased again. Now there were more than twenty.

I thought I must have been cutting them myself, but I had no recollection of doing this.

I felt I must be forgetting something terrible and important, and I felt uneasy. Could someone be messing with my memories? I looked down at the fallen chisel, and from its sharpened tip I sensed something eerie, something that could drive annoying people completely over the edge.

4.

It was just after dinner. Kazuya was lying on the carpet in the living room watching a baseball game on TV. With one hand he was propping up his head, and with the other he was nibbling on some snacks. His legs were stretched out every which way, and every few minutes he would bend them and stretch them again, over and over. His chest heaved with every breath.

I would have to kill him. That was the thought that came to me. I went to my room and closed the door, sat in my chair, and waited for it to get dark. As always, a fetid odor wafted from my desk, as if I had hidden the body of a dead pet in the back of a drawer. My hands were shaking rapidly. I tried to control my agitation, but I didn't do very well.

I kept telling myself that I mustn't have a second of hesitation about killing him. If I could not do this, then I wasn't worth anything. His steely gaze could see right through my flesh, and no matter how I tried, I couldn't get his laugh of derision out of my mind. I shut my eyes tight and held my hands over my ears, but there he was, pointing his finger and digging around in my ugly heart.

To achieve peace, I had only two options: I could remove myself to a world where no one else existed, or I could remove him from my world.

A few hours passed. I shivered with fright as I left my room and went down the squeaky hallway, heading for my brother's room. I stood before his door, the hall light casting my shadow in front of me. The fact that my shadow still resembled that of a human being surprised me.

I pressed my ear to the door to confirm that he was fast asleep. I put my hand to the cold doorknob and opened the door a crack. I held my breath as I squeezed my body into the room, leaving the door open behind me. It was dark in his room, but that was okay. The light from the hall was enough for me to see.

He was a restless sleeper, and I noticed that his blankets were all tangled up in a big ball. As I got closer, I confirmed that his eyes were closed and that he was sleeping. Light seeped into the room, but my body blocked it, throwing a shadow over his face. I put my mouth close to his ear and was about to whisper some words about death.

In that instant he stirred and the bed creaked. Slowly waking up, he groaned a little and opened his eyes. He looked toward the open door at first, and then noticed me standing beside him.

"What are you doing here?" he asked innocently with a slight smile on his face. I put my two hands on his throat and felt his slim shoulders, like a girl's, as he sat up in surprise. I concentrated all my powers in my voice, saying, "You-u-u wi-i-ill di-i-ie!"

His eyes bulged with fear, his delicate fingers grasped for help and found none. But then I noticed something odd. Whenever I had used the words before, I had always felt an explosion deep in my sinuses. This time there was nothing. I didn't experience the automatic nosebleed either.

I took my hands away from my brother's throat. Strangely, he didn't cough and gasp. He did not reproach me, he simply closed his eyes and lay down, as if it had all been a dream. I found his behavior to be incomprehensible. As I left his room I looked back and saw he lay in the embrace of a deep, peaceful sleep.

Feeling like my head was about to burst, I returned to my room as if some kind of switch inside me had been flipped. Looking at my desk, I saw a cassette deck I had never noticed before. It was small and cheap. Beside it was a big pile of batteries. The cassette player was the kind of model made to run only on batteries. I couldn't understand why I had never seen this before, and it seemed strange to me that I might have overlooked it somehow.

There was already a tape in the deck. I had a strange feeling that I shouldn't listen to whatever was recorded on the tape. It was like a secret order planted deep down in my brain. Nonetheless, my finger went straight to the playback button. I couldn't help myself.

Through the tiny clear plastic window, I could see the tape as it started to turn. From the speakers came my own voice, tense and trembling.

Things have gotten complicated.

How many times have I played back this tape? Even I, as I am recording this now, cannot imagine.

You who are listening to this must be the me of several days or even years from now.

No matter. As you are listening to this tape now, you probably have no recollection of what has happened to you. That is because I am recording the necessary words on this tape so that you will forget everything, and I am trying to start a life where I will be able to overlook a lot of things.

That is the only reason I have prepared this tape. So that the me of the future, leading a normal life, having forgotten about everything, will be able to know what he did in the past.

There is even a reason why you felt this sudden irresistible urge to play the tape. It is because I have recorded these words at the very end of the message:

"If ever you feel the urge to kill someone, or to commit suicide, you will see the cassette deck on your desk, and you will listen to the tape that's in it."

As you listen to this tape, I do not know whom you thought you would kill, or how you thought you might kill yourself.

But the fact that you are listening to this tape means that one or the other is true. And that is evidence you were unable to live a peaceful, happy life, and for that I am sad.

But there is something I must tell you. There is absolutely no need for you to feel that you must kill someone, or to want to kill yourself. The reason for this is very simple: a long time ago, virtually everyone else stopped moving. Your father, your mother, your brother, all your classmates and teachers, everyone you never met, none of them are alive anymore. In all likelihood, the only people living on the earth are you and perhaps a small handful of others.

When was it that you tried to figure out a way to become invisible to everyone else in the world? You remember that, don't you?

When that dog died, the very next morning I put on my ugly smile and went down to the breakfast table to eat breakfast. Kazuya, as usual, was rubbing his eyes, but he was there, and Mom put down a plate of fried eggs in front of him. Dad was frowning at the newspaper. As he turned the page, the rest of the paper brushed against my arm. On the TV, there was a commercial for a cleanser that gets things really clean. All of a sudden, I couldn't take it anymore, and I decided to kill them all.

I used the following words: "In one hour, everything from your neck up will fall off."

To this I added the following order: "When your head falls to the ground, it will be a signal to everyone else to obey the very same words."

Of course I also added other words that would protect me from the effect of the first words. I also did some more things to affect their memory. I made them forget they had heard my voice, and I made them leave the house.

One hour after I spoke the words to my family, I was on my high school's campus. There was a sudden uproar in Kazuya's classroom. I went to see what was going on and I saw my brother's head on the floor, surrounded by a pool of blood. All the students and the teacher were as white as could be.

It was a magic head that would, within the hour, cause the death of everyone who had seen it. I walked past the screaming mob of students and thought about my parents. I was confident that the same thing was happening to them, wherever they were.

One hour later, dozens of people who had seen Kazuya's head fall to the ground suddenly lost their own heads as well, plop, plop, right in front of the assembled policemen and assorted neighbors. No screams this time, just an armload of heavy objects dropping to the ground. The vision of falling heads would continue to be seen again and again by more and more people.

A riot of fear and confusion broke out. TV cameras arrived on the scene about an hour later, and the image of headless bodies was broadcast around the world. That is when my words became electrical waves that could chop off the heads of the entire human race.

That evening, the town was very quiet. In the silence, the setting sun cast very long shadows. As I walked through each neighborhood, all of which smelled red and raw, I saw many people horizontal and quiet. Strangely, animals and insects also seemed to have been affected, so I saw a lot of headless cats and dogs and even beetles and flies lying on the ground.

There had been numerous accidents around town, and I could see black smoke here and there. The TV was showing mostly nothing, but on some screens I saw images of headless newscasters slumped over their desks.

At some point, all the electric power in the whole town went out. The electric power plant had lost the people it needed to maintain control, and once it encountered an excessive load, it was no longer able to supply power. I imagined the same thing would be happening all over the world.

As I walked around the town, I became convinced I was the
only living thing left in the whole world. This depressed me. I
could find no place where there wasn't a person stretched out
on the sidewalk.

I saw a motionless driver who still had his head on, slumped
over the wheel of a crashed car, spewing smoke. In this case, I
thought, the accident must have occurred before the driver saw
a fallen head.

The stars came out in the peaceful night sky. I sat down on
a pedestrian bridge and looked up. Strangely enough, I had no
inkling of the deluge of the pangs of conscience to come until I
saw *her*.

As I looked up at the stars, I heard soft footfalls, and from
somewhere I heard a voice calling for help. Looking down from
the pedestrian bridge, by the light cast by the still-burning auto-
mobile, I could see a young girl approaching perilously close to
the fire. In complete disbelief, I called out to her. As she looked
up at me, her face filled with an expression of relief. It was like
she hadn't heard another voice in a long time.

It was at that moment that I understood why she still had a
head on her shoulders. She was blind.

To me, this young girl was bad luck. I shuddered and ran away.
A feeling of complete and utter shame filled my heart. And the
world would never be the same again.

For a long time I suffered. The earth was covered with dead
and rotting people. I had the strong feeling I would no longer be
able to tolerate this world.

I decided I would have to forget everything. I decided to blind
myself to the current state of things. I needed to live in the illusion that the world was normal, just like it had been before. At
the end of this tape, I recorded the following words.

"Each time you carve a new gouge in the desk with the chisel,
you will return to the feeling that you are living once again in the
normal world, the way it was before. You will continue eating,
and sleeping, and doing the things you need to do to continue

living, but you will remain completely unaware of this. You will remain intent in your perception that your life is simply going on as it always has."

The desk in my room is the only thing excepted from this condition. "Your five senses will not be able to trick the desk." In other words, I think I am living my normal life, but the desk is my only actual connection to reality.

Listening to this tape, you may be feeling some remorse. You may be thinking you wish you could forget everything and return to the you you were before listening to this tape. If that is true, feel free to carve another gouge in the desk and perhaps you'll feel better.

The desk is not part of your dream. The number of gouges in the desk is a record of how many times you have listened to this tape and afterward erased the memory.

The monologue went on after that. It seems the me of the past had managed to use the tape to use the words on myself, to manipulate my own memory. I leaned my face down close to the desk and sniffed. From the gouges carved by the chisel, or perhaps from deep in the drawer, from the far side of some deep hole where the light could not reach, came a strange, damp, rank smell. From the real world on the far side, only this smell was able to penetrate my world, through this drawer of the desk.

I sat on the edge of the bed and was lost in a reverie. In a world whose surface was covered in rotting flesh, I was the only person still going back and forth to school, still dressed in my school uniform. At the railway gate I still showed my commuter pass to prove I had paid the full fare for my trip, as I had vowed. I wondered if I walked along the tracks to school, pretending I was riding the train, gently swaying. Approaching the school gate, I must have had to step around lots of soft things that had rolled to earth. I must enter the uncleaned classroom still wearing the fake smile that protects me from being hated by others. I must imagine the teacher is still shouting at my rowdy classmates to get them to be quiet. The truth, though, is that I persist in sitting down at my school desk where all has gone utterly still. My hair grown long, my eyes vacant, I was still smiling my fake smile, looking more animal than human.

There was a knock at the door. I answered, and my mother opened the door, a cactus in her arms.

"Are you still awake? You should go to sleep soon," she said, expressionlessly. She seemed to be alive, but I knew she was really lying dead somewhere.

I am the only person in the whole world. As I think that, some nameless emotion comes burbling up inside of me, and I cannot stop it.

"Why are you shaking? Why are you crying? Are you not feeling well?"

I shake my head, and I mumble a heartfelt apology. If I am crying it is not because I feel ill. It is because I am at peace. I have finally arrived in the world I have sought for so long, where I am completely alone. Realizing this, I make my peace.

SEVEN ROOMS

Day No. 1: Saturday

When I first awoke in that room, I did not know where I was, and I was afraid. The first thing I saw was a dim, yellow-tinted light bulb casting its feeble light out into the darkness. Gray concrete walls surrounded me. There were no windows in the rectangular room. I lay on the floor, as if I had fainted.

Propping myself up on my hands and lifting my upper body from the floor, I could sense the unforgiving hardness of the concrete surface. As I gazed around the room, my head hurt so much I thought it had split in two.

Suddenly behind me I heard a groan. My older sister lay beside me holding her hands to her head.

"Sis, what's up? You okay?"

I shook myself. My sister lay on her side with her eyes open. Like me, she was looking around the room.

"Where are we?"

"I don't know," I said, shaking my head.

The naked light bulb hanging from the ceiling was the only thing in the gloomy room. Nothing else. Neither of us could remember how we got there.

All I could remember was walking with my sister along a tree-lined street in the suburbs near a department store. She was taking care of me while our mother did some shopping. This was unpleasant for both of us. I was ten years old already and didn't need to be babysat. My sister, of course, had better things to do than look after her kid brother. Our mother, however, wouldn't allow us to split up and go our own way.

And so we walked down the street not speaking to each other. I remembered that the square bricks of the street were set in a pattern, and the nearby trees formed a ceiling of branches over our heads.

Now and then my sister and I would bark at each other:

"You should have just stayed home!"

"You're just selfish!"

My sister was almost in high school, but I could already hold my own with her in an argument. I thought there was something strange about that. As we were walking along, I could hear the bushes rustling behind us. Before I could turn my head and see what was going on, I felt a terrible pain in my head. The next thing we knew, we were in this room.

"Somebody must have hit me from behind. And while I was unconscious, whoever it was brought us here."

My sister got up and looked at her watch.

"It's Saturday! It must be three in the morning!"

She was wearing an analog wristwatch with a silver face and a tiny display window for the day of the week. She loved it so much she would never let me touch it.

The room measured about three meters in length, width, and height. In other words, it was a perfect cube. The bulb's dim light cast shadows on the room's hard, gray, undecorated surface.

There was a steel door with no handle or anything like that. It was just a heavy slab of steel that looked like it was embedded in the concrete wall.

At the bottom of the door was a five-centimeter gap through which a light from beyond the door spilled onto the floor.

I knelt down to see if I could get a glimpse of anything beyond the door.

"Can you see anything?" my sister asked expectantly, but I just shook my head.

The walls and floor around us were not very dirty. Apparently someone had cleaned recently because there wasn't a speck of dust anywhere. The thought came to me that we had been locked inside a cold gray box.

The only light came from the single electric bulb hanging from the middle of the ceiling. As my sister and I walked around the room, our shadows came and went along the four walls. The bulb was very dim, and the corners of the room remained shrouded in darkness.

There was one very odd thing about this room.

A trench, perhaps fifty centimeters in width, split the room in half. Facing the wall with the door, the channel extended from the base of the left wall to the base of the right wall, straight across the middle of the floor. The water in the trench was murky white and had a strange odor. Flowing left to right, the water had stained the edges of the trench a disgusting color.

My sister was pounding on the door and shouting, "Hello? Anybody!"

There was no answer. The door was thick, and no matter how hard she pounded, it would not budge. The sound of her pounding on the slab of heavy steel echoed around the room; it was an absolutely pitiless sound that declared our absolute desolation. I stood stock still with sadness. How would we be able to get out of here? My sister's bag was gone. She had a cell phone, but it was in the bag, so we couldn't even call home.

My sister pressed her cheek to the floor and yelled through the gap beneath the door. Trembling and bathed in sweat, she yelled as loud as she could for help.

This time, from somewhere far off, we could hear a muffled sound like a human voice. My sister and I looked at each other.

Someone other than the two of us was not far away. The voice was not clear, though, and we could not understand what it might have been saying. Even so, I felt some relief.

For a while, we continued pounding and kicking on the door, but it was no use. Eventually we got tired and gave up. We snuggled together on the floor and fell asleep.

At around eight in the morning I opened my eyes.

While we slept, a plate with a single slice of bread and a bowl of clean water had been slipped under the door. My sister split the piece of bread in half and shared it with me.

We wondered who had delivered the bread. Without a doubt it had to be the same person who had shut us up in here.

While we were asleep, the water in the trench had continued to flow uninterrupted. It still smelled like something rotten and it made me feel nauseated. Dead insects and food scraps floated on the water's surface as it made its way from one end of the room to the other.

I had to go to the toilet. I told my sister and she shook her head as she looked toward the door.

"There's no way we can get out of this room. You'll have to do it in the trench."

We were sitting around waiting to be released from the room. But no matter how long we sat there no one ever came to unlock the door.

"Who in the world put us in here and why?" my sister grumbled, crouched in the corner of the room. I squatted over the trench and relieved myself. The gray concrete wall, the light and shadow of the electric bulb, my sister's tired face . . . everything made me sad. I wanted to get out of the room as fast as possible.

My sister yelled again through the gap beneath the door. From somewhere, we could hear someone answer.

"I knew it. Someone is out there."

Again, we still could not understand the answer.

No more food came through the door. It appeared that we would only be fed in the morning. I complained to my sister about how hungry I was. All she could do was yell at me. I would just have to put up with it, she said.

There was no window in our cube so it was hard to tell for sure, but my sister's watch said it was six in the evening. From the far side of the door, we could hear the sound of footsteps approaching.

My sister, who was still sitting in the corner of the room, looked up. I moved away from the door.

The footsteps came closer. We thought someone was coming to our room. We were confident that the person would explain why this was happening to us. We both held our breath as we waited for the door to open. But the footsteps just went right by. The blood drained from my sister's face as she fell toward the door.

"Wait!" she cried.

The person continued walking and ignored my sister's pleas.

"I think whoever it is has no intention of letting us out of here," I said.

"That just wouldn't be right," said my sister. She was obviously as frightened as I was.

A full day had gone by since we had awakened. In that time we heard the sound of a heavy door opening and closing, the sound of machinery, and the sound of human voices and footsteps. Locked up in our room, though, none of these sounds was clear. Everything sounded like the grunting of giant animals—nothing more specific than a vibration of air.

The door never opened once. Eventually we collapsed on the floor and fell asleep.

Day No. 2: Sunday

When I opened my eyes, a piece of bread was again in the gap beneath the door. This time, however, there was no fresh bowl of water. The empty bowl from the previous day was still there. My sister thought that maybe no one had put water in it because we had not pushed it out through the gap.

"Damn!" said my sister, picking up the bowl. She raised it above her head as if she were going to slam it down on the floor. If she broke it we might not get any more water ever again. I bet that was what she was thinking.

"We have to get out of here somehow."

"Yeah, but what can we do?" I asked meekly. My sister glared at me for a second and then looked down at the trench extending across the floor.

"Clearly this waterway is meant to be our toilet."

The water continued to flow uninterrupted from the base of one wall under the base of the opposite wall.

"The stream is too small for me to access," she said, "but I bet you're slim enough to get through it."

Looking at my sister's watch, I knew that it was around noon.

What my sister wanted me to do was lower myself into the trench and squeeze under the wall and out of the room. If I could make my way out of the building, I could find someone and ask for help. Even if I couldn't get out of the building, at least I could find out something about our surroundings. That's what my sister was thinking.

I didn't like it.

In order to get down into the trench, I would have to strip down to my underwear. I didn't like that. I would also have to push my way through whatever might be hidden in the murky water, and I didn't like that either. My sister was sympathetic.

"Please! You can do it!"

I was still hesitant as I put one foot into the shallow water. The soles of my feet hit bottom right away. It was slimy and really slippery. The water did not even reach my knees.

At the base of the wall, where the water exited the room, there was a dark, rectangular hole. It was small, but I thought I could get through it. I was the smallest kid in my class.

I brought my face down close to the surface of the water hoping to see what lay ahead. Right away the foul smell attacked my nose and made my eyes tear up. It was awful. I was unable to see beyond the rectangular hole. The only thing to do was to dive under the water and take a peek.

I was worried. What if I got caught on something in the tunnel under the wall? It was dangerous. I might not be able to get out.

Thinking about this, my sister strung all of my clothes together—including both of our belts—to make a lifeline. She tied this to my foot with a shoelace so that if I got stuck she could pull me back out. That was the plan.

"Which way should I go?" I asked, looking first at the left wall, then the right. Upstream or downstream? Left or right?

"Go whichever way you like," she said. "But if it looks like the tunnel is going on for a long time, you should definitely come right back."

I decided to go upstream first. In other words, I went toward the hole on the left side of the door. I stepped up to the wall and dove down. The filthy water gradually covered my entire body. I felt like tiny insects were invading my body, gnawing away at me.

I held my breath, shut my eyes tight, and plunged headfirst through the rectangular hole from which the water was emerging. The ceiling was low and it was a tight squeeze. The back of my head immediately hit the ceiling of the tunnel.

The rectangular concrete tunnel was just barely big enough for me to squeeze my body through. It was like passing a thread through the eye of a needle. The water was not flowing very rapidly, so it was not that hard to fight my way upstream.

I only had to go about two meters through the waterway before I sensed that my head and back were no longer bumping the ceiling. The trench had emerged into a wider space again. I quickly lifted my head and stood up.

I heard a scream.

I didn't want to get the dirty water in my eyes, but I couldn't help it. I had to open them. For a minute, I thought I was back in the same room I had just left behind. It was exactly the same, a small cube of gray concrete. The same trench ran straight across the middle of the floor. I thought I had entered the upstream tunnel entrance and emerged from the downstream exit.

But I hadn't. Instead of seeing my sister, I saw someone else. A young woman, perhaps a little bit older than my sister, with a face I had never seen before.

"Who are you?!" she screamed. She was obviously afraid and scrambled to get as far away from me as possible.

I explained to the frightened girl that my sister and I were being held in the next room, on the downstream side. I detached the rope from my leg, and decided I would proceed upstream. And I discovered two more identical concrete rooms.

That is to say, ascending the stream that flowed through the trench from the room where my sister and I had been, there were three other rooms. And in each room there was a person.

In the first room was the young woman.

In the second room was another woman with long hair.

And in the room furthest upstream was a woman whose hair was dyed red.

Every one of these people was being held captive without knowing why. All were grown-ups except my sister and me. I think my sister and I were in the same room because I was still small, so we were kind of a brother-and-sister set. I guess I didn't count as a whole person.

An iron grate blocked the trench in the room containing the woman with dyed red hair. I could go no further, so I went back to the room where my sister was and told her everything.

Even after I dried off, the stench of the water clung to my body. There was no clean water to wash with so the whole room got smellier. My sister, to her credit, did not complain.

"So . . . the room we're in is the fourth from the upstream end," she mumbled, thinking something.

There were many rooms in a row. Locked in each room was a person. That surprised me. It made me feel braver. I found it encouraging that other people were in the same situation.

When they first saw me, each one of them was puzzled, but then their faces brightened. It seemed as if each of them had been there for days and had seen no one the whole time.

The doors did not open, and the people inside did not know where they were, or what lay beyond the walls surrounding them.

Their bodies were not small enough to pass through the trench and there was nothing they could do.

As I dove through the trench from room to room, each person begged me to come back and tell her what I had seen.

Who had locked us in here? None of us knew. We did not know what this place was, and we all wanted to know when we would be able to get out of there.

After I reported back to my sister about what I had seen upstream, I prepared to reenter the trench and head downstream. Just like upstream, I discovered a series of dimly lit concrete rooms.

The first room downstream was the same as all the others.

In it, I found a girl who looked like she was about the same age as my sister. When she saw me she was startled, but when she heard what I had to say her face slowly brightened. Like everyone else, someone had brought her here, and she had no idea why she was being kept prisoner.

I took a breath and headed downstream again.

I emerged in another rectangular room. But this one was different. It was configured the same way as all the others, but there was no one there. It was an empty space, with another feeble electric bulb barely giving off any light. In every other room I had found someone, so it was strange to not see anyone.

The trench continued beyond the farthest wall.

From the empty room, I went to the next. There was no one to hold the rope for me, but I wasn't worried. I was sure that downstream as well would be a series of small rooms, so I left the rope in the room with my sister.

In the third room downstream was a woman about the same age as my mother.

She was not startled to see me emerge from the trench. I could tell right away there was something strange about her.

She looked haggard as she crouched in the corner trembling. My first impression, that she was about the same age as my mother, was wrong: she was younger, maybe.

I looked ahead. There was another iron grate at the base of the wall. I could go no further. This was it. I was at the downstream end of the line.

"Are you . . . is everything all right?" I asked, concerned. The woman shrugged her shoulders. With fear in her eyes she stared at me.

"Who . . . ?"

Her voice lacked spirit, any trace of strength.

She was clearly different from the women in the other rooms. The concrete floor was covered with hair that had fallen out from her head. Her face and hands were sweaty and dirty. Her eyes and cheeks were sunken, and she looked like a skeleton.

I explained to her who I was and what I was doing. I sensed a spark of light in her dark eyes.

"So you're saying there are living people upstream from here?!"

Living people? I had trouble understanding what she meant by that.

"You saw them, right? There's no way you couldn't have seen them! Every day, at six in the evening, corpses float down this trench!"

I went back to my sister and told her about what I had just learned.

"So altogether there are seven rooms. Hmm . . ."

As my sister spoke, I numbered the rooms to make various things easier to explain. Starting from the room furthest upstream, the room my sister and I were in was number four, and the woman in the last room was in room number seven.

Then I waffled about whether I should tell her what the woman in the seventh room had said. Even I thought it was kind of crazy. As I was thinking about this, my sister seemed to notice my indecisiveness.

"Was there something else?"

And so, with trepidation, I told my sister what the woman in room number seven had said. I told her about the dead bodies and how they floated down the channel every day at six.

I thought it was strange when I heard that these bodies would be able to get through the narrow tunnels. I mean, in room number seven, on the downstream side, there was an iron grate blocking the trench. How could they get through there? If a corpse came floating into the room, wouldn't it just get stuck?

But that's what the wild-eyed woman had said.

She told me the dead bodies were all chopped up so that they could pass between the bars of the grate. Sometimes a piece would get stuck, but that was about it; mostly they went right through without a hitch. From the very first day of her captivity she had seen pieces of dead bodies floating down the stream through her room.

My sister listened to this, staring intently at me.

"Last night too?"

"Yeah."

The night before, the two of us had not noticed any dead bodies floating down the trench. How could you not notice something like that? There was no question—we were still awake at six p.m. No matter where you were in the room, the trench could not be ignored. If something strange had been floating in it, there was no way we wouldn't have noticed.

"What about the person in room number three? Did she say anything about that?"

I shook my head. The only person who had said anything about dead bodies had been the woman in room seven. Had she been hallucinating?

But I could not put her face out of my mind. Those sunken cheeks, the dark rings under her eyes, the eyes themselves so dark she looked like someone already dead. She had the expression of someone in a state of unrelenting terror. There was no doubt in my mind she had experienced something particularly awful.

"What she said, do you think it's true?" I asked my sister, but she just shook her head as if to say, "I don't know." I was so scared I didn't know what to do.

"When the time comes, we'll know. For sure."

My sister and I sat down and leaned against the wall. We waited for the watch on my sister's arm to say six p.m. After a while, the big hand and the little hand formed a single straight line from the twelve to the six. The silvery hands reflected the electric bulb in the middle of the room, telling us the time had come. My sister and I held our breath and gazed at the trench. On the far side of the door, it sounded like someone was either coming or going. Hearing these sounds made us fidget. Could there be some connection between the time and the sound of these footsteps? My sister did not call out. She probably knew that it wouldn't help.

From somewhere far away we could hear the sound of a machine. But no bodies came floating by—just murky water and countless dead flying insects.

Day No. 3: Monday

When we opened our eyes again it was seven a.m. Our breakfast, once again a single slice of bread, had been thrust through the gap beneath the door. Yesterday we had pushed the empty water bowl back through the gap. And today it was back and filled with water. Maybe the person keeping us here, when he or she brought around the bread for breakfast, also carried a jug of water. I imagined this faceless person going from door to door: one slice of bread and a bowl of fresh water for each room.

My sister tore the piece of bread in two and gave me the bigger half.

"I have a favor to ask you," she said. She wanted me to go back through the trench and ask everyone something. I didn't want to do it, but she threatened to take back my bread, so I guess I had no choice but to do what she wanted.

"There are two things I want you to ask everyone. How many days they've been locked up in here and whether they've ever seen any dead bodies come floating through the trench. That's what I want you to ask them."

So I did.

First I went to the three rooms upstream from ours.

Everyone in these rooms was relieved to see my face. I asked each of the women the questions my sister told me to ask.

Each of these rooms was a space without windows or anything else, so it was hard to know how long we had been locked up. But each woman had a pretty good idea how long she had been there. Some had no watch or anything, but something to eat arrived once a day, so all you had to do was keep track of the meals.

Then I went downstream. And there I found something strange.

In the fifth room there was the same young girl from the day before.

But in room number six, which had been empty, there was now a woman I had never seen before. When she saw me emerge from the muck, she started screaming and crying. She seemed to think I was some kind of monster. Explaining everything to her was a pain in the neck. But once I told her everything I knew, and how I could fit through the tunnel and swim from room to room, she seemed to calm down a little bit.

It seems she had come into this room just the day before. She had been jogging along a levee and she noticed a parked white station wagon. The car pulled up beside her, and the next thing she knew something hit her over the head and she blacked out. She kept her hand pressed to her head as if it still hurt.

I continued on to room number seven. Just yesterday the haggard crazy woman had been there, the one who had told me about the dead bodies. Now there was no one in the room. She had disappeared, and there was nothing but a cold, stark concrete space. The bare bulb from above illuminated nothingness.

Another strange thing I noticed was that the room seemed cleaner than when I had been there the day before. It didn't seem like anyone had ever been kept in there. The walls and floor were spotlessly clean—just plain, flat gray surfaces. The woman I had talked to yesterday, had she been a hallucination? Or could I be in the wrong room?

I went back to the fourth room and told my sister everything I had seen and heard.

Concerning the first question my sister wanted me to ask, the answers were as varied as could be.

Today was the sixth day of captivity for the woman with dyed hair in room number one. She was positive that she had eaten six meals so far.

The woman in room number two was on her fifth day, and the woman in room number three was on her fourth. My sister and I were in the fourth room, and it was our third day. For the woman in room number five it was day number two. In the next room was the woman who had been nabbed by the white station wagon the night before. So for her, this was day number one.

How long had the woman in the seventh room been there? She was gone before I had a chance to ask her.

"I wonder if she was able to get out?" I asked my sister, but she said she didn't know.

In response to the second question—"Have you ever seen any dead bodies come floating through the trench?"—everyone simply shook their head. Not one had ever seen a corpse come floating down the stream. But the question rattled them the minute they heard it.

"Why do you ask a thing like that?" asked each woman. They all seemed to think I had access to some sort of inside information. And of course they were right. No one except me was able to go from one room to another and gather information. All they could do was imagine things. Being shut up in a room, it was easy to spend your time imagining what was on the other side of the wall. It could have been a TV studio, or an amusement park, or something like that.

"I'll explain everything later."

I wanted to make the rounds and ask the questions quickly, so I cut everybody off just like that.

"That's not acceptable. I won't let you pass through here. Maybe you're part of the gang that's holding me in here. Why should I believe you when you say there are other rooms and other people locked in them?"

The person in room number one said this to me as I was about to leave. She stood firm in the trench with her back to the downstream wall. Her feet were blocking the tunnel and I could not get past her.

There was nothing else I could do, so I told her I was following my sister's orders and asking everybody about the things I had heard the night before. She turned white as a sheet and called me an idiot. She said there was no way anything like that could be true. But in the end she got out of my way.

No one said they had seen any dead bodies. All I could think was that the woman in the seventh room must have been dreaming or hallucinating or something. That's what I thought.

She said she saw dead bodies floating by at a certain time every day. But the rest of the women I talked to said they didn't know anything about that. I just couldn't figure it out.

I drew a deep breath and used the rope to wipe off the liquid filth from my body. My sister and I had made the rope using my shirt and pants, and for days I had been wearing just my underpants. Even so, the room was warm enough, and I wasn't worried about catching a cold. I had no use for the rope anymore, so it was just lying in a corner of the room. I only used it when I needed a towel.

I threw myself to the floor and curled up in a ball. Clutching my knees to my chest I went to sleep. The surface of the bare concrete floor rubbed hard against my ribs. It was painful, but there was nothing else I could do.

Although my information was often incomprehensible, I felt compelled to make the rounds from room to room and talk to all of the women. They were isolated and afraid.

But on the other hand, talking to me might make them even more confused. I began to reconsider my daily visits. I was unsure whether they did more harm than good.

My sister sat in the corner of the room, staring fixedly at the line formed where the wall met the floor. All of a sudden, she grabbed something in her hand.

"A hair fell off my head," she said, surprised by a long hair that hung from her pinched fingertips. I could not for the life of me figure out why she was saying that.

"Look how long it is!"

She stood up and held one end of the hair in each hand. She was trying to gauge how long it was. We guessed it was probably around fifty centimeters long.

Finally, I understood what she was trying to say. Neither my hair nor my sister's hair was that length. Which meant, of course, that the hair on the floor had come from someone else.

"I wonder if somebody else was held captive in this room before we got here?"

She turned pale, and her words came out in little moaning bursts.

"It must be . . . no . . . maybe . . . This may be a stupid idea, but . . . Did you figure this out too? The people upstream from us have all been here longer than we have. From one room to the next, the person has been here one day longer. That means we've all been put in here in order, starting from the far end."

My sister concentrated on each room and the person in it, and how long they each had been here.

"So, who or what was here before?"

"Before the people were put in here? Don't you think it was empty?"

"That's right. It was empty. But what about before that?"

"Before it was empty, it was still empty, don't you think?"

My sister was walking around the room, moving her head from side to side.

"Think about it. Yesterday was the second day we woke up in this room. For the person in the room next to us downstream, room number five, it was her first day. Room number six was empty—in other words, day zero. But what about the person in room number seven? Based on the order, it was day

minus-one, wasn't it? Have you learned about negative numbers
yet in school?"

"Well, I know that much anyway."

But, the truth is, this was all too hard for me to understand.

"Don't you get it? On day minus-one there's nobody there.
That person—and this is just a guess on my part—as of yesterday
was on her sixth day since coming here. She must have come the
day before the person in the first room."

"So where is she now?"

My sister stopped circling our room and stared at me with a
shocked look on her face. After hesitating for a few seconds, she
explained to me that, more than likely, that person was no longer
part of this world. She was probably dead.

So, the person who had been there yesterday had disappeared,
and a new person appeared in the empty room. I thought about
what I had observed, moving along the trench from room to
room, and compared it with what my sister was saying.

"As each day goes by, the empty room moves one room downstream. When it reaches the downstream end, it starts over again
at the upstream end. There are seven rooms, one for each day
in the week . . ."

One day, one person killed in one room and left to float down
the trench. And then someone new brought into the adjacent
empty room.

Put to death, in order, and then replaced by someone new.

Yesterday there had been no one in room number six. Today
someone was there. Someone new had been kidnapped—a new
body to fill the empty space.

Yesterday there had been someone in room number seven. Today
there was no one. Disappeared. Flushed down the trench.

My sister bit down on her thumbnail and mumbled something
that sounded like an unpleasant magic spell. Her eyes focused
on nothing in particular.

"That is why the person in the seventh room saw the dead
bodies floating in the water. With the order that people are put

in the rooms, even if corpses are put into the trench, no one up-stream from that room will ever see them. That would explain what the woman in room number seven saw. She wasn't dreaming or hallucinating. I think what she saw were the dead bodies of the people who had been in the other rooms."

As of yesterday, the only person who had seen any dead bod-ies floating down the stream was the woman in room number seven. That is what my sister explained to me. All of this was very complicated and hard to understand, but I believed that what my sister said was true.

"It was a Friday when we were brought here. I think on that day the person in room number five was killed and dumped into the trench. The next day the person in room number six was killed, and someone new was put in the fifth room. When you saw the empty room, it was after the person who had been in there was killed. Then on Sunday the person in room number seven was killed. Even if we had been watching the trench the whole time, we never would have seen any dead bodies because they don't float upstream. Today is Monday . . ."

The person in the first room is going to die.

I hurried to get to room number one.

I found the woman with the red hair and I explained to her everything my sister had said. But she didn't believe me. She scrunched up her face and said there was no way anything like that could be true.

"But if there was even a chance it might be true, wouldn't it be a good idea to try to find some way to get out of here?"

But none of us had any idea how to do that.

"I don't believe you!" she yelled at me angrily. "What the hell is this place anyway?"

I stepped back into the trench and made my way back to the room where my sister was. On my way I had to pass through two other rooms. In each room I had to answer questions about any news I might have heard. I wasn't sure if I should say anything. So I decided it would be better to say nothing for now. I just told them I would be back soon.

My sister was sitting in the corner of our room, hugging her knees. As I got out of the trench, she motioned for me to come closer. Paying no attention to the fact that I was covered in filth, she hugged me tight. Her watch told us it was six p.m.

All at once, we noticed streaks of red streaming down the waterway. My sister and I stared, speechless, as something small and white came floating through the rectangular hole in the upstream wall. At first we couldn't tell what it was, but as it bobbed up and down in the water, we could see a row of teeth. It was a piece of a lower jaw. It passed through the room, floating to the surface and then sinking a bit, until it was sucked through the hole on the other side. Ears, fingers, bits of tendon and bone soon followed. On one finger there was still a gold ring. A mass of dyed hair floated by. Looking closer, we could see that this was not just a matted bunch of hair; there were bits of scalp attached.

I knew it was the woman from room number one. In the murky water, countless pieces of her body were flowing past. It hardly seemed like something that had been a human being. It made me feel very strange.

My sister pressed her hand against her mouth and groaned. She vomited in the corner, but there was very little in her stomach. I spoke to her, but she did not answer. She was silent and dazed.

One by one we were being quarantined into separate gloomy, rectangular rooms. We were being given a bit of time to contemplate our solitude, and then our lives would be nipped in the bud.

"What the hell is this place?" That is what she had yelled at me—the woman in room number one. Her shrill, trembling voice was burned into my brain and I could not shake it out. I had the sense that these locked rooms were more than just a place to hold us. I thought they must be something more important, locking up our very lives and souls, isolating us, stripping even the light from us. This was a prison of the soul. This room had taught me a true loneliness of a kind I had never seen or experienced before, and the meaninglessness of a life without a future.

My sister had curled herself up in a ball and wrapped her arms around her knees. She was sobbing. I thought to myself, this is what the true human form must have been like, way back when, long before we were born, long before the beginning of history. Crying in a dark, damp box, just like my sister was doing right now. I counted on my fingers how many days it would be before my sister and I would be killed, on the sixth day of our captivity, on Thursday at six p.m.

Day No. 4: Tuesday

After several hours, the red finally disappeared from the water in the trench. Near the end, the water became soapy, like someone was using the trench to clean a mop. Perhaps someone was cleaning the upstream room? When somebody gets murdered, there's bound to be blood. And somebody needs to wash it up, right?

The hands of my sister's watch reached twelve. It was now midnight, the start of Tuesday, the fourth day since we had been brought here.

I dove into the trench and headed for room number one.

Both women in the two rooms I passed asked me for an explanation of what they had seen flowing through the trench. "Later," I told them. I was in a hurry to get to the first room.

As I expected, the woman was gone. The room looked as if it had just been sprayed down with a hose. Someone had obviously cleaned it—just as I thought. I had no idea who that might be. But I was certain it was the same person who was keeping us prisoner here.

I was equally sure that the long hair my sister had found in our room belonged to a woman who had occupied, and died in, our room before we got there. Somehow the single strand of hair had escaped the aftermath of scrubbing.

I wondered what sort of person brought us here to these killing rooms. He (or she) was a total mystery. From time to time we could all hear the sound of footsteps on the far side of the door. We were sure these footsteps came from our captor.

That person was killing one person a day in these rooms. That person enjoyed putting people into a room for six days and then cutting them into pieces.

We had still not seen that person. We had not heard that person's voice. But we were certain that person was there, walking past the other side of the door. Every day that person brought bread and water, and death. That person had designed and built these rooms and created the rules of killing.

We couldn't help but fall into a depressed stupor. At some point, my sister and I would be killed. We had no way of meeting our executioner until immediately before our death.

The killer was none other than the God of Death. My sister and I—and everyone else—were trapped in this madman's creation. Our death sentences were certain.

I returned to room number two. I told the woman, now in her sixth day of captivity, all the things that my sister had realized the day before. She did not tell me this was stupid speculation. She had seen the remains of the woman from the first room as they flowed through the trench. She seemed to understand that she would remain a prisoner here and never see the outside world again. After she heard what I had to say, she was silent, just like my sister.

"I'll come back later," I said, and headed for room number three, where I gave the same explanation again.

The woman in three was scheduled to be killed the following day. Until now, she had been at a complete loss as to how long she would have to remain locked in that room, or what would happen to her. At least now she had a clear idea.

Not unexpectedly, the woman pressed her hand to her mouth and started to sob.

I don't know, is it better to know the exact hour you're going to die, or not know? It might be better to know nothing. You'd spend your days watching anxiously as the corpses passed before your eyes, and then one day suddenly the door opens and someone you've never seen before comes in and kills you. Looking at the woman crying in front of me, I remembered the emaciated woman who had been in room number seven. All of these women had the same expression on their faces.

Desperation. To be shut up for days in these rectangular concrete rooms—I was having a hard time believing this could be somebody's idea of a game. To know that the God of Death would come and call your name . . . well, it was certainly a terrible thing to think about.

The woman in room number seven had to watch every day as chopped-up bits of human bodies came floating down the trench, wondering the whole time if she would be next. She had no way of knowing when she would be killed. I remembered her frightened face and felt a terrible pain in my heart.

In rooms two and three I delivered the same explanation, and then I went on to do the same again in rooms five and six.

In room seven there was someone new. When she saw me rise from the trench, she screamed.

I returned to my sister in room number four.

I was worried about her. She sat motionless in the corner of the room. I got close enough to look at her watch. It was six a.m.

On the far side of the door, I could hear footsteps. A single slice of bread slid through the gap beneath the door, and I could hear water being poured into the bowl we had put outside.

Light leaked in through the gap beneath the door. In that one spot, the gray floor looked whiter. At this moment, there was a shadow there, and it was moving. Someone was standing directly in front of the door.

On the other side of the door was someone who had killed many people, who even now was holding us captive in this room. Just thinking about this, I could feel that person's black, ominous power seep through the closed door and press on my chest until I could no longer breathe.

My sister stood up as if she had been yanked by a string.

She flung her body at the gap beneath the door, pressed her

lips to it, and yelled, "Wait!" Desperately she squeezed her hand through the gap, but it caught at her wrist and would not yield. "Please! Listen to me! Who are you?!"

My sister yelled with all her might, but the person on the other side of the door gave no indication that he heard her. Within seconds that person was gone. The sound of footsteps faded into the distance.

"Shit . . . Shit . . ." my sister mumbled, and leaned her back against the wall beside the door. The steel door had no handle, and judging by the placement of the hinges, it was made to swing into the room. The next time it opened would be when we would die.

"I'm going to die," I said to myself. Many times in my life I had cried because I was away from home. Never before in my life had I shed tears because I thought I was going to be killed.

What did it mean to be killed? I had trouble understanding the concept.

Who was going to kill me?

I was sure it would be painful. Once I died, what would happen to me? I was afraid. But the most terrifying thing was that my sister might be even more terrified than I was. Watching her as she glanced anxiously around the room, I didn't know what I should do. Involuntarily I shuddered.

"Sis . . ." I said as I stood by her side. She just sat there hugging her knees. She looked up at me with hollow eyes.

"Did you tell everyone about the rules of the seven rooms?"

I nodded, but I was confused.

"You did a cruel thing."

"I didn't know," I tried to explain, but my sister seemed not to be listening.

I headed back to room number two.

The woman in room two looked relieved to see me and broke into a smile. "I was worried that you might never come back, and I was wondering what I would do."

It was a rather feeble smile, but it warmed my heart nonetheless. It had been a while since I had seen anybody smiling, so her face looked to me full of both light and warmth.

But it was strange, too, to wonder how she could smile knowing she was going to die that day.

"That yelling I heard a little while ago, was that your sister?"

"Yeah. That's right. You could hear her?"

"Not well enough to understand what she was saying, but enough to wonder if it was her."

Then she started to tell me about her home. She said I looked like her nephew. Before being locked up in here, she told me, she had worked in an office, and she liked to go to movies on her days off, and things like that.

"When you get to the outside, I would like you to give this to my family." She removed her necklace from around her neck and fastened it around mine. It was a silver chain with a small cross attached. For her, this was a protective symbol. Every day since she came here, she had gripped this cross tightly in her hand and prayed.

I spent that whole day with her, and we became friends. We sat next to one another in the corner of the room with our backs against the wall and our legs stretched out relaxed in front of us. We talked the whole day, standing up once in a while to stretch. During these moments, the dim ceiling light cast giant wiggling shadows against the far wall.

The only other sound came from the water continuously flowing through the middle of the room. It suddenly occurred to me that I was probably a smelly mess from swimming back and forth across the waterway. And so I moved a little further away from her.

"What are you doing, moving away?" she said right away with a smile. "I haven't had a bath in days myself. My nose is no longer functioning. The whole time I've been in here I've been thinking, if I ever get out of here, I'm heading straight for a nice, long bath. I wanted so badly to get clean again."

As we talked, she smiled from time to time. I found this rather strange. "If this is the day you are going to die, why aren't you crying and wailing?" I asked her. I'm sure the look on my face showed my confusion.

She thought for a minute and then said, "Because I have accepted it." She looked like a statue of a goddess in some church, both kind and lonely at the same time.

When the time came for me to go, she clasped my hand.

"So warm," she said.

I returned to my room before it turned six p.m.

When I explained to my sister about the necklace around my neck, she hugged me tightly.

When, finally, the trench turned red, I saw the eyes and hair of the woman who had sat before me just a short while ago, now flowing through the trench across our room.

I approached the channel and saw her finger floating by. Gently, with both hands, I plucked it from the filthy water. It was a finger from the hand I had last squeezed before I left her room. It had no warmth left in it whatsoever. Now it was just a little chunk of flesh.

Pain ran through my chest. Inside my head was stained as red as the water in the trench. The whole world turned red, hot, and I could hardly think of anything at all.

When I came to myself I found I was crying in my sister's arms. She was stroking the hair that was plastered to my forehead. My hair was stiff from repeated drying and wetting in the filthy water.

"I want to go home," my sister said, in a voice that was totally sweet and kind, and totally out of place in that gray concrete room.

I nodded back at her.

Day No. 5: Wednesday

Somebody kills. Somebody gets killed. The rules governing these seven rooms were absolute. Under ordinary circumstances, only the person doing the killing would be aware of these rules. Those of us being killed would be clueless.

But this time, an exception had occurred.

The person who brought all of us here had put me in the same room as my sister. Because I was still a child, I did not count as a whole person, I guess. Maybe the killer considered my sister a half-person too. She was, after all, just a teenager. Maybe the killer thought that the two of us together made a whole unit—a kind of sibling set.

Because I was small, I was able to move back and forth through the trench and visit the other rooms. And that is how we were able to deduce the rules that had been set down by the killer. What the killer did not know was that we, those who were to be killed, had figured out the schedule.

The killer and the to-be-killed. There was absolutely no way we would be able to turn the tables. The rules that governed these seven rooms were absolute. They may as well have been sent down by the gods themselves.

But my sister and I started to think of a plan of how we might be able to live through this.

Our fourth day here was over, and Wednesday, our fifth day, had started. The person in the second room had disappeared and had been replaced by someone new.

The rules of the seven rooms lay in the repetition of this pattern. We had no way of knowing how long this had been going on. How many people's bodies had passed through the trench?

I was able to pass under the walls and speak to everyone. Understandably, no one was very cheerful. Still, whenever I left, they all seemed to want to see me again. Each of them would be left alone in her room, forced to face her own solitude. No one could really survive that.

"But you, you can move from room to room, and the killer may never catch you," my sister said to me as I prepared to enter the trench tunnel once again. "The person who has locked us up in here has no idea you are able to do that. Tomorrow, even if I am killed in this room, you can slip away to another room. As long as you keep moving from one room to another, you won't be killed."

"Yes, but eventually my body will get bigger and I won't be able to go through the trench anymore. And the killer won't forget there are two of us locked in here. If he doesn't find me here, he'll look for me."

"At least," said my sister in total desperation, "you'll be able to live a little bit longer." I thought this scenario would merely buy me a fraction more time to live. But my sister seemed to think it might provide an opportunity to escape.

I was sure there would be no such opportunity. There was no way of ever getting out alive.

The young woman in room three talked with me until right before she died. Her name was a little unusual, and when I first heard it I didn't know how to write it. She drew a notebook from her pocket, and in the feeble light showed me. It was the kind of notebook that had a little pencil attached to it. The person who had put us all in here had apparently neglected somehow to take this away from her, and so she still had it in her pocket.

The tip of the pencil had countless little teeth marks, and the lead jutted out. It seems that when the lead got worn down, she would retrieve more by gnawing off some wood.

"You know, because I live in the city by myself, my parents are always sending me food. I'm an only child and they worry about me. They send me cardboard boxes full of potatoes and cucumbers. The deliveryman brings them to me, but I'm always at work, so I'm never home to get them."

Even now, she was worried about the deliveryman standing at her front door with an armful of packages from her parents. Her eyes turned to the murky water where clumps of maggots floated by.

"When I was a girl there was a little brook that ran near my house. I liked to play there."

The water in this brook was very clear, so you could see the pebbles on the bottom. Hearing her talk about this, I pictured the stream as if in a dream world. Sunlight reflected off the surface of the water, a bright world flickering and glinting in myriad facets. A blue sky spread high overhead—an unending sky, where a body could fall ever upward against the pull of gravity.

I was starting to become accustomed to being shut up in these tiny rooms, with their gray concrete walls and the smell of rot wafting up from the trench. I started to forget the normal world that I had inhabited before coming here. I grew sad remembering the world outside where the wind blew and the air was fresh.

I wanted to see the sky. Never before in my life had I ever wanted anything so badly. Before being shut up in here, why had I not spent more time gazing at the clouds?

Just the day before, I had sat beside the girl in room number two and we had talked the very same way.

She did not wail and rail against the injustice of it all. She just sat and talked with me, completely normally, as if we were spending an afternoon on a bench in a park. For a short while, she allowed me to forget the hard gray walls that surrounded the little room.

The two of us sang songs together, and I wondered why this person—my new friend—had to be killed. And then I remembered that I myself was also going to be killed.

I tried to think of a logical answer to my questions, but I kept coming back to the same conclusion: I was going to be killed simply because the person who brought me here wanted to kill me.

The woman got out her notebook again, and she closed my hand around it.

"If you ever get out of here, please give this notebook to my parents. Please."

"But . . ."

Get out of here? Would I ever be able to do that? Just the day before, the woman in room two had hoped that I would be able to get out, and had fastened her cross on its chain around my neck. But none of us had any reason to believe I would ever be able to get out of here.

Just as I was about to say that, I could sense that someone was outside the door.

"Oh, no!" she said, her face stiffening.

It was six p.m. I should have left earlier, but time had slipped away from us. She had no wristwatch, and we were having such a good time together I became careless.

"Get out of here! Fast!"

I jumped up and dove into the trench and through the rectangular tunnel that headed upstream. It was the downstream tunnel that would take me to the room where my sister was, but I was closer to the upstream tunnel.

Just as I dove into the hole, I could hear the sound of the heavy steel door opening behind me. For an instant, the inside of my head grew hot.

The person who had imprisoned us appeared. I already thought of that person as a taboo vision, something I was forbidden to see until just before my death. I was in awe of the image of this God of Death.

My heartbeat grew distant.

I passed through the tunnel and stood up in room number two. As expected, it was empty. I stood in the trench and breathed deep. I put the notebook I had been given on the floor.

At this moment, the person who had shut us in these rooms was in room number three killing the woman who was there. Suddenly a thought took hold of me. My whole body trembled with fear. What I was thinking would be dangerous. But I had to do it.

My sister and I would have to flee from here. I was racking my brain to think of how we could do this. To be able to see the sky again, I had to search for clues that would allow us to crawl out of here.

To do this I would have to get a look at something that was still blotted out in a black riddle and tell my sister what I had seen.

I would have to get a look at the person responsible for trapping us in here, and I had to see how he was killing us. I had to ascertain his *modus operandi*.

I steadied myself to get ready to go back to room number three. Of course, there was a risk that if I were discovered in that narrow room, I too would be killed in the wink of an eye. My plan was to stay in the trench while observing as closely as I could. Even so I was so tense I felt giddy. If the person discovered me watching, he would not wait until the next day to kill me.

At the base of the wall on the downstream side of room number two, the long, narrow rectangular hole led to room number three. I now knelt before that hole from which I had just emerged. The flow of the water struck at the back of my thighs, and I let myself be sucked into the rectangular hole.

I breathed deep and entered, careful not to make a sound. The flow of the water was gentle. As long as I was careful, I could stay in control. If I used my hands and feet, I could even go against the current. I knew this from all the times I had done it before. The concrete walls were slippery, covered with a slimy film. I would have to be very careful.

In the rectangular tunnel, there was very little space between the water's surface and the ceiling. In order to see what was going on in room three, I would have to lurk in the tunnel and open my eyes under the water.

I cringed at the thought of having to do this in the filthy waste, but I opened my eyes anyway.

Using my hands and feet, I stopped myself just before I entered the room. Water poured over me and rushed ahead. Through a froth of bubbles, I caught a glimpse of a narrow rectangular slit of dim light.

Mixed with the sound of the rushing water was the sound of a machine.

Because the water was murky I couldn't see well, but I could see the black silhouette of a person moving.

A clump of something rotten, festering with maggots and insects, brushed past my cheek.

Trying to see better, I inched closer to the mouth of the tunnel.

I lost my grip. My fingers slipped and left a racing stripe-like pattern on one side of the trench. I focused all my strength to brace myself again. Luckily my body finally came to a stop. My head was jutting out of the tunnel.

I looked.

The woman I had been speaking with just a short while ago was now a pile of blood and meat.

The steel door, which until now I had only ever seen closed, was wide open. While the inside was unadorned, on the outside I could see a bolt. This was the bolt that kept all of us locked up in these rooms, alone, until the instant of our death.

There was . . . a man. He was standing in front of the red pile that could no longer even be called a corpse. His back was to me. If he had been facing me, he would have seen me right away.

I could not see his face, but in his hands he held a chain saw that made a terrifying noise. I realized this must be the machine sound that we sometimes heard from the far side of the door. The man stood ramrod straight, emotionless, as he worked his way through the pile before him, cutting the pieces into even smaller pieces. Flesh was flying in every direction.

The entire room was red.

Suddenly, the sound of the saw disappeared from the room. The rippling sound of the water was all that stood between the man and me.

He started to turn around.

I dug my nails into the slippery sides of the tunnel and quickly pulled myself back. I believe the man did not see me. If I had hesitated an instant longer, our eyes would have met.

I went back to room number two where no one else was. I was hardly safe here though. Someone new would be put in here, and

I had no way of knowing when the door would open. I picked up the notebook I had left and headed for the first room. There was no way I could go through room number three to the room where my sister was.

I sat down next to the woman who was now in the concrete prison.

"What did you see?" she asked me.

My face must have looked awful. She had been brought here last night, the newest arrival. I had already told her about the rules of the seven rooms, but I was unable to tell her what I had just seen.

I opened the notebook that the woman in room number three had given me and looked inside. The notebook had been through the water, so the pages were wet and stuck together, and it took some effort to separate them. The paper was wrinkly, but the writing was legible.

There was a long letter addressed to her parents. The phrase "forgive me" was repeated often.

Day No. 6: Thursday

I was so afraid of seeing that man again I was unable to go back to room number four. I spent the whole night in the first room. The woman was so happy for the company that she gave me most of her breakfast bread. As I was eating it, I realized my sister must be terribly worried about me.

Slowly I was able to bring myself to return to the room where my sister was. I made my way through the tunnel, and someone new was in room number two. Just like everyone else, she was startled when she saw me emerge from the trench.

Room three was empty, and the blood had been cleaned up. I searched for even a faint whiff of the person who had sat and talked with me just the day before, but there was not a thing— just a vacant concrete room.

When I returned to my room, my sister gave me a big hug.

"I thought he found you and killed you!"

Even so, my sister had not eaten her bread. She was obviously waiting for me to return.

Today, Thursday, was our sixth day in lockup. It was the day my sister and I were supposed to be killed.

I told her that I had been in room number one, and that I had shared that person's meal. I told her I was sorry, and that she could eat the whole slice of bread because I had already eaten. Her eyes were red from crying and she called me a dope.

And then I told her about the person in the third room and how she had been killed, and that I had hidden myself in the trench and tried to see the killer's face.

"Why the hell did you do something so dangerous?" she yelled angrily. When I told her about the door, though, she grew still and listened intently.

She got up and ran her hand over the steel door. Once she even pounded on it with her fist. The sound of soft flesh striking metal echoed through the room.

"Really?" she finally asked. "On the other side of the door there's a bolt?"

I nodded. Looking at the door from inside the room, there were hinges on the right. The door was made to open into the room, and from my place in the tunnel I had clearly seen the outer side of the door. The bolt was very solid, the old-fashioned kind that slid horizontally. I looked again at the door to our room. It was not exactly centered in the wall, but set a little to the left.

My sister stared at the door with a frightened look on her face.

According to her watch, it was already noon. Only six hours were left until evening when the killer would come to slaughter us.

I sat in a corner of the room looking at the notebook. Because the woman had written to her parents, I began thinking about my own parents. I was sure everyone was worried about us. During nights when I had trouble sleeping, my mother would warm some milk for me in the microwave. Perhaps because I had opened my eyes in the dirty water the day before, they hurt, and the tears flowed easily.

"I can't just let it end like this . . . not like this!" my sister sobbed, her voice full of rage. Her hands were shaking violently. When she turned back to look at me, her face was magnificent, and the whites of her eyes gleamed fiercely.

These were not the powerless eyes of the day before. This was a face that had a fearsome decision written all over it.

Once again my sister started to ask me about the killer's build and his electric saw. I realized that when the killer came to attack us, she meant to fight him.

The killer's chain saw was half as long as I was tall, and it roared like an earthquake as the blade spun around in a loop. How did my sister intend to fight a man who had a weapon like that? But what choice did we have? If we didn't fight back, we would surely die.

My sister looked at her watch.

When it was time, he would come, and he would kill us. Those were the rules of this world we were now in. It would surely come soon. Certain death was in our future.

My sister told me to go through the trench once again and talk to all the others.

Time would soon be up.

How many people's bodies had already passed through this trench? I dove into the filthy water and swam through the rectangular concrete hole to the other rooms.

Besides my sister and me, there were five women being imprisoned by that man. Of these, the only ones who had seen the water turn red and frothy and the pieces of what had been a person flowing by were the three in the rooms downstream from us.

I went to their rooms, one by one, and greeted them. They all knew today was the day for my sister and me to die. They all pressed their hands to their mouths and were sad for us. One of them even suggested I should just run away to another room and save myself.

"Take this," said the woman in room number five, handing me her white sweater. "It's warm in here. I don't need it anymore."

And then she hugged me hard.

"I wish you good luck, you and your sister," she said, her voice quavering.

Soon it would be six o'clock.

My sister and I sat in a corner of our room, the spot furthest from the door.

I sat right in the corner, and my sister sat beside me, pressing me up against the wall. We stretched out our legs. Her arm brushed my arm, and I could feel the warmth of her body.

"If we get out of here, what's the first thing you want to do?" she asked me. "If we get out of here . . . " I had too many answers to that question.

"I don't know," I said, but really I knew I wanted to see my parents. I wanted to breathe in deep. I wanted to eat chocolate. There were countless numbers of things I wanted to do. If this wish came true, I would cry. I told my sister this, and she made a face that said, "I knew it."

I glanced at her watch for a second. My sister looked at the electric bulb on the ceiling. I looked at it too.

Until we were shut up in this room together, my sister and I did nothing but fight. Sometimes I even wondered why I had to have a sister. Every day we would shout insults at each other; if one of us had candy, the other would steal it.

But that was then. Now, just the fact that she was there made me feel stronger. The warmth of her body proved to me that I was not alone on this earth.

My sister was different from the other women in the other rooms. I had never thought about this before, but my sister had known me since I was a baby. That was something special.

"When I was born, what did you think of me?" As I asked her this she looked at me in an odd way. She probably thought it was a weird thing to ask at that moment.

"'What the heck?' is what I thought. The first time I saw you, you were on the bed. You were very small, and you were crying. Honestly, I couldn't see that you had anything to do with me," she said.

And then we were silent again for a while. It wasn't like we didn't have anything to say to each other. There in the concrete box dimly lit by the electric bulb, with the water flowing quietly by, I felt as if, somewhere down deep, my sister and I were chatting away nonstop. That thing called death was pressing up right beside us, but our hearts were calm.

I looked at the watch.

"Are you ready?" my sister asked, inhaling deeply. I nodded and tensed my nerves. It would be soon. I pricked my ears, straining to hear any other sound but the gurgle of the flowing water.

After a few minutes passed like this, I heard faint footsteps approaching. I touched my sister's arm to let her know that it was time.

I stood up, and my sister got up too.

The footsteps sounded louder and clearer.

My sister put her hand gently on my head and touched her thumb to my forehead. It was a quiet sign of parting.

My sister had come to the conclusion that even if we fought the man with the chain saw, there was no way we could win in the end. We were just children, and he was an adult. This was a sad thing, but it was the truth.

A shadow fell across the gap at the base of the door.

My heart felt like it was going to burst. My entire insides were trying to come up through my throat. My heart was full of both sadness and fear. The days we had spent locked up in here came back to me, with the echo of the voices and faces of the people who had died.

From the far side of the door, we could hear the sound of the bolt being thrown back.

My sister knelt with her back to the corner furthest from the door and waited. She looked at me. Death was on its way.

The steel door creaked heavily, opened, and there stood the man. He entered the room.

I couldn't see his face clearly. In my eyes, his face appeared out of focus, like a shadow. He was just a black silhouette, administering death, and bringing it to us.

The sound of the chain saw started up. The entire room was engulfed in a clamorous, violent vibration.

In the corner of the room my sister spread her arms defiantly before her, showing that she would not turn her back on her attacker.

"You will not lay one finger on my brother!" she yelled, but her voice was almost entirely drowned out by the sound of the saw.

I was so frightened I wanted to scream. I tried to imagine what sort of pain I would feel at the instant of death. What would pass through my mind as I was being ripped apart by the spinning blade?

The man spotted my clothing, partly hidden in my sister's shadow. He drew up the saw and took a step toward us.

"Back off!" she shouted, thrusting out her arms and protecting her back. Her voice was still drowned out, but I knew that's what she said. For whatever reason, that's what she had decided in advance she would say.

The man took another step toward her and struck her outthrust hand with the spinning blade. For an instant, a mist of blood hung in the air.

I was not able to see all of this too clearly. The shape of the man and the instant when my sister's hand was clipped by the chain saw were hazy to me. I was seeing it all though murky water.

I crawled out of the tunnel where I had been hiding and ran out through the open door. I quickly slammed the door shut and bolted it.

The closed door muffled the sound of the electric saw. My sister and the killer were alone in the room.

When my sister had put her hand on my head and pressed her thumb to my forehead, that had been our parting sign. In the next instant, I hurriedly plunged feet-first into the upstream tunnel. The upstream side was closer to the door than the downstream side.

This was the gamble my sister had planned. She would be in the corner of the room with my clothing behind her. She would lure the killer as if she were protecting me. In that instant, I would spring through the door. That was the plan. That was it.

We had to make it look as if my clothes had something in them. To do this, we collected clothing from everyone and used it for padding. It was just a simple little trick, and I had doubts about whether it would work, but my sister encouraged me by saying it would buy us at least a few seconds. My sister pretended to be protecting me, but all she was really protecting was my clothes.

She stood in the spot furthest from the door and enticed the killer toward her, distracting him so that he wouldn't see me crawl out of the tunnel.

When the killer was close enough to my sister to hit her hand with the blade, I was to jump up out of the tunnel and out the open door . . .

As soon as I had bolted the door, my body started trembling. I had left my sister to be killed. I alone was able to escape. To give me that chance, my sister had made no attempt to escape the chain saw. She had stood in the corner of the room and played her part.

On the far side of the door, the sound of the saw ceased.

Someone was pounding on the inside of the door. Since my sister's hand had been cut, I was sure it was the killer.

Of course, the door did not open.

From inside, I could hear the sound of my sister's laughter. It was a high, piercing sound—the sound of victory. She was undoubtedly thrilled that her simple plan had worked.

I knew that my sister would likely be shredded by the killer. Locked in that small room together, he would ravage her with a more heartless method than he had ever used before. Even so, my sister had outmaneuvered the killer to give me a chance to get away.

I looked left and right. Standing in a long hallway with no windows I was positive that we were all underground. Seven doors stretched before me.

I unbolted and opened all the doors except to room four. I knew there would be no one in the third room, but I opened it anyway. Many people had been killed in that room as well, so I felt like I had to do it.

The people in the rooms all nodded quietly when they saw my face. Not one of them was truly happy. I had told them all about my sister's plan. The fact that I had been able to escape to the outside meant that my sister was at this very moment being killed. We all knew that.

The woman from room number five hugged me tightly and cried. And then all of us gathered in front of the one closed door.

Inside we could still hear my sister laughing.

The sound of the electric saw started again. We could hear the sound of metal on metal as the man tried to cut through the steel door with the saw. We were confident that he would never be able to free himself.

No one suggested we should open the door and try to save my sister. My sister, using me as her mouthpiece, had explained to everyone that if we were able to get out of the rooms, we should all run away, or else the man would hunt us down and kill us.

And that was what we did: we ran away, leaving my sister locked in the room with the God of Death.

We ran down the corridor. At the end of the hallway we could see stairs going up. At the top was the sunlit outside world. We had escaped the gloomy, comfortless rooms where solitude reigned.

I could not hold back my tears. A necklace with a cross hung from my neck, and in one hand I held a notebook filled with apologies to a woman's parents. On my wrist was a memento from my sister: her watch. It was not waterproof, so it had been ruined when I hid in the water. The hands had stopped moving—they pointed straight to six o'clock.

ABOUT THE AUTHOR

 Born in 1978 in Fukuoka, Japan, Otsuichi won the Sixth Jump Short Fiction/Nonfiction Prize when he was seventeen with his debut story "Summer, Fireworks, and My Corpse." Now recognized as one of the most talented young fantasy/horror writers in Japan, his other English-language works include the short story collection *Calling You* and the Honkaku Mystery Prize-winning novel *Goth*.

HAIKASORU—The Future Is Japanese

The Lord of the Sands of Time
Only the past can save the future as the cyborg O travels from the 26th century to ancient Japan and beyond. With the help of the princess Miyo and a ragtag troop of warriors from across history, O has a chance to save humanity and his own soul, but will it be at the cost of his life?

All You Need Is KILL
It's battle armor versus aliens when the Mimics invade Earth. Private Kiriya dies in battle only to find himself reborn every day to fight again. Time is not on Kiriya's side, but he does have one ally: the American super-soldier known as the Full Metal Bitch.

ZOO
A man receives a photo of his girlfriend every day in the mail...so that he can keep track of her body's decomposition. A deathtrap that takes a week to kill its victims. Haunted parks and airplanes held in the sky by the power of belief. These are just a few of the stories by Otsuichi, Japan's master of dark fantasy.

Usurper of the Sun
Schoolgirl Aki is one of the few witnesses to construction on the surface of Mercury. Soon an immense ring has been built around the sun and the Earth has plunged into chaos. While the nations of the world prepare for war, Aki grows up with a thirst for knowledge and a hunger to make first contact with the enigmatic Builders. Winner of Japan's prestigious Seiun Award!

And soon:
Battle Royale: The Novel
The best-selling tour de force from Koshun Takami in a new edition, with an author's afterword and bonus material.

Brave Story
The paperback edition of the Batchelder Award-winning fantasy novel by Miyuki Miyabe.

Visit us at www.haikasoru.com